Soldier Tales

by

John O'Brien

DORRANCE PUBLISHING CO., INC.
PITTSBURGH, PENNSYLVANIA 15222

The contents of this work including, but not limited to, the accuracy of events, people, and places depicted; opinions expressed; permission to use previously published materials included; and any advice given or actions advocated are solely the responsibility of the author, who assumes all liability for said work and indemnifies the publisher against any claims stemming from publication of the work.

Although this book is lighlty based on true events all the characters featured in this book are fictional, and any resemblance to persons dead or alive is entirely coincidental.

Dorrance Publishing Co., Inc.
701 Smithfield Street
Pittsburgh, PA 15222
Visit our website at www.dorrancebookstore.com

ISBN: 978-1-4349-3031-6
eISBN: 978-1-4349-3582-3

To all, who have lived and passed under
the grace of the shadow of the tower,
none more so than.... "The Families".

Table of Contents

KITS IN BITS

It was the morning of the kit inspection, and I was not looking forward to it at all, and to make matters more complicated the rain was pouring down from the heavens. It had been raining all the night before, and right into the morning, and looked like it was going to stay that way for the remainder of the day. The floors the lads had shined the night before, and this morning they had to be rebuffed every time a body walked in from the rain. Patience was starting to wear thin, as little arguments started to develop among the troops. The kit inspection takes place in number five block, which houses the quarters for the lads that live in barracks. The block itself has an iron stairway at both ends that lead up to two billets on each end. The toilets are communal and are situated at the opposite end of the entrance hallway. Just before the entrance to the toilets, there are two doors left and right, each one leading to a long hallway with six live-in cubicles, three on each side of the hallway that house two men to a cubicle. At the end of the hallway that runs to the center of the block there is a door that opens to a white tiled shower room and hand basins. In the shower room there is another door which is locked to block off the other cubicles on the other side of the block. The door is there in case of a fire, and has keys on both sides in little glass boxes and can only be opened in emergencies, or for billet and kit inspections. At the other end of the block the layout is identical with no comparisons to the structural organization. Number five block has four billets in all, of which I am in charge of one. The other three billets are also under charge of Corporals, and between the four of us, we are responsible for the upkeep and cleanliness of the block.

It was now ten-to-nine, and the kit and locker inspection was at nine-o-clock, and everything was in order. The lads had their lockers opened, and their kits laid out on their beds. All the kits looked very good, laid out on tight crisp white sheets spread over the mattresses, with the bed blocks at the head of the bed. On top of the bed blocks were the number one uniform and great coat, folded in a military orderly appearance. Just in front of this was the squared off kit, and right down along the rest of the bed was all the military paraphernalia that one was issued with.

There were just two snags. One was, Jessie Dunne had lost the key of his locker, and the other one was Jimmy "Twitchy" Fagan was absent, and the door to his room was locked. After he had finished his inspection of the kits and lockers in the cubicles at the far side of the hall, I now handed over my cubicles to Quartermaster Feeney, otherwise known disparagingly by the Troops as "The Weasel" because of his slight frame, and pigeon chest. Lurking behind the pale dreary face was a cutting dry sarcastic wit, and an intense manner to all below his rank. After handing over, I fell in behind him as we entered the first cubicle. The occupant of this cubicle was Timmy Walsh, who had an annoying habit of repeating the person's name that he would be talking to. Timmy was a small lad with a lot of scars on his face and a bad wheezing chest. Both of these inflictions came from a car accident two years previous. Timmy's roommate was on leave, so this left Timmy to do all the cleaning of the room before the inspection.

"Ah, Welsh," said Feeney, "the only man I know that would be the healthiest man in the world if brains were a disease, is that not right Welsh?"

"Q....Q....ye know yourself, Q, if brains, Q, were a disease then we would be able to hang around together, Q, ye know yourself, Q," wheezed Timmy.

"Shut the fuck up, Welsh, and don't hand over your kit to me as you have ear fucked me enough already, just talk when asked," retorted a stern Feeney. Looking at a list on a board that he held in his hands, Feeney started the kit inspection. "Green shirts?" queried Feeney.

"Two, Q—Q, two." answered Timmy.

"I see only one in your kit; where's the other one, Welsh"?

"It's in the laundry bag in my locker, Q."

"Take it out and give me a look at it," said Feeney. Timmy went to his locker, and took out a blue laundry bag, and after a little root around inside it, he pulled out the other green shirt. It was as black as the ace of spades from the dirt of it. Timmy held it up by the collar, and with a look of sheer disgust on his face Feeney told him to throw it onto the floor.

"Cream shirts?" asked the Quarter, who was still looking at the green shirt on the floor, with utter astonishment on his face.

"Three, Q."

"I see one in your kit, Welsh, and you're wearing one, so where's the other one?"

"Q—Q, it's in the laundry, Q."

"Show it to me, Welsh, I can't wait to see," said Feeney with an air of anticipation. Timmy once again went to the laundry bag and pulled out the cream shirt that was even mankier than the green one. The collar was filthy, and it had what looked like a dried soup stain down the front of it. Feeney's face now turned from sheer disgust to revulsion, and with his head down and rubbing his eyes he told Timmy to throw it on top of the so called green one.

"Vests, I see one in your kit; no, hold on, Welsh, don't tell me, the other ones are in the fucking rag pool in your locker?" said Feeney. Timmy nodded, then turning to the laundry bag, he produced a vest that was so unpleasant looking that even I took a step back. The Quarter never said a word; he just motioned with his hand for Timmy to put the vest on top of the other dirt on the floor. Feeney just stood there and looked Timmy up and down in disbelief.

He then looked back down at his board to the next item on the list, and without realizing he uttered, "Underwear," and terror set in immediately. The blood drained from his face, and in a slow and vicious voice, and without losing a breath he growled at Timmy, "For-fuck-ing-get-about-it, do ye hear me? For-fucking-get-about-it, end of fucking story." He turned and walked from the room. He crossed the hall into Jessie Dunne's room and paused for a moment to look back at Timmy's room, giving a shudder of his shoulders in doing so. He now turned his attention to a calm looking Jessie who came to attention and informed the Quartermaster that he had lost the key of his locker, and therefore he could not lay his kit out for inspection.

Feeney walked over to Jessie's locker, and after casting his eye's over the lock, he said, "I'd open that lock with my flute, Dunne." He then reached into his pocket and produced a bunch of keys. He ran the keys through his fingers to find the right size to fit the lock, and then without deliberation he chose a small key, and inserted it into the small lock. Snap! The lock opened first time of trying. It was only a small cheap lock, but to look at the triumphant elation on Feeney's face would give the impression that he had opened the mysteries of the universe. Looking at Jessie I could see he no longer looked calm, as he now had small beads of sweat on his forehead, something was not right. Feeney then removed the lock from the hole in the locking latch, and flung open the two doors of the locker, and luckily in doing so he took a couple of paces backwards away from the locker. There was a loud thud from a large heavy object hitting the floor, and landing at Feeney's feet. It had violently emerged from Jessie's locker.

"A fucking motorbike engine," said Feeney in a disbelieving voice, while shaking his head. "What in the name of jasus are you doing with the engine of a motor——oh holy fuck," said Feeney peering into Jessie's locker. "He's got the whole of the bastarding motorbike in there," gasped the Quarter as he lowered his head into his hands. Walking over to the locker, I could see a wheel and handlebars on the floor of the locker, and on top of these was a frame of a motorbike a bit broken up and stuffed into the locker. I wondered what kind of a motorbike it was, and I turned to Feeney saying, "What is it?" meaning what make was it.

Feeney took my query up the wrong way, and looked at me with his mouth wide open for a few seconds before he retorted in his own sarcastic manner. "What is it?" he conducted in a voice of mimic. "Well let me see here, it could be a large jigsaw puzzle, or wait a minute, it could be a fucking Meccano set he got for fucking Christmas." He paused, placing his hands on his hips. "It's pieces of a piggy motorbike that is stacked up in the Minster's property, which that dilapidated brainless bollix is using as a mini fucking garage. Now does that answer your stupid question, Corporal?" said Feeney, and not waiting for my answer he walked over to Dunne and stood with his face almost touching Jessie's face. "Now listen to me, Dunne, and listen to me very careful like, because if you give me a smart answer, I will kick seven different kinds of fucking shit from you, do you understand?" said the Quartermaster, taking a step back away from Jessie. There was a nod of the head from Jessie, and then Feeney said, "What is that shit doing in your locker? And where is your kit?"

"I lost it, Quarter." replied Jessie, in a quivering voice, and an air of apprehension about him.

"So, Dunne, your telling me that you lost your kit; is that right?"

"Yes, Sir, I lost my kit."

"Well, Dunne, how did you lose it? Maybe you left it behind on a bus, or maybe you lost it through a hole in the back of your fucking locker. How in God's name did you lose it?" asked Feeney.

I nearly fell out of my standing when Jessie answered Feeney. "I lost it through a house of kings, when this other chap from the F.C.A. (part time soldiers) had four Queens. Having no money left to see him, he let me bet my kit, and I lost the whole fucking shebang, Quarter." explained Jessie, now becoming a little braver. I could understand the F.C.A. guy letting Jessie bet his kit, because the F.C.A. at the time were inadequately equipped of clothing and webbing gear, and a regular soldier's kit was like gold dust to them. Feeney now made a fist, and placed the first knuckle of his left hand between his teeth, and bit down on the knuckle. Then after a few seconds he took his knuckle from his mouth, and then pouting his lips, he let a roar that came deep from his lung's in a single breath, " Jasus!!!"

He then pulled his right fist back to pulverize a now trembling Jessie, but then thinking better of it he put his fist down. He walked to the door, and stepping out into the hall he called out to Cpl. Rankin, who was in charge of the billet at the other side of the entrance hall, to come to him and to bring with him two Troopers. When Cpl. Rankin and the two Troopers entered the room Feeney told the two Troopers to fall in back and front of Jessie. He then told Rankin that he, the Quartermaster, was placing Trooper Dunne under arrest, and Rankin was to march Trooper Dunne to the guardroom under escort, and to keep him there until the C.O. was ready to deal with him. Just as Rankin was about to march Jessie to the guardroom, Timmy Walsh came out of his room, and curiously asked Feeney, who was standing out in the hall next to Timmy's room, "Eh, Q-Q, what's going on, Q?"

"Nothing that concerns you, Walsh, now go back in—no! Hold it there for a minute, Walsh." said Feeney as he raised his hand to stop the escort. Standing there, the Quarter's icy stare went from Jessie to Timmy, and back to Jessie again, and then he could not resist one last show of derisiveness towards the two lads. "Let me ask you, Dunne, just by the off chance, did Walsh happened to change the oil in that engine for you and was he wearing a cream shirt at the time? Because it's either that or he is a mucky swine of an individual." Timmy glared at the grinning Feeney.

"Q-Q-Q, there is no call, Q, for saying that about me, Q," protested Timmy with an agitated voice. Feeney moved to the side and placed his mouth about two inches from Timmy's right ear, and in a voice that was unequivocal, said, "There was certainly a call for what I said, so listen to me, sonny, you double Dutch fuck, back the fuck off into your room because you're contaminating the clean air that is around me. Move it!" He kept his posture until Timmy retreated into the room. He was standing there within an air of silence, and thinking to myself of what a vile man Feeney was, when out of the blue the silence was broken by a threatening feminine voice coming from Twitchy Fagan's locked room

"If ye spoke to me like that, ye would be shoving your toothbrush up your arse to clean your teeth, or what's fucking left of them." said the voice, with intensity.

Feeney, having a look of disconcertion about him, looked at me, and quizzically asked, "Was that a woman's voice I heard coming from Trooper Fagan's room?"

"Either it's that Quarter, or Fagan's dick is caught in his zip," I quipped. Banging hard on the door, Feeney demanded that it be opened immediately. From behind the door, the female voice had its own demand, "Go away!" she yelped. "Go on now, fuck off, shag off with yourself, or I will go out there, and kick your living bollix up into your throat, d' ye hear me now?" she growled, and then went silent. I had to duck onto Timmy's room, as to not let Feeney see me laughing. Now, she could only be either drunk, or a head case, but knowing Twitchy, and his past conquests, it was more than likely both. Stepping back out into the hall I could see Feeney's face was as red as a beetroot from anger, and after rummaging through his overcoat pocket he pulled out a bunch of keys. These keys were the spare ones he always carried with him on inspections should he want to investigate any rooms that were locked. I walked toward him as he placed the spare key into the lock. The sight the Quarter and I were to behold when he unlocked and opened the door would live long in the memory. Twitchy was lying on his bed bollock naked in a drunken sleep and was dead to the world. The only way that we could tell that he was alive was that he kept pushing, pulling, and scratching at his nether regions. Just across from Fagan's bed, and standing in front of the wall heater that was situated under the window was a small, and obese woman who was naked except for a pair of grey Army socks that were pulled up to her knees. Her breasts were so large they came down onto her stomach, and thank God for small mercies, her stomach covered her private parts. To tell her age was quite difficult as she had long dark unkempt hair with long streaks of grey running through it. She had a pair of soccer eyes, one away, one at home. All in all, I think Cinderella was missing one of the ugly sisters. The room was in a heap with flagons of cider, and several empty vodka bottles strewn around.

Feeney looked the woman up and down with a look of disgust on his face, he then pointed at her, and with an informative air, and speaking to me, he said, "Do you know that we used to put things like that on display in the fucking Congo? I mean, what in the name of fuck is it?" he then turned his attention to Fagan, still lying there in his pelt, mauling himself. There was still not a word from the she troll by the heater. "Corporal," said Feeney, "stop that man interfering with himself."

"I'm not going to stop him interfering with himself, or nothing like it, Quarter, you stop him interfering with himself." I stated defiantly. Feeney looked at me for a moment, and then told me to cover him up, which I did. Feeney then left the room, and went back down the hall, and into Timmy's room. He returned with Timmy who was carrying his great coat over his arm. Timmy started to laugh when he clasped eyes on the scene that confronted him when entering the room.

"Shut the fuck up Walsh, and take your over-coat and cover up that monstrosity over there," ordered the Quarter, pointing at the nude encroacher.. Not liking what the Quarter said about her, she gave him the finger sign, and turned her back to us.

"Be the lamp lighting divine fuck," said Timmy. "Would ye look at the size of that arse, it must be breathing on its own."

"I'll stop your fucking breathing, Walsh, if you don't keep quiet, now throw the coat—wait a fucking second, what in the name of jasus is that?—is that what I think it is? It bastardingwell is, it's a web-belt I see around her back," said a squinting and disbelieving Feeney.

Spotting the web-belt before Feeney, I stayed quiet, hoping against hope that he would not see it.

The reason none of us could not see the web-belt from the front was that the folds of her stomach were hiding it. Feeney had enough, he grabbed the overcoat from Timmy, and as he was crossing the room he pointed at Twitchy in the bed, and conversing to me, said, "No matter what you have to do, Corporal, I want that sick bastard woken up, and placed under arrest. I'll see that he gets the digger (military prison) for using military equipment to get his sick fucking gratification." He now stood facing the woman's back. He threw the overcoat over her shoulders, at the same time telling her to get dressed, and she would be escorted from the barracks. The overcoat slipped to the floor, and as he bent down to retrieve it, he just got about head high level with her arse when she let out this fucking huge screamer of a fart. I think Feeney must have felt the heat from it alone, never mind the smell. She gave an evil cackle, and at last she started to get dressed. With his hand over his mouth, and his body giving heaving motions, Feeney rushed out the door. Timmy and I were in convulsions laughing.

Timmy stopped laughing long enough to stick his head out the door, and shout after Feeney, who was heading for the toilet, "Here Q-Q, d' ye think her arse could do with an oil change?" More titters.

Feeney came back a while later with the barrack Orderly Sgt., and two barrack policemen, but the woman had gone by now. Twitchy was arrested, and was locked up in the guardroom.

"How did she go?" inquired Feeney.

"She put Dunne's bike together, and fucked off, Q-Q." Timmy was arrested.

HERO TO ZERO

Celebration day, most of the Squadron was in the N.C.O' s mess to congratulate the General Purpose Machine Gun (G.P.M.G.) team who had just won the All Army shooting competition that afternoon. Everyone was in high spirits, not just for the G.P.M.G. victory but also for the free write off of booze for the troops, and the filling of the winning cup. All in all it was going to be one big piss up, on that you could be certain. The first person I encountered on entering the mess was Darby Kylie, and I just knew that it was going to be a very unusual and, most likely, intoxicating day. Darby was on the small side in height, and had blue eyes and a smile that could bring a graveyard to life. He was far from old, but had that cunning, old sweat persona about him, with a silver tongue and the gift of the gab. He was a good friend, and we were like birds of a feather; we liked a bit of crack and exceptional gargle.

I joined Darby at the bar and asked fat Paddy, the barman, for a pint. I was not surprised to see fat Paddy was already sweating profusely as the place was packed, and because of the free beer, the lads were a lot quicker getting back to the bar than they normally would be if they had to pay for it.

Fat Paddy put my pint down in front of me, and then with his elbow on the bar and his arm leaning forward and pointing down at the crowd in the mess, he said to us, "By fuck lads, are they not the greediest shower of bastards that ye ever met in your life? I have been watching this one little muck savage that's been up and down more times than the knickers of an overworked fucking streetwalker, and he isn't even belong or from the barracks." He then wiped the sweat from his forehead.

Darby looked at him and with the right eye half closed said, "Will ye shut the fuck up, Paddy; if you were not working and were on this side of the bar you would drink them off a fucking conveyor belt, not to mention the barrel that ye are more than likely hiding somewhere out the back and will sell later on for yourself," giving fat Paddy a wink. "For the love of divine will ye shut the fuck up, Kylie, you never know who in the name of jasus is listening to ye."

"Now will I put you on another pint," said Paddy wiping the counter.

"Ye can and one for himself," replied Darby, pointing at me. Darby and I were lashing back the pints and having a great crack at the bar, when to the left of us the winning cup was placed on the bar for filling with whiskey and cider. The honor of filling the cup went to the C.O. of the Squadron, Commandant Hook and Squadron Sgt. Gerry Wall. It could have been Ben Bollix the Blacksmith filling the cup, as the lads did not care who filled it as long as it was filled. The cup was so big; it took a lot of whisky and cider to fill it. Just as the C.O. was pouring the last drop into the cup, the door of the mess opened and in walked four U.S. Marines in battle dress uniform. When stepping through the entry door to the mess, the bar presents itself immediately on the left. The Marines were standing in the doorway with their sleeves rolled up and looking very gung-ho.

Commandant Hook looked at them for a few seconds and then turned to the Squadron Sgt. And, nodding at the cup, said, "Here, Gerry, give them fuckers a drop of that, and tell them that we are on our coffee break." He was smiling as he said so. Gerry Wall did exactly what the C.O. told him to do, and the Marines got the joke and the ice was broken. A shout came from somewhere among the lads, "Come in, lads, for fuck's sake and get a drink for yourselves, and spread out, one grenade and your all fucked." Laughter rang all around. I could see by the smiling expressions on their faces that the Marines felt right at home with the atmosphere that was generated throughout the mess. The Marines were over from the States on a visit to give lectures throughout the Defense Forces, and they were billeting in the block behind the N.C.O's mess. They introduced themselves to the C.O. and the Squadron Sgt., and then were promptly asked and served a drink of their choice by fat Paddy.

Of the four Marines, one was a black guy. They all sported the old fashion crew-cut and were all of the rank of Sergeant, and all of them over six feet tall. Darby and I felt like the hobbits, Bilbo and Frodo fucking Baggins as we stood next to them, so we went and sat down with the rest of the lads for the passing round of the cup. Just as the Squadron Sgt. called for order to allow the Commanding Officer to make the victory speech and to blow bubbles up the arseholes of the G.P.M.G. team, the Marines came over to the tables where most of our lads had congregated and ventured to ask if they could join our company.

Gerry Burnley jumped to his feet and said, "Of course ye can, lads, now sit down there and take the weight of your new desert boots and join in the craic," with his hand beckoning to the vacant seats around the table. One by one, we all introduced ourselves and vice versa. They had real wholesome all American forenames which were: Brad, Doug, Dillon, and Toby. When I heard their names I remember thinking to myself that they should be drinking a glass of milk and eating cookies with names like that. Well here they were in Ireland swigging back a whole shit load of drink, and, as they would say, having a nice day. The cup finally got to me, and I took a good gulp from it. I then passed the cup to Darby, who took three big swigs from it.

He then gave the cup to Doug the Yank, who was sitting next to him, and said, "Just hold on to that for a second and don't let it pass on to the next man, just a second." Then taking a green plastic mug from his pocket, he said, "Now be a good man, Doug, and pour some into the mug, and keep pouring until I say when, good man." Darby held out the mug and Doug poured. The roars and whinges of the lads at Darby and the Marine, who did not have a clue as to what was going on. Darby took a drop from the mug and lifting it in the air said, "Bite the butt end of me bollix, the lot of ye. When I was stuck out the back of the ranges this morning doing range sentinel and freezing me balls off, not one of you fuckers brought me out tea. So ye see, me good green Army mug might not have got any tea in it this morning, but by jasus there's something in it now that will keep me grand and fucking warm." He then stood up and, putting the mug in the air, roared, "Ye fucking ha." Then he took a drop from the mug and sat down. There were cheers and laughter from the lads and the cup got passed on. Darby, winking at Doug, said, "It never fails; ye see I was nowhere near range sentinel this morning, as a matter of fact I was lying on the bed in the billet while all this range shit was going on." Then with a devious smile on his face he embraced the mug and took another slug.

Doug smiled at Darby and said only one word, "Hustler," and then the two of them laughed and shook hands. The rest of the day went well. There was great banter between the Marines and ourselves, and everything was going grand until the inebriation kicked in and set off a dramatic sequence of events. The free bar had finished a good hour ago, and I was up at the counter to get a round in when I notice that fat Paddy and Brad the Marine were having a tit for tat at the end of the bar. I went over and asked them if there was a problem.

Brad, dropped his head and then rising it, slowly said, "Yeah, man, my name is Brad, and this barkeep here, all day, keeps insisting on calling me Joe, and another thing, I seemed to have been overcharged for the last round of beers I got from lard ass here." He was now holding onto the bar with both hands to keep from going sideways.

Fat Paddy was quite for a moment, then leaned across the counter and spoke, "Listen, Joe, the reason I call you and your friends Joe, is because all you assholes are G.I. Joe to me, and I did not overcharge ye. Maybe you're that drunk that you think your back home in the land of milk and honey at a happy hour in the Full Metal Jacket bar on fucking base. Now listen to me, if you ever call me lard ass again, I'll kick your Yankee-doodle arsehole all the way back to heartbreak ridge or whatever other fucking shit hole you came from; now, have a nice day." He walked away to serve and left the Marine with his mouth open. I went and got Toby, who was not that far gone with drink as the other three lads were, and he gave me a hand to bring Brad back to his seat before anything else kicked off between fat Paddy and himself. I went back to the bar and got the pints for Darby and myself, and told fat Paddy to stop messing the

Yank around, and he agreed. I then returned to our table of mayhem just in time to witness another ludicrous occurrence on behalf of Gerry Burnley. Gerry was a man's man; he liked to fish, hunt, and rugby ran in the family. Gerry and the black Marine, Dillon, were in deep conversation entirely about American football and rugby, which both had heated indifferences about each other's sports. At some stage in the debate, Gerry lost the rag and turning away, he swiped his left arm in the air as a sign to Dillon that the exchange of opinion was over. At the same time, he said, "Will ye go away, Dillon; ye know fuck all about rugby, end of story." He then turned and began talking rugby to Doug, Darby, and myself. Dillon was just out of earshot of our conversation, and I could see him leaning over to try to hear if Gerry was still going on about American football and rugby.

Just then Doug asked of Gerry, "Why, as being Irish, don't you drink the Guinness?" He was pointing at the half pint of stout in front of himself.

Gerry, who had turned away from Doug's Guinness question in exaggerated disgust was now face to face with Dillon, and without time to think, blurted out, "I can't stand the black shit." His face shriveled with embarrassment. Gerry put his hands over his face and then put his head in his lap, and that was when he missed Dillon winking at us. Bringing his head up from his lap and looking at Dillon, he made a sign of the cross with his finger on the middle of his throat, and with an apologetic voice said, " I swear to God, Dillon, I was talking about Guinness." He was looking at Dillon for a good reaction.

Darby moved forward in his chair saying, "That's right Dillon, he said that you looked like a pint of Guinness without the fucking head." He was trying to keep from laughing.

Spits were flying from the mouth of Gerry as he spluttered out, "Don't believe a word out of that lying bastard's mouth." Pointing at Darby he ranted on, "Will ye stop throwing petrol onto the flames, ye little bastard of a row riser?" He then turned and looked at Dillon. Gerry wised up when he saw Dillon in fits of laughter, "Ye knew all along I was talking about the Guinness, ye basketball dribbling shit head, though I have to admit I was caught. Yeah, I was caught alright, ye shower of fuckers," he said as he put his hand in the air. Dillon jumped up and smacked his hand off Gerry's hand, giving him a high five. The rest of us were slapping the tables and stamping our feet, and giving Gerry some stick.

After having the crack with Gerry and giving him a right slagging we settled back down. One of the lads from the other side of the mess broke into song, and sang a ballad, and we all joined in. When the song was finished, Darby got to his feet and shouted across the mess to the lad who had sung the song, "Ye sang that well, Higgins, considering ye were singing it through your arsehole." The whole mess was in laughter again. Just when I thought to myself that nothing worst could happen, Darby came up trumps.

Doug had just got back from the toilet and noticed fat Paddy collecting empty glasses from our table; he said to him, "Hey, buddy, what time is the bar over at." He then belched and excused himself.

"Well Douglas old boy the bar's not over until the fat man sings, and I don't have a fucking note in my head. Does that answer your question, buddy old pal?" said fat Paddy with sarcastic overtones in his voice. He then trudged his way back to the bar.

"What the hell time is it. Darby; I can't see this timepiece of mine, damn it," slurred Doug, who was by now completely pissed out of his military mind.

Darby put his arm around Doug's shoulder and said with a chuckle, "Bed, it's time to put your big helmet fitting head on your Marine pillow, and dream of taking a bullet for the President or running bollix naked through a paddy field, now come on, there's a good man," trying to get Doug to his feet.

Pulling away from Darby and pointing at his watch, he said, "Do you see that watch Darby; that watch cost me over three hundred bucks."

Then he mumbled something, and I said, "What's that he said, Darby?"

"I'm not really sure; I think he said he got the watch in ding-yang, dang-yang or ding fucking dong or some stupid fucking place like that," replied Darby, now pulling up his sleeve to reveal his own watch. "What do you think of that one, Doug?"

"Nice, really nice, man; is it Army issue, Darby?"

"You could say that, Dougster old man, but it is not of this Army. There is a chilling story behind how I came to have this watch, yes, Doug, a suspense story," said Darby as he scrunched his head down between his shoulders and shook them as if he had got a sudden shiver up his spine. Either Doug was just being kind to Darby or he was blind drunk, because there was nothing about Darby's watch that was remotely nice, in fact it was the ugliest displayer of time I have ever seen, ever. It was just a green digital with a short narrow cut that displayed nothing else but numbers. I was convinced that the scientific profession designed it to give you the exact time to commit suicide.

Sitting up in his seat and with a look of interest on his face, Doug enthusiastically pleaded, "Tell the story, Darby; come on, buddy, tell the story." He pulled his chair closer to Darby.

Taking a mouthful from his pint and then wiping his lips Darby began, "Your lads," and he pointed at Doug, "were in the Lebanon at the same time as I was. They were situated in Beruit, and I was up in the hills in a place called Tibnin, a safe haven for the warring factions in Lebanon, if you follow my meaning. I was on patrol this day when we received news that the Marines in Beruit had been ambushed and had taken a lot of casualties. We were then told that the group that was responsible for the attack was heading into our Area of Operations, and we were to set up mobile checkpoints at sporadic locations."

"And did they come into your area?" inquired Doug.

Darby vented his frustration, "Will ye fuck up and let me finish the piggy story, for fuck's sake. Now, we were only on our first mobile checkpoint on the outskirts of a small village when around the bend in the road came two B.M.W. cars loaded to the bollix with the dissidents who had attacked the Marines. They were not for taken; they leaped from their cars with their weapons, and a fire fight ensued. We won the fire fight in the end, and they took a lot of casualties but not before I took a Kalashnikov round in the knee." He pulled up the left leg of his slacks to reveal a scared and shattered knee, or what was left of it. There were gasps all round, except for myself, as I had seen that kneecap so many times in different circumstances. Darby continued, "I was put in a U.N. ambulance alongside one of the Arabs, and he was bleeding very bad. Now this is the strange part, as he was lying across face on to me, he stretched out his arm towards me and pointed at his watch and said in a small eerie whisper, 'MARINE!' and then he fell into unconsciousness. I reached across and yanked, forgive the pun, the watch off his wrist and thought to myself, that fucking watch will be a memory of what I did to help the U.S. of A. Marine Corp. That, my friends, is the story in a nutshell as seen through the eyes of this humble soldier." He then lowered his head very slowly. I think I would have cried at that moment if I had not known Darby better than that. Applause and pats on the back all round for Darby. Putting his hands in the air for hush, Darby said, "Doug, I would be honored if you would accept this watch to remind you that your buddies were not over there on their own in that foreign land."

"I will gladly except, but only if you accept my watch as a token of respect for a hero," said Doug as he stuck his chest out and at the same time removed the watch from his wrist.

The smile on Darby's face was short lived as a voice from behind us bellowed, "You were never in the Lebanon, Darby, and your busted knee was down to a land rover accident; do you not remember, Darby?" It was Dozy Davies. Of all the people to stop and listen to the story, it would have to be Dozy. He would say things without thinking, and to make matters worse he was pissed.

In an instance Doug had his watch back on his wrist. "Shut fucking up, Davies, ye claw hammer; what are ye drinking, fucking truth serum?" said Darby showing Davies a fist. Davies went away fairly rapid.

Doug shook his head and said, "Buddy, you have just gone from hero to zero in my eyes." And then there was silence. At that moment a voice came from under a table at the far side of the mess, "I'm not singing through my fucking arsehole, Kylie." Everyone laughed. The Marines called Darby a cheeky bastard and a silver tongued hustler and all was forgiving.

I asked Darby why did he say the Arab said, "MARINE?"

He retorted, "Yeah, I thought of that myself; I should have said that the Arab eerily whispered, "Royal Canadian Mounted Police." Would you ever fuck off?" He gave a grin. Darby then put his arm around Doug in comrade fashion and slipped the badges from his jacket.

WHO'S THAT MAN?

The Company Sergeant walked to the front of the parade and pulled the cords on the hood of his military parka jacket to their limit to fend off the driving rain. Company Sgt. Finch was a balding, middle aged, red cheeked disciplinarian, who most often would be seen walking with his head bowed, as though he was fretting or in deep religious thought, which made me wonder if he would have been more suited to the role of Brother Superior in a Christian school, or an Abbot in a monastery. He did not seem to be cut out for the Defense Forces, as I detected when I was attached to his Company for two weeks last year, as part of an armored car crew involved in a Command exercise. He was totally inept when military tactical procedures came to the fore. His position of rank was down to his essence of discipline over others.

He was now standing on the camp square in front of a combination of troops from various Units of their Command, who were supplied as a labour force to carry out menial tasks in the camp in support of troops that would be taking part in a military exercise in and around the surrounding area of this County Cork based camp, for the next four days. His face was showing fine creases from the tightening of the cords, with heavy raindrops dripping from the end of his nose down onto his lips to mix with saliva that was ejecting from his mouth as he started to speak with speed and aplomb. "The sooner we get this over with, the sooner we get out of the rain. After ye put your gear into your allotted billets, which are directly behind where you're now standing, ye can make your way over to the dining hall where there will be a hot meal to eat. Now, let me tell ye? I will stand for no nonsense for the next four days that we are here; we have a job to do, and we will carry it out to the best of our abilities, and let me tell you that I will make sure that we do? Now fall out and get out of this rain," said the Company Sgt., who was already scurrying away to get shelter.

Wilforth Camp is a small military outpost in County Cork, which is mostly used for billeting, and replenishing training troops on tactical exercises in the area. The billet buildings in the camp mainly consist of wooden structure with old pot-bellied stoves as the only means of heating, which I have to say that I have experienced before, and found to be sufficient to keep a wooden billet warm. The only solid constructions are the cookhouse and dining hall and a small house that is used to accommodate officers when in camp. There is also a guardroom made from bricks and mortar that is inferior in quality and made all the more unattractive in appearance by the corrugated tin roof that covers the top of the building. We were not in the camp as part of the work detail; by we, I refer to one Sergeant, two Corporals (of which I am one), and six Troopers from the Cavalry Corps.

Our purpose in the camp was security, which consisted of one N.C.O. and two troopers carrying out an armed duty in the guardroom over the next four days, which will be shared between us on a twenty four hour basis. The duty would commence as soon as we had settled in and had something to eat. We made our way to our allotted billet and were pleasantly surprised to find that the potbellied stove had already been lit, and the room was snug and warm, with the fuel bin filled to capacity with turf. Putting my gear on top of the bed that I had chosen, I looked over at the burning, bulbous cast iron stove, and could not help but wonder who had and for what reason, contributed their time to make us comfortable on our arrival, as it had never happened before. Not even in the dead of winter when we were attached to these sort of camps, did we have fires lit for us, so why now I asked myself.

Just then the answer presented itself in the form of Coy-Sgt. Finch, who had hastily entered the room rubbing his hands together. "Everything in order, Sergeant?" asked the Coy-Sgt., as he walked past us towards the far end of the room, and stopped in front of a neatly made up bed which had a blue civilian quilt gracefully covering the army blankets that lay beneath.

"Grand," replied Lenny Lewis, the Sergeant that was in charge of our section. "It's grand and fucking warm," enthused Lenny, as he threw his bed block onto the floor.

"There will be no swearing in this billet, or in my presence for the next four days from yourself Sergeant, or your underlings, do you understand that Sergeant?" said the Company Sgt. in an almost confessional-box whisper. He began fluffing his pillow while staring up the room with a demanding expression on his face for Lenny to answer in compliance to his forceful request. Although the Sergeant possessed a beguiling innocence and youthful face and a lackluster attitude, he was in fact in his thirties, and was deliberate and intense in nature. Before Lenny could answer, the billet door was flung open with a devil may care manner, and entering through it was Trooper Eddie Smith.

"I'll tell ye one thing, boys; I'm only basteringwell lepping with the fucking hunger. I'd mill a fucking kangaroo's bollox done in batter this minute, because I'm only fucking starving," bellowed Eddie, as he dropped his carrier bag to the floor. As I looked at Eddie standing there pushing his round rimmed glasses upwards onto the bridge of his long pointed nose, and with his long skinny frame, I could not help but wonder that with his immense appetite and all that he eats, why he never puts on weight.

"What the fuck is wrong with ye lot? What in the name of jasus are ye looking at? By the way you're looking at me ye think I had pissed in your fucking pockets or something; what in the lantern fuck is wrong?" inquired Eddie, with a touch of anxiety in his voice as he lifted his bag from the floor, and moved to a vacant bed to his right. Ben McGahan was the first to break out laughing, and with the exception of Sgt. Lewis and Coy-Sgt. Finch, the rest of us in the room joined in.

"Well Sergeant Lewis, are you going to do something about this?" said Finch, raising his voice over the laughter.

Lenny placed his chin into his hand, and thought for a moment before saying, "I am, C.S.—right everybody fall in outside." He then walked to and out the door with the rest of us following behind. Being the last out, I turned to close the door and could see Finch sitting on the side of his bed with a book in his hand, and a pretentious smug grin on his face. "Right!" said Lenny, as he walked away rapidly up and along the small road outside the billet. "Come on, lads, were going to get something to eat, and leave that stainless tongue asshole of a C.S. to himself." he spewed, as he now headed in the direction of the dining hall, much to the delight, and most certainly a relief, to Smithy. Lenny was still mumbling to himself about Finch as we entered the dining hall, and took our place in the queue to get something to eat.

Squeezing my right shoulder with his enormous hand, and placing his head over my left shoulder, Ben McGahan enthusiastically said, "Will ye look who's dishing out the grub, are we going to be in for a right laugh down here with him on board, or what?"

"Who?" I said, as I looked along the inside of the queue towards the serving area where the cooks were dishing out the food.

"Slick," chuckled Ben, just as my eye's fell upon the conspicuous and somewhat daunting figure of Private Leonard Halligan. He was known to officers and men alike by his nick-name "Slick" because of his love of hair-oil which he would use in abundance to comb back his red hair, which was beginning to show signs of premature greyness, as he was only in his early thirties. There was other distinguishing characteristics about Slick that would make people who were unacquainted with him feel anxiously apprehensive when he would first enter their immediate vicinity, like, overgrown red colored eyebrows that matched long thick sideburns that ran down the side of his face. He had large gleaming eyes that seemed to be in direct competition with his mirrored hair, and a deep gruff voice that was orally intimidating when put into use, to which he was now doing at present to a skinny Private that was three places in front of me in the queue for food.

Slick had placed a shriveled rasher that resembled a small ear onto the skinny Private's plate, and with the rasher being the first of the food served onto the large plate, it seemed to look smaller than it was. "What kind of a rasher is that?" asked the disgruntled Private, and at the same time lifting the plate in an upward motion towards Slick.

"It's a fucking back rasher! If ye don't want it, give it fucking back—now move on," snarled Slick. The embarrassed Private awkwardly pulled his plate back toward himself in the knowledge that the lads in the queue that were in earshot of what had been said were laughing.

"Well will ye give me two rashers, will ye?" asked the Private, trying to save face.

"I will," said Slick, "one today and one tomorrow." He then gestured with his hand that was holding the serving spoon, for the skinny Private to move on, which he did, to the amusement and delight of the lads that were following after in the queue.

"Jasus, will ye look at the drunken head on the fat fucker?" pointed out Smithy, who also underlined the fact that Slick's stomach was resting on the hot-plate in front of him.

"How's it cutting, Slick?" I asked with no real meaning, as I now stood in front of him to be served.

Slick looked up at me, and then glancing down the line behind me at the rest of the Calvary lads, he said, " Ah lads! It's great to see ye all down here. I'll tell ye this. There is fine gargle in the boozer down the road; I'll see ye all there in an hour, and we'll have a right laugh. Here have a few of these, their small." He placed three rashers onto my plate.

"That's bloody favoritism," said a smiling Harry Bentley, the Cook Sergeant, who was serving out the food alongside Slick. Harry, being the same age as Slick, was much fitter and trimmer looking, and due to his head of black thick hair, and his complete abstention from alcohol made him look younger than his cooking counterpart. Turning my head sideways with a smile on my face I could see that the skinny Private who was filling his cup from the tea container at the other end of the tray running rail was staring intensely at the three rashers that had been put onto my plate. He stopped filling his cup, and returned it to his tray which he then began to push hastily along the running rail back towards a confrontation with Slick, it would seem.

"How come he got three fucking rashers-why the hell is that?" inquired the Private of Slick, in a shaky and flustered voice.

"Right!" said Slick, sticking out his hand towards the skinny Private. "Will ye give me your plate, please?" requested Slick in a mannerly tone. The Private handed his plate of double sausage, egg and chips, with a measly rasher, over to Slick, with a look of satisfaction on his face. Reaching out his hand Slick took the Private's plate, and placed it over the container that held the chips. In one felled swoop he removed almost half the chips on the plate into the container, and then handed the plate back to the wide-eyed Private. Slick then pointed the serving spoon at the Private, and growled, "Go on, ye covetous greedy bastard ye, go on fuck off before I go around there and kick what's left of your chips up your bony fucking arse, one at a time."

"That's right Slick, with fucking tomato sauce on them," cried out Smithy. Everyone suddenly went quiet and stared at Smithy, with the exception of the skinny Private, who was still looking at Slick, in a state of apprehension.

"What?… What?" said Smithy, looking a bit bewildered.

"Tomato sauce—tomato—fucking sauce!… Just shut up Smith, just stay the fuck quiet," expressed Lenny, rolling his eyes upwards, and shaking his head.

Smithy took a few paces to where I was standing, and first pointing at the cook Sergeant, and then at the private, he said, "Either ye hurry the fuck up, or I will take a bite out of his skinny arse, and right now it would only be the bone of his arse that I would leave—because I'm only starving with the basteringwell hunger, now can we put a move on, for fuck's sake?" He then walked back and took his place in the stillness of the queue.

It was Harry Bentley who broke the icy atmosphere. "Right!" Harry shouted, as he reached over and took the stunned Private's plate, and lavished it with chips, and gave a short unalloyed apology. After giving the Private back his replenished plate, and sending him on his shattered way, he told Slick that his presence was needed in the kitchen. The two of them disappeared into the kitchen for what apparently was a rollicking for Slick, and pressure for the red-faced, and overheated young cook that Harry left on his own to dish out the grub. With a cup of tea in his hand, Harry Bentley made his way across the dining hall, and taking a chair from the table adjacent to ours, he placed it at our table, and sat down with us. He put the cup of tea on the table, and then after rubbing the weariness from his eye's with the palms of his hand's he hesitantly told us that Slick had stormed out after he had words with him concerning his behavior towards the skinny Private.

"Slick being Slick, he'll more than likely head straight for the pub up the road—what's it named?" uttered Lenny, with head back and eyes closed, trying to recall the name to mind. Before Lenny so much as got a mental image of the pub, Harry informed him that it is called "The Watering Hole," and that is where Slick has been since he landed with the advance party last Friday evening.

"Yeah! It's a watering hole all right! That big fucker that owns the hole, waters down the drink, and it's a fucking hole alright, but the only shit hole around for miles." interjected Ben with a touch of hostility and resentment. When asked what he was going to do about Slick, by Lenny, Harry said that he was going to do nothing, as Slick and he go way back to when they both started their careers in cooking. He told us that he would just have to cover Slick for the next four days, and hope against hope that Slick would not get into trouble. Lenny spilled half of his tea down the front of his jacket, as he took the cup down from his mouth rapidly and placed it on the table on hearing Harry was going to cover Slick.

"Harry! Are you out of your chef's fucking head or what? I think you're eating too many of your own fucking sour sausages. Look, Slick is a lovely guy and all, but there is no surer thing that Slick will get himself into trouble, the drink will see to that, and when he does, it's you who will get it in the neck for covering him. For fuck's sake Harry, think about it, what?" said Lenny, now dabbing at his jacket with his cap. Harry stood up from the table, and after picking up his cup he gave Lenny a wry grin. Without saying a word he turned and walked towards the kitchen looking somewhat forlorn in appearance.

On returning to the billet, Lenny informed us that Troopers Kelly, Harrington and himself were going to take the first guard duty, and that he would make out a duty roster for the rest of the week, and later on, he would stick it to the back of the billet door so everyone could see when exactly they were on duty during the week. "In any case I have to get out of here tonight, as I could not spend the first night listing to Vatican fucking jaws over there," said Lenny, pointing to the empty bed-space of Company Sergeant Finch.

"I wonder where he is?" I asked Lenny.

"More than likely he is in one of them fields out there self-flaying himself for his fucking sins of the day," expressed Lenny.

"Yeah, and probably pulling the handle out of his fucking stomach at the same time—the dirty gic-head," Smithy inserted to Lenny's comment. Lenny laughed the loudest of the lot of us, and was still laughing as the two lads and he headed out the door for the guardroom. Lenny and the two lads had only just left when into the room walked Trooper John "Gudser" Knight. The reason for Gudser been so late was that he was designated back in our home Unit by Lenny (who had a distaste for Gudser) to the task of driver for the pompous, and utterly presumptuous Captain Shovelin—the Camp Commandant for the next four days. Looking at the hung-over head and the still bleary eyes of Gudser from the night before, and by the speed he was changing out of uniform at, I could tell that he was heading straight for the pub, and giving the dining hall a miss. John "Gudser" Knight was insolently antagonizing to superior ranks, and when the fancy takes him, playfully rude to all else. Lenny would often say of him, that he was a short arsed twenty-eight year old going on sixty who could change the atmosphere of a sauna to that of an igloo with his cutting and derisive remarks from a mouth that could only be described as a shite-pot. Most of the troops liked his devil-may-care attitude, and paid no heed to a verbal volley that he would send their way.

Tightening the belt on his civilian slacks, and pushing, and trying to squeeze his foot into his shoe hastily at the same time, Gudser said, "Is any of ye shit heads going for a pint, or do I have to drink on me own?" He now stood on one foot while jerking his other foot from side to side trying to squeeze it into his shoe. Smithy jumped off his bed, and he and I told Gudser that we would join him, but we wanted to have a quick wash first. "Well hurry up for fuck's sake," wheezed Gudser, as he had lost the battle of getting his foot into his shoe, and was now holding it, trying to untie the lace. Smithy stopped as he was walking by Gudser's bed, and placing his washing gear down upon it, he took the shoe from Gudser's hands and said "Give the fucking thing here ye useless piece of shit ye." He then took the lace by both ends, and dangling the shoe across his chest he pulled as hard as he could, and in doing so he tighten the shoelace into a knot that was so small that it looked like it had been welded together, and was not for opening. "Now!" said Smithy, with a mischievous smile on his face, as he handed the shoe back. "Will that keep ye busy until we have a wash?"

"What kind of an arse hole are you? Ye dick head," shouted Gudser, as Smithy and I went laughing out the door. When we returned from the wash-room Gudser had gone. Ben told us that Gudser told him to tell us that he could not wait, and that he would see us down in the pub and that was where we next met him. On walking through the door of the bar, I could see Gudser sitting at the counter beside Slick, who was standing, but not at all to steady on his feet.

"Ah jasus lads, what are ye having?" said Slick, inhaling the words as he spoke, as he laid his half-closed eyes on Smithy and myself. "Here, Jacko! Give the lads a brace of pints, me good man." ordered Slick, of the very tall and overweight barman, and owner of the roadhouse. "Give them a pint each of that Aussie stuff," said Slick, as he adjusted his trousers back up under his beer belly. "No! For fuck's sake I can't stand the bleeden stuff," cried Smithy, who was physically flinching.

"Why? What's wrong with it?" I inquired.

"Yeah! Like what ails ye boy?" asked Jacko, the barman. Smithy looked around at the three inquisitive faces looking at him, and a drunk and stupefied facial expression from Slick, which urged Smithy to start and begin to explain.

"I walked into this bar a while back, and just as I walked in, there was this ad on the telly about this Aussie beer, and it showed an Australian geezer holding a pint of the stuff, and it had a big white frothy, mouth-fucking-watering head on it. Then the geezer said, 'It's like a heavenly angel crying on your tongue,' ye know—with one of those Aussie fucking " gadaay" accents, and the fucker was right. It was absolutely gorgeous; it was… like a heavenly angel crying on your tongue. What they failed to tell in the ad….that, the next morning it was like a load of hell's fucking angels walking all over your bas-tering head. So no thanks, I'll have a pint of the black." said Smithy, pulling out a stool, and sitting up on it next to Gudser. We all had a laugh, except for Jacko, who just scratched the back of his head as he walked away to pull two pints of stout, as I also opted for a black one. "How in the name of jasus did ye get that lace open?" Smithy, asked Gudser.

"Easy," was Gudser's reply.

"Easy, my-bollocks; Houdini wouldn't have opened that fucking thing—who are ye trying to cod," said Smithy, tapping the side of his pointed nose with his index finger. Leaving the two lads to get on with their petty row I ventured over to Slick, who was by now, well passed his pissed by date; he was having a murmuring argument with the beer tap in front of him. Cautiously I approached him and asked him was he all right. He told me that he was tired, and that he was going back to the camp for a kip. He then ordered an-other pint, coming to a decision that he would stay; he did not think that he had fulfilled his quota. Thinking of the busy main road that passed outside this pub, and the stretch of hard shoulder on the road as being the only means of a path to walk on in order to get back to the camp, which was about three quarters of a mile from the roadhouse, I decided to walk back to the camp with Slick when he was ready to leave. Turning around to go back to my pint and leave Slick to get on with his one sided embroiling debate with the beer tap, I saw that Quartermaster Mick Jevins had arrived on the scene, in civilian attire, and standing next to him was Ben McGahan. Mick was an unusual Quartermaster, unusual, in comparison to the normal grumpy and rigorously enforcing Quartermasters that was to be encountered throughout the Army. He was in contrast a very endearing and sensitive man, with a cheery and amiable temperament who was small in structure, but big in heart.

"I thought the C.S. would be with ye, Mick?" inquired Gudser of the Quartermaster. Placing his pint down on the counter and wiping his mouth with the back of his hand, he told Gudser that the C.S. was in a foul mood because he forgot to pack and bring his civilian shoes with him to the camp.

"Now, ye know him, he's a stickler for rules and regulations; he would not wear his army boots with his civvies, and therefore he opted to stay in camp. Fucked if I'd go without me pint," said Mick, taking his pint in his hand, and after giving it an endearing, but somewhat creepy look, took a large gulp from it. He then, keeping his pint in his hand, walked away towards a group of lads from the fatigue party in the camp that were playing darts at the far end of the pub. "I bet Finch did bring those shoes with him, didn't he? You took those fucking shoes, didn't ye?" asked Smithy, with an accusing glint in his eye's towards Gudser.

"Eh no, I didn't my sack take the pricks shoe's, and what brought ye to that conclusion? Ye bony fuck."

"Because me good man, Gudser! The lace that I tighten earlier on was not leather, and the ones that ye have in your shoe's now are. Can ye explain that?" enthused Smithy, with an air of exultance about his shoelace detection.

"Bite the butt end of me bollix," was Gudser's reply to Smithy. Gudser stood up and told us he was going for a game of darts and walked off to the other end of the bar.

"I'd bet any money that he robbed that shit head's shoes, and if Finch finds out that he did not leave them at home but were stolen instead, well he will only crease the whole fucking lot of us, all because that fucker gone down there to play darts, needed a lace," complained Smithy, to Ben and myself. Sitting up on the stool that Gudser had vacated, Ben told Smithy that he did not give two fucks about Finch's shoes or laces or anything else about him for that matter; he was here to enjoy his pint, and that's all that mattered. Smithy went into a huff when I told him that I agreed with Ben, and that he should forget about the whole thing. On returning from his darts game a short time later, Gudser bought Smithy a pint, and all was forgotten. "Here! Suss out that fat bastard behind the bar, and see can ye squeeze a few bob out of him." said Smithy, nudging Gudser. "Go on ask him for a lend of twenty until Friday; he won't have a fucking clue that we are leaving on Thursday. If he lends it, then I will hit him for a few bob tomorrow night—go on, go on for fucks sake," urged Smithy to Gudser, as he gently pushed him slightly down the bar to lay in wait for Jacko to serve down this end of the pub. He did not have to wait that long for Jacko to waddle towards our position at the bar, because I raised my hand in the air, and signaled to him that I wanted a pint; I just had to see the outcome between Gudser and Jacko. Smithy, conveniently departed for the toilet as Jacko approached, and took my order.

Gudser, standing at the bar in front of the pump that the barman was now pulling my pint, said, "Here Jacko, would ye give me a score till Friday?"

"Certainly," replied Jacko, not looking up from the pint he was pulling. But looking at his raised eyebrows and puckered lips gave me the impression that Gudser was in for a rude awaking. With two fingers hitting the handle of the tap in an upward and snappy motion Jacko brought the flow of the beer to a stop. "Cork—one goal and five points....Kerry...three goals and fifteen points. Now! How's that for a fucking score, because that's the only fucking score that ye will get from me, boy, de ye understand like?" retorted Jacko, who then took my three quarter pint of stout, and placed it on top of the beer tray to settle, before he would then top it off to the finished article.

"Well fuck me, what?" said an embarrassed Gudser, who, after placing what was left of the beer mat that he had nervously torn to shreds onto the counter, continued, " you're a real cute Cork fucker—all right."

"No! For fuck's sake, no! Jacko is a cute Kerry fucker; he hails from Kerry," interceded, a now revitalized Slick, on behalf of the fat barman. "That's right boy, I'm a Kerry man taking the money from the not so cute Cork men—how about that then, boy? And I'll have ye know that I am a descendant of Daniel— the liberator—O' Connell, from Cahirciveen in County Kerry—come up for fucking air now, me Kildare boyo," expressed Jacko, braggingly, more so to anyone in earshot rather than directly at Gudser, with hands on hips, intrusive chest, and an air of triumph about him. Coming back from his visit to the toilet, I noticed Smithy siding up alongside Slick, rather than return to where Jacko and Gudser were having a heated discussion. "What's the story, Slick? What was that fat fucker of a barman saying to Gudser?" I heard Smithy ask Slick.

"Didn't hear it all." said Slick, whose moment of revitalization had somewhat deteriorated rapidly, as he now had one eye closed, and was squinting at Smithy with the other one. Smithy asked him again what Jacko had said to Gudser? " Jacko...Jacko told Gudser that...that he had a cousin that goes way back...who was a collaborator and a fucking sleeveen from Kerry, and has the same name as that fucking eejit of a country and western singer from Donegal. That's all I can fucking tell ye, Smithy-eh-Smithy," varyingly explained Slick. Seeing me laughing, Smithy broke out laughing, and then Ben McGahan, who had also been listening to what Slick had said, also went into the kinks. Gudser was standing at the bar looking at us with a fierce scowl on his face; he must of thought that we were laughing at him. He then turned and called out to Jacko, who was walking away from him.

"What ails ye, boy?" asked the barman, as he turned around to face Gudser.

"Have ye any ham sandwiches left?" inquired Gudser.

"I have a pile of them left," replied Jacko, as he walked over towards the glass cooler. "Well, that's your own fucking fault for making so many ye fat sappy bastard," spewed Gudser, who then turned to look at us with a big self-redeeming smile on his face. Very quickly Smithy and I were off our stools to lead Gudser away from the now fuming and red faced barman. "That's right lads, take the little fucker of a weasel away and out the front door with him, before I go around and kick his fucking arse, go on—away with him now," instructed Jacko, to Smithy and myself. Shrugging his shoulders, Gudser freed himself from my grip, and announced to all that he was leaving peacefully.

"But before I go can ye tell me something?" he asked Jacko. Without waiting on Jacko to say yes or no, he continued, "Looking at the obese nature of your body, and the way you speak to people, well I was wondering if your arse has its own set of teeth; it seems to me, looking at that oversized stomach—" we quickly started to walk him away "—that ye eat and shite from both fucking ends—ye big lard arse fucker," he shouted back over between Ben and Smithy's shoulders, as they were reversing him towards the pub door. In a way it was a blessing in disguise that Gudser got barred from the pub, because Slick, sliding off his stool and picking up a white bag from the counter, shouted to Gudser (who was being squeezed out the door screaming a string of expletives) that he would walk back with him. At least now I could enjoy the rest of the night in the knowledge that Slick would get back to the camp, safely.

The remainder of the night went quite enough, except for Mick Jevins; every time he walked by where we were sitting, and without stopping he would constantly tell us that he seen nothing, nothing at all. Getting back to the billet that night we were careful, and very quiet when entering so as not to wake Finch, or Mick Jevins for that matter, who had left the pub a good bit before us.

"Here! Gudser is not in his bed, I wonder where he is?" whispered Smithy, across the room to me. Looking across the darken room I could make out Gudser's bed with the help of the glow coming off the potbellied stove. His bed block was still on top of the mattress along with his carrier bag. So, I put two and two together, and I quietly told Smithy that Gudser would more than likely be across in Slick's room, drinking. I told him that I was sure that there was a takeaway of drink in the white plastic bag that Slick took away from the pub, for his morning cure, and that they were probably dug into it right now. There was no reply from Smithy who I thought must have fallen asleep, until I was just nodding off myself when I heard, "Jammy fucking bastards!" coming from his bed space. The next morning I awoke with a seedy head from the proceedings of the night before, and looking around the billet to get my bearings, my eyes fell on a gruesome sight. There, lying face down on top of his bare mattress was Gudser, wearing only his white army issued y-front underpants, which—to the weakening of my already queasy stomach—had several "skid marks" imprinted into them. Shaking my head and diverting my eyes from the chocolate runway I got out of bed, and walked over to look at the duty roster that Lenny had pinned to the back of the billet door.

"Check for me, will ye?" Smithy called out to me as he sat up in his bed rubbing the sleep from his eyes, before putting on his glasses. Smithy smiled and seemed to be happy when I told him that he, Johnson, and I were taking over guard room duty from Lenny and the lads at nine this morning, until nine tomorrow morning. Returning from having a shower and a shave Smithy and I entered the billet to find Finch and Quartermaster Jevins standing at the end of Gudser's bed debating.

"No!" said Mick Jevins, to Finch. " I will not charge him, I mean, what do ye want me to charge him with "soiling government property" if you want to charge him then go ahead, but I'm not charging him, Terry, and that's for sure. I mean most men from time to time have a few skid marks—don't you, Terry?"

"No, I bloody well don't. Besides skid marks is one thing, but to look at that," Finch said, pointing at Gudser's jocks, "you would think he went out of control with the bloody handbrake on."

"Well I'll leave it in your hands as I have to go and carry out an ordnance check, I'll talk to ye later," said Mick, who then scurried out the door.

"Right Corporal, wake that man, and tell him to get dressed, and most certainly to put clean underwear on," Finch conveyed to me. He then told me that if Gudser was still there, and not gone to his place of employment when he returned in a quarter of an hour, that he would find something to charge him with, he then walked briskly from the room. What a relief! Just as I turned around and was dreading going into the shitty bed space, Gudser turned over and sat up in the bed, reaching and taking a cigarette from its box, he lit it up. Looking at the head of Gudser, I could tell that he was still half-cut.

"What's wrong with that bastard of a C.S.? And where did he get skid marks from?" asked Gudser, who then tried to mimic Finch. "Ooh skid marks, ooh bloody handbrake—fucking nance prick. Does he not know unadulterated shite marks when he sees them?" he said, with a pleasant expression on his drunken face. "Come on! Let's go for our breakfast before that fucker puts us off it," said Smithy to me, who was already moving very fast from the room. On our way up the camp for breakfast we met Ben who was with Tommo Johnson, they had just come from finishing their breakfast. I told Ben to make sure that Gudser had not gone back to sleep, and I also told Tommo that Smithy and myself would meet him outside the guardroom at ten to nine. After the breakfast the two lads and I relieved Lenny and the lads on taking over the camp duty.

Before Lenny left he educated me on what tasks had to be carried out on the duration of the duty, and what times of the night that the patrols were to be executed. "Right so, I'm off to my bed," Lenny informed me. "Oh, By the way, did that fucking eejit Knight get out of the bed? Because he has to collect Captain Shovelin at nine, and drive him out to where the exercise is going on; he wants to see how they are all getting on, as they went straight out on the ground yesterday evening." said the Sergeant, yawning out the last part of the sentence. Through the chicken wire of the locked compound gate I told

Lenny that Gudser was awake when I went for my breakfast, but as I came straight to the guardroom from the dining hall I could not say for sure if he had not gone back to sleep. "He had better fucking not have, for his sake," said Lenny, as he then walked away whistling tunelessly.

Turning away from the gate I started to walk towards the guardroom when a familiar voice shouted, "Good morning." to me, it was Slick. He was coming out the door, and down the three steps of his billet which are located about five yards or a little more, directly in front of the compound gate, with the remainder of the billet running adjacent with the wire fence of the guardroom compound. Going back to the gate I asked Slick if he was all right. He told me that he will be as soon as he got down to the "Watering Hole" for a cure, and off he went on another drunken escapade. No sooner was I through the guardroom door, and putting on the kettle when I could hear Lenny shouting my name from outside the gate.

"What's wrong, Lenny?" I asked as I opened the gate to let him in to the compound. Walking through the gate, Lenny had his right hand fully extended covering his eyes, and the left one holding the back of his head. "Did something happen to the back of your head, Lenny?" I inquired curiously.

"No-no, it's that fucking asshole Knight. Go over to the room and place him under arrest; if I would have stayed there I would have fucking killed the little bastard. Go over now and arrest him before I change my mind and murder the fucker. Go on! I'll stay here until ye get back," said a ferocious looking Lenny, as he took the gate key from my hand. Taking Smithy from the guardroom to act as arrest escort to Gudser we both headed out the gate, and made tracks to carry out the unsavory task over in the billet. Walking down the path that led to the billet we encountered C.S. Finch who was also headed in that direction. He asked me if Trooper Knight was in the billet, as the Camp Commandant was getting impatient waiting for Trooper Knight to drive him out to the location of the exercise. The question he posed seemed quite pointless as he pushed his way passed Smithy and myself without waiting on my reply, and walked down the path and into the billet. Following him into the billet I observed a sight that would be etched into my memory for the rest of my life. For there, hunched down on the wooden floorboards that ran down the middle of the room, was Gudser. He was being rigorously scrutinized by a silent and scrunched up ghastly faced C.S. Finch, who was directly behind him, and in front of Smithy, and myself. The reason for the contortion on the face of Finch, was the image he could see before him of Gudser heating up a mess tin of stew on a small portable, and lightweight metallic military issued Hexi Cooker that was being fuelled by Hexamine tablets, wearing only his skid marked underpants, and the fact that his testicles were hanging out from one side of them did not help the sight. The C.S. did not acknowledge our presence as Smithy and I moved alongside him, as he was too engrossed with Gudser's next action. Gudser placed his hand between his legs, and proceeded to scratch his hanging testicles for a brief moment before tucking them neatly back into his ill-fitting underwear.

"Slam that fucking door, Smithy, will ye? There is a ferocious fucking draft going up between the crack in me arse," said the shitty chef, who then took up a fork from the wooden floorboards, and began to stir the stew with it.

"This is a funny time of the day to be eating stew, Trooper," snarled Finch.

"What? Stew—fucking—stew," retorted Gudser as he turned to his right and picked up the empty tin that the stew had come from and stared at the label on the front of it. "Well fuck me, I really need to get glasses, because I could have sworn, C.S., that it said scrambled eggs, beans, and two slices of toast on the front of the label."

"Right!" growled the C.S. I am placing you under arrest, Trooper; do you hear me?" He then turned to me, "Corporal, I am arresting this man…."

"I'm afraid Sergeant Lewis has beaten you to it, C.S.," I said, interrupting him. "That is why Trooper Smith and I are here; we've been sent by Sergeant Lewis to arrest him and march him to the guardroom where he will stay until the C.O. can deal with him," I explained. Finch nodded his head in agreement, and said that he would see Sgt. Lewis to inform him that he would be adding to the charges. Placing my hand on Gudser's shoulder I officially told him that he was under arrest, and after he got dressed he was to fall in outside to be marched to the guardroom. Gudser then walked over to his bed space, and proceeded to get dressed, while I told Smithy to extinguish the hexamine tablets.

Finch moved across to the foot of Gudser's bed, and said, "Do you know that you have a drinking problem, a serious drinking problem; do you know that, Trooper?"

"Yeah, C.S. Finch, I do know that," replied Gudser, who was now buttoning up his shirt. "That's right, C.S. I have a drink problem, ye see I have two hands, and only one fucking mouth—now that's my fucking problem, ye know what I mean C.S.?" he said, sarcastically, before winking at Smithy and myself. Looking down I could see Finch's knuckles had gone pure white from squeezing his hands into unbounded fists, through restrained violence. He then walked out of the room with head down, mumbling to himself. This was Smithy's cue to go into a convulsion of laughter as he had bottled it up for fear of Finch. After the laughing had ceased, Gudser gave me a pleading look, and then turned his eyes down to where a unopened can of beer was lying in his half opened backpack. Telling Gudser that he had three minutes to get fell in outside, I went and waited out front of the billet, leaving Smithy with him. After about two minutes Gudser fell in on the road outside the billet, and thanked me; we then proceeded to the guardroom.

"What are you doing here?" I asked Ben McGahan, as he unlocked the compound gate. He told me that Lenny took Tommo Johnson off duty to drive Shovelin out to the exercise, in place of Gudser, and as he was returning to the billet because he forgot his cigarettes when the lads and he were sent to clean the cars; he got nabbed for duty by Lenny as he passed the gate. The rain started to fall as I went into the guardroom, leaving Gudser outside, and who was by now showing a lonely and dejected outward appearance, which I thought I could ease a small bit by having a word with Lenny. Inside the guardroom Lenny and Finch were in deep conversation, about Gudser. Interrupting their verbals, I explained to them that I could not contain a prisoner in a guardroom that had not got an enclosed structure to place him in, and therefore could not hold him in the guardroom because of the danger of the guard's loaded rifles, and not knowing the prisoner's state of mind. To my astonishment they agreed with me, and they came to the conclusion that Gudser would be placed under open arrest, and report to the guardroom every hour on the hour. After Lenny had a few words with him, Gudser was let out the gate to go and work with the rest of the lads, cleaning the cars. Finch went about his business, and Lenny went over to the billet to catch some needed sleep. Peace at last, I thought to myself as I sat down to have a cup of tea with Smithy and Ben, but little did I know at the time that it was the calm before the storm. Later on that morning Ben and myself went for a short patrol around the camp.

Having a splitting headache from a combination of the drink the night before, and this morning's Gudser calamity, I stopped off and went into the medical hut to see if I could get something to ease the pain. Sitting down on a wooden bench inside the medical hut when we walked in were four Privates and a Corporal from the fatigue party who were on the morning sick parade. Emerging from a small shabby looking wooden cubicle from across the hut came a frightfully looking medical orderly. Frightful was in his demeanor, which consisted of a long stick like body, and a head that was the most alarming to the observer. He possessed thinning, red hair that was combed over from one side of his head to the other in a vain attempt to hide the premature balding of his bonce. He was enormously bug-eyed, and had very large protruding top teeth that were overreaching his thin-lipped mouth.

"What ails you, boy?" the medic asked, a sickly looking Private sitting on the bench. Though he was listening to the Private telling him about what he thought his suffering most probably was, the medic was scrutinizing Ben and me with his bulging eyes as we stood with our backs to the closed door. Reaching up to a jar on a shelf the medic took a thermometer from it, and began shaking it. "Here!" he said, placing the thermometer into the Private's mouth. He then told the Private that the doctor would be coming shortly, from the City of Cork, as he had to finish off a clinic there, and that is why there is a delay. The fatigue party Corporal was next, and he informed the medic that he had something wrong with his knee. "Pull up the leg of your pants and give me a squint, boy," ordered the medic, to which the Corporal complied. With a hand around both sides of the Corporal's knee, and with his thumb's resting on the kneecap, he began to forcefully press in on the kneecap to require validity for the complaint, which was verified by the Corporal's short yelp. "That's one vicious fucker." said Ben, with a frown. After having finished with the last of his sick parade, the medic crossed the room to where we were standing. The medic now stood right in front of Ben, looking him up and down. "What ails you, boy?" asked the medic. When Ben was not forthcoming with a reply, the medic said, "Did ye not hear me, boy? What ails you like, boy? I have to tell the doc when he comes in like, what your ailment is, boy—so what's wrong with ye boy?"

"It's my private part," said Ben, bowing his head down in the direction of his groin area.

"Drop the slacks and the underwear—like, I'll have to see so I can tell the doctor when he arrives, boy," said the medic, who was already bending down on one knee to inspect Ben's private region. Ben unbuckled his belt, and at the same time as he was doing this he turned his head slightly and gave me a devious smile. Then, in one swift movement he pulled down his battledress trousers to reveal to all in the hut that he was not wearing underpants.

"Fucking hell!" exclaimed one of the Privates on the bench, who seemed to be filled with awe at the sight of Ben's manhood, whilst the rest gazed on in fascination. The medic, who was eyelevel with Ben's enormous genitalia got the biggest shock of all; he flinched, and in doing so his bottom lip disappeared due to the fact that his large jutted teeth dropped.

"His father worked across the water as a nuclear chemist in Sellafield," I said smilingly, as I pointed at Ben, which turned the uneasy atmosphere that was prevailing in the hut, to that of laughter.

"Sure there is nothing at all—at all wrong with that, like—boy, not a scratch boy," said the restored medic.

Ben leaned over, and placed his face inches from the now standing medic's face, and jubilantly said, "No! But wouldn't it impress the loving fucking shit out of ye—wouldn't it?"

"Sure not at all, boy, sure haven't I seen bigger and a lot cleaner than that, boy," replied the medic, laughingly.

"Are you fucking gay?" inquired Ben of the medic, abruptly.

"Sure not at all, boy—for fuck's seek, sure am'ent I going out with a dolly bird from the town beyond. For fuck's seeks boy, there's some fucking allegation coming from the likes of you—ye big fucking pin-up fucking nancy boy, like," protested the overly blushing medic.

"He's only joking," I said to the medic, trying to defuse the situation before it got completely out of hand.

Ben told the medic that he was only having a bit of crack, to which the orderly replied, "Sure you're an awful man—an awful man altogether, so ye are boy." He then started to laugh and scratch the side of his head while retreating to the sanctuary of the small wooden cubicle. Giving him a few moments to compose himself I went over and knocked, and then entered the cubicle to ask the medic for something for my headache, for which he gave me a few paracetamol tablets to take. The doctor was coming in the door as Ben and I were going out. On closing the door behind us I could hear the doctor announcing to the sick parade that there could not be that much wrong with them, for the laughing among them. On the way back to the guardroom I asked Ben why he thought the medic was gay.

"Well, his teeth gave him away, didn't they?" he said. Stopping in my tracks I gave him a quizzical look.

"What do you mean, his teeth gave him away? How does having protruding teeth make you think he is gay?"

"Well let me explain," said Ben. "I think at one time he thought he was ready to tell everyone that was close to him that he was gay, so he came out. Then at the last minute he became panic stricken, and went back in that fucking fast he forgot to tell his fucking teeth, and besides, did ye see his eye's pop out of their fucking sockets when he seen the snoozing gladiator," he said, as he placed his opened hand over his groin, and holding a straight face for a few seconds before the two of us began to roar with laughter. Travelling back towards the guardroom we were still laughing and joking.

"You're a homophobic asshole, McGahan," I said with a serious face; knowing full well that Ben was not homophobic, as he had a brother and cousin who were of the gay community.

Leaning slightly forward Ben cupped his hand around his ear, and said, "What? What did ye say? Ye want me to phone a homo for an asshole, have ye got that number? Because it will come in dead handy tonight as I'm staying in until tomorrow morning," he jokingly said, as the two of us broke out laughing again. The laughter did not last very long, because as we rounded the cook's billet for the guardroom we came upon Captain Shovelin, who was standing outside the main gate of the compound with hands on hip, and tapping one foot in a show of impatience. "Do you want to get in to go to the toilet, Sir?" I quipped, as I walked up to him, and gave him a formal salute, to which he did not return. "No I fucking well don't want to go to the toilet, Corporal," he answered, in a gruff voice which displayed his surly manner. "I mean how long does it take to patrol the camp, Corporal? I'm standing here at this gate waiting a bloody age on you to return from your slouch around the camp," he moaned, raising his eyebrows and started to tap his foot again, in a gestured signal for an immediate answer. After I had explained to him that I had stopped off in the medical hut to get tablets for a headache, his self-centered and overbearing character came to the fore as he told me to shut up as he did not give two fucks about my headache; he had a more pressing matter to contend with. The heated and concerned Captain snappily removed his cap, and began slapping it very anxiously off the side of his leg. The front of his wiry red hair was stuck to his forehead with damp sweat, and his eye's seemed to be glazed in his somewhat deep eye sockets. The reason for these obvious tensions became apparent to me when he revealed his more pressing matter, which was in the form of a Colonel from Command H.Q. visiting the camp, today. The worry seem to stem from about a year ago when Shovelin was passed over for promotion to the rank of Commandant, it going instead to a Captain, one year junior to him. It was common knowledge that Shovelin had dirtied his bib when in charge of a range shoot. On the day of the range practice Command H.Q. carried out an unannounced inspection of the firing range, and found there to be several irregularities, such as lads not wearing their helmets whilst firing, and a range sentinel sitting down on the grass smoking a cigarette. This flaw in his track record was what had lost him promotion to a junior, and it has gnawed him, and by that he has left nothing to chance ever since. There was another explanation doing the rounds among the troops at the time of his missed promotion, and that was he lost out because Command was aware of his obstinate and tactless nature.

"Jasus Sir, your sweating there like an Iraqi brickie, are ye ok?" said Smithy, who had come out of the guardroom, and was now at the gate with the keys in his hand.

"Get back into your fucking shit hole until you're called for, Trooper," the Captain roared at Smithy. With a satisfactory smile on his face from the service of his smart remark to Shovelin, Smithy retreated to the guardroom. Shovelin stood silently watching Smithy until he disappeared into the guardroom.

He then turned his attention to me with an air of resolution about him, and firmness in his voice, he said, "This man will be here in the camp around the two o' clock mark, all I want from you, Corporal, is…."

"I'm reporting in Corporal," inserted Gudser, talking over and suspending the captain's words, as he appeared from behind him.

"Could you not see that I was speaking, Trooper, you fucking igno- ramus…what form of a fucking pig are you?" raged the extremely dis- gruntled officer.

"Are you related to the Dolittles by any chance, Sir?" asked Gudser, sar- castically. With a shake of my head and a look of concern on my face, and knowing full well that Gudser's renowned antagonism could cause an embar- rassing situation, I immediately, and before the officer could reply, sternly told Gudser to go for his lunch. Seeing the earnest expression on my face, Gudser got the message and walked quietly and swiftly away, and out of sight as he rounded the corner of the cook's billet.

"What was that he said? What was that comment he made?" confusingly inquired, Shovelin.

"I don't really know what he said, Sir? Now! What was that about the Officer coming to the camp?" I evasively said, as I changed the subject, but to no avail: the mouth McGahan cut in.

"I do! Sir, I know what the comment meant, Sir."

"Do you indeed, Trooper, enlighten me—if you would?" said the Captain, as he returned his cap to his head.

"Well Sir, it was the way that ye talked to him—the way ye talk to most people, Sir…."

"And your fucking point being, Trooper?" voiced Shovelin, halting Ben's utterance.

"Doctor Dolittle, Sir, Trooper Knight was telling ye in a roundabout way, Sir…..that ye talk to people like ye were taking to fucking animals—excuse my French, Sir," Ben concluded his dig at Shovelin, and then stood there solemnly waiting on Shovelin's abusive condemnation, but it did not come.

The Captain instead turned his eyes away from Ben's icy stare to address me. "Have that fucking guardroom gleaming when this man comes, or I will lock the whole fucking guard away—do you understand Corporal?" he growled, as he began to walk away, and not waiting on my response. Walking away he cleared his throat and spoke aloud to himself, but his words were for Ben and me to absorb. "Doctor fucking Dolittle indeed, I don't talk to animals, but I walk and fucking live with animals, and if any shit heads have a complaint about me—then they should take it up with the fucking I.S.P.C.A.," said the concerned officer, as he walked hastily away and down the camp. Waiting on Smithy to open the gate, Ben had a big smile on his face, he told me that he had enjoyed telling Shovelin the truth, and that he gambled on Gudser and himself not being brought up on charges.

"I mean what was his evidence going to be? That we called him Doctor fucking Dolittle. No! Because he knew he would be the laugh of the barracks. Jasus did ye see his face? I tell ye it was well fucking worth it." he said enthusiastically, rubbing his hands together.

"Yeah, I was listening from inside the guardroom door, and it was music to my ears. I detest the bastard; well done, Ben." said Smithy, who arrived to unlock the gate. Shaking my head and smiling, and thinking how harmonious the two of them were when it came to abusing the hierarchy. Taking the keys off Smithy I told the whimsically uninhibited duo to go for their lunch. The two of them headed off to the dining hall, laughingly talking about the ludicrous occurrence involving the Captain. After lunch we gave the guardroom and the compound a good clean up, and then played cards to pass the time away while we waited the arrival of Shovelin and the Colonel. The guardroom bell rang, bang on three o clock. Taking the keys from off the table I walked out the door, and headed for the gate to admit the two officers into the compound. Approaching the gate I could see that the Colonel was a small cranky faced and elderly looking man, who seemed to be nearing his retirement age. He sported a grey pencil moustache, and had age creases on his face like a badge of a hard, prolonged and tiring career. "No-no, Corporal, we shan't be going in—thank you Corporal." said the Colonel, abruptly. "Well I think I've seen all that I want to see Captain, everything is in order. The camp is in fine shape, you've done a very good job indeed Captain," expressed the satisfied Colonel.

"That's very kind of you, Sir; nothing escapes me, Sir. I take the running of the camp to my own high standards, Sir," said the beaming, and overly conceited Captain. Just as the Colonel was about to walk away, the door of the cook's billet opened, and out from it staggered Slick onto the top step in all his ginger nudeness, except for an undersized tattered white vest that had dried beer stains imbedded into it, that only covered half his bloated stomach; the end of the vest was above his massive navel. He also increased the clarity of his nakedness by adorning his feet with a civilian pair of leather shoes that had the laces missing from them. The two officers did not say a word; they just stood in silence staring at Slick as he drunkenly negotiated the three steps leading down from the billet.

"What in the name of jasus is he doing? His out of his fucking tree," whispered Gudser to me through the wire, as he arrived for his hourly showing of the face. Regaining his balance from a stumble on the last step down, the red-headed, hair-oil drunk now stood directly across from the two stunned officers, unashamedly exhibiting his stubby one eyed organ, and large loosely hanging testicles surrounded by a mass of fiery pubic hair.

"Lads!" said Slick, in a deep throaty voice to the still silent and mesmerized officers. Slick then turned right, and moved to the side of the billet placing one hand on it to keep his balance, and then proceeded to relieve his bladder against the side of the building. Standing behind the officers, Gudser and I were in the throes of bladder trouble ourselves, trying to keep in the laughter. The officers now had a rear view (literally) of Slick's big ginger hairy arse, and slightly bleeding open ulcers that ran down the backs of both his leg's, which were an encouraged development of his excessive drinking. After shaking himself the ginger binger turned around, and made his way to the bottom of the steps, and then with the clop of each shoe he went up them. Turning around on the top step to look down at an astonished Colonel, and a gaping mouthed Shovelin,

Slick, again in a throaty voice said, "See the pair of yis for a frothy one in the hole shortly; don't fucking start without me." He then turned back to face the door, and let off an unmerciful fart before disappearing through the billet door. That was it; Gudser and I were now hunched over in convulsions of laughter, as Shovelin turned his head to look at us, and then turning it back to look at the disfeatured faced Colonel. "Who's that man?" rigorously inquired the Colonel of the Captain. Wiping the tears from my eyes, I could see a muted Shovelin staring with a blank expression at the raging face of the Colonel. With no utterance forthcoming from the Captain, the Colonel raised his voice, "Are you bloody well listening to me, Captain? Who's that man?"

"It...it's the cook! Sir," gasped an ashen faced Shovelin. The Colonel went slightly backwards with shock, and gripped the compound wire to steady himself.

"The cook! The fucking cook.....the fucking cook!!" roared the Colonel, who then released his grip on the wire, and roughly pushed passed the soon to be "passed over Captain" once again. With the Captain now gone chasing after the Colonel, Gudser stopped laughing.

"Seeing them fucking shoes in the daylight I should have charged that fat fucker Slick more than twenty," said the lying and thieving Trooper Knight, as he made his way up the steps to the cook's billet.

CHRISTMAS SPIRIT

B eing a most bitter frosty morning I was not looking forward to the annual Christmas soccer match that will take place this morning at ten thirty between the officers and the men. The match, "officers versus the men," takes place every year on the day of the breakup of the troops for the festive period. All the troops looked forward to the break up day, due to it being the last day in barracks before the festive holidays, and for the mostly, free booze up in the Mess that afternoon. Everyone, from the modest trooper to the crankiest Quartermaster all the way up to the brass, was of a jovial state of mind on this day of the year. This was immediately evident when marching out for the nine o clock parade; the lads had to be shouted at by the Orderly Sgt. to keep it quiet in the ranks quite a number of times before they reached their designated area on the parade ground. The parade was taken by the Squadron Sergeant, who, because of the day that was in it, gave us insignificant and trivial jobs to carry out around the barracks, or in other words, take it easy until the break up session in the afternoon. Tony "Pebbles" Thomson and I were sent down to the old Quartermaster's store to tidy up the junk that was now stored there since the Quarter moved to the newly refurbished number seven block at the top of the square. The rubbish that was now kept in the old store consisted of defunct locker's, and other items that were either broken or had outlived their use. Walking down to the old store I could see that Pebbles was in an elevated and cheerful mood as he kept rubbing his hands together and had a permanent smile on his chubby face. His face did not imitate his body, which was robust in constitution, and which by, made him look conspicuously peculiar. He had an acute tendency to aggravate people intently with his tomfoolery and idiotic, but sometimes amusing pranks. I was about to witness one of those pranks. As we neared the bottom of the square he turned and called out to the Hook O'Neal who was standing talking at the top of the square. The Hook is the cook Corporal in the N.C.O. Mess., and he got his name because he liked to box, inside, and more often outside the ring.

The cook turned and looked at Pebbles, and then pointing to his chest, shouted, "Me?"

"Yeah! That's right, you! I've got an important message for ye," cried Pebbles.

"What fucking message have ye got for him?" I asked.

"Oh, the message that he fucking creased me last week scrubbing fucking pots in the kitchen," said Pebbles, puckering his lips and giving that mischievous wink of the eye.

As I was moving a safe distance away from him I warned him, "You've got to be fucking joking? I hope his in the festive mood, or he will upend you." The hook came walking down the square, which was a good distant walk to where we stood. Getting that little bit closer to us I could see just what a hardy man he was. He was not that big in height, but had muscles protruding through his white cook's uniform. Under his grey, brylcreem slicked hair was a face that was a plastic surgeon's nightmare, with a flat boxer's nose, and scars covering scars.

After his long walk the Hook now stood in front of Pebbles. "What's the important message Pebbles?" inquired the cook, with his eyebrow's raised.

"The message, Corporal O'Neal," began Pebbles, "is from Captain Kirby; he told me to tell you that you've to proceed to the Quartermaster's store, and draw a gas cooker, and then you've to bring it up to his office and name the parts to him?" said Pebbles, saying the last few words with a chuckle. Standing there stuck to the ground, I did not even think about laughing, as I did not want to get on the wrong side of the Hook. Pebbles was having a right laugh, but the cute antagonist was running at the same time.

"I'll get ye, Thomson; you'll have to come into my kitchen sometime, ye little prick, and then you can name the parts of yourself that are black, blue and fucking broken. Ye little shit head, ye," roared Hook at Pebbles, as he disappeared around the corner of the old store. The Hook, thanks be to jasus said nothing to me, but just turned and walked back up the square, and oddly enough, he was laughing to himself. Pebbles had bolted the door of the store, and it took me five minutes to convince him that the Hook was not outside, waiting to pounce.

Pebbles was laughing his head off, until I said, "What are you going to do about going to the Mess for a gargle? Because the Hook will be there. You're going to be uncomfortable drinking your pint through a straw, thickhead."

He stopped laughing, and kicked a door on an old locker. He then placed his fist to his mouth, and pulling it away again, said, "Holy shit! I never thought about that—-ah fuck him, besides I don't think he is that fucking hard."

"Is he?" he asked worriedly.

I had to contain myself from bursting out laughing, as I said, "Hard!, hard is not the word, did ye know that when his wife was having a baby, he went in with her, and when the baby was born the doctor slapped it, and the doctor ended up in traction for six fucking months, now ask yourself is he hard or mad? Either way you're fucked. Not hard, my bollix."

Starting to laugh I told him that I was only kidding, to which he replied, "I knew that, do ye think I'm a fucking eejit?, or what?" He started to laugh. "Yeah I was only kidding, Pebbles, the doctor was only kept in hospital overnight, as a precautionary measure, that's all," I said, keeping a straight face. He stopped laughing, and started surveying my face with his eyes to find any sign that I was joking, which I was not about to let happen. After a few moments of staring at me he quickly turned, and in his haste, almost tripped over as he headed for the door. "Where are you off to? We haven't finished here yet!" I said, still keeping a straight face.

"Fuck here! I'll tell ye where I'm going, will I? I'm going up to the Hook and apologize to him, and see if he needs any pots washed or floors scrubbed. I'll tell ye, I would rather get a box in the mouth now!, while his sober, than wait until later on when he gets drunk, and he fucking de-balls me with one of them butcher knives he has in the kitchen. I know what?" he was now talking more to himself, that to me. " I'll tell him, that in a way of an apology I'll buy him a pint and a double of whatever he wants, yeah that's what I'll do," he said, looking very flustered indeed. He then disappeared out the door to carry out his apologetic and obsequious mission for mercy. There was not that much tidying up to do. It took me about ten minutes to leave the store in a neat and orderly state. After I had finished in the old store I headed for the billet to get changed into my football gear for the Christmas match, which I now had a change of mind about, and was looking forward to playing in it. Aggressiveness, and no quarter given by either side was how the first half of the match went, but the second half was of the uninhibited kind, mainly due to the half time refreshments which consisted of paper cups of whiskey, for players, referee and spectators alike. During the second half Sid Braddock came on as a substitute for the men's team, and a short time later pandemonium ensued. Sid carried an excessive amount of weight for a lad in his early twenties. He had blue, beady eyes embedded in his abundant face that seemed to be always dancing, owing to the jolly and exuberant nature of the guy. Bright and pleasant he may be, but just to mention the name of the officer's goalkeeper, Captain Coulter made him cringe. Sid had a resentful hatred of the man, and his obnoxious, immorally affected behavior, as did most people that came into contact with the arrogant Captain. Although Coulter hails from county Cavan, he had the facial features of East Asian descend, that being, it must have come from somewhere along the line. The main distinct characteristic of his face being the stretched and narrowing of the skin running along the eye recesses, which gave him the oriental look. Sid had a run in with Coulter during the summer when he entered Coulter's office, and saluted in a quick and casual way unbeknownst to himself. Coulter lost the head, and told Sid that the boy scouts could salute better than he had done, and that he wanted the action carried out in the correct manner, when Sid was leaving the room. Sid being Sid, when he went to leave the room he jokingly raised his right arm, and placed the back of three finger's to his forehead and said, "Dib-dib-dib," giving a salute any scout would be proud of. Coulter duly charged Sid, and brought him up before the Commanding Officer, where he was found guilty of insubordination, and was confined to the barracks for fourteen nights, as punishment, and that was something Sid was harboring at the back of his mind when he came onto the field of play. He was only on the pitch five minutes when our team got a corner kick. the ball came across from the corner kick, and seeing the flight of the ball I ran in front of Coulter to get my head to it, when in the blink of a eye I was face down on the ground a couple of yards from where I had been standing, with Coulter's body in a heap on top of me, gasping for air. I could feel the pain around my rib cage caused by the impact of Coulter landing on me. Coulter got to his feet, and without speaking a word, due to the fact that he was still out of breath, shook his fist in the direction of Sid, who was standing on the edge of the box with the ball in his hand's, smirking. Standing there absorbing the pain in my ribs I was told by one of the lads, that when Coulter and myself leaped for the ball together, Sid, with no intentions of going for the ball had jumped knees first into the back of Coulter with such force that it repelled him into me, and consequently sending the two of us sprawling onto the grass. Let alone Coulter, but to everyone's surprise, the referee awarded a penalty, thinking the Captain went into the back of me as I went for the ball. Oddly enough, the only person arguing with the referee over the decision was Coulter, which brought home to me the animosity that everyone, and including his fellow officer' s, held for him. After an interval of arguing with the referee, Coulter reluctantly and grudgingly accepted the decision, and then walked over and readied himself between the posts for the forthcoming penalty kick. Crouched on the goal line, and ready to pounce left or right for the penalty, Coulter's whole posture nearly crumbled when he seen who stepped up to take the penalty. When Sid placed the ball onto the penalty spot it was like rubbing salt into the wound for Coulter.

"Give it all you've got you big fat shit." rapped Coulter. After placing the ball on the spot, and not speaking a word Sid walked backwards a good distance to take the shot, he then stopped, and lifting his hand he pointed at Coulter standing in the goalmouth. Thunderously charging like a demented elephant was how Sid ran up to strike the ball, and all the time he was running, Coulter repeatedly shouted, "Show us what you're made of, you fat lump of shit; come on lard arse." Then he fainted with the pain, falling backwards into the net. Just before Coulter collapsed Sid had reached the ball to strike it, but his foot went over the ball missing it completely. His football boot left his foot, and flew through the air with great speed hitting Coulter, with the stud end up, in the dead center of the face rendering him unconscious immediately. Only a few of the lads went to help the Captain, but everyone on and off the pitch were in a heap laughing.

Walking over to the side of the goal mouth to where Sid was replacing his boot, I asked him, "Did your boot come undone, Sid, did it?"

"Like fuck it did, and fuck the pun, but that was a little eye opener for the slant eyed fucker. I must say though, that was some fucking shot for something I had to do but never fucking did practice for. I think I should make the barrack team after a shot like that, what do ye think? Now I had better see if he is all right, and see if I can help him in any way," he said with irony in his voice, and a wry smile on his face. Coulter came to his senses and had to be restrained from getting to Sid, by a couple of the officers. Sid was quickly ushered away by some of the lads across the grass of the plains, and up the hill to the back of the barracks, the match was over. Sid and Coulter were the talk and laugh of the barracks for the rest of the morning, and on into the break up session in the Mess in the afternoon. At two o' clock that day the N.C.O. Mess was jampacked with officers and men alike, and all in an uplifting Christmassy state of mind. There was slapping of backs and Christmas wishes, and pleasantries to each other, and passing of the same onto each other's families. There were all sorts and every sort, and all in their own groups just making merry, and having the craic in general. There was the fitter staff, and the administration and transport staff, the Quartermaster with his work force, and over in a small corner of the Mess sat the lads of the Equitation School. In their company were a couple of nurses and officers that had been out on horseback with them on the Christmas ride out across the Curragh plains, that morning. The officers and nurses would be regulars at taking horses out to ride during the year, and this day of the year was when they showed their appreciation by giving presents, and buying drinks for the lads from the horsey yard for all their help during the year. Each was to his own group at the moment, but as the day moved on, and the drink flowed, they will all fall into the melting pot. Standing at the bar, I was having a great laugh mainly because I was having a pint, and in conversation with Sgt. Jimmy "Old blue eye's" McGrane. Jimmy was just your run of the mill thirty something kind of guy, not to tall and not to small, but he had two outstanding features that made him curious to the stranger, his eyes and his hair. The eyes were the blue color of a heat wave sky that shimmered in his head, and the brown hair was a comb over that sat on his head like a large toupee that looked like it was being fed with fertilizer. Jimmy was one of the few gentlemen that were left in the Unit who was a great conversationalist, and liked nothing better than a good laugh. Jimmy and I were doing just that, having a good laugh at Sid and Coulter's expense, when a red headed torment by the name of Matt Kinsella barged his way in between us. Matt always seemed to be carrying the world around on his shoulders, and was forever agitated about one thing or the other. Matt was a Corporal in the Quartermaster's store. He wore a large black rimmed pair of medical prescription glasses on his narrow face which made him look like a leading figure in the Irish "Buddy Holly" fan club. What is typical of him is his repeating behavior of placing his finger onto the nosepiece of his glasses, and pushing upwards weather they were down his nose or perfectly on the bridge.

"What ails ye, Matthew?" Jimmy questioned. Matt stood there with shoulders shrugging, and his head submissively bowed, bowing to Jimmy's question. "Come on," said Jimmy. "What's wrong?"

Jimmy then put one arm around Matt's shoulder giving it a gentle shake. Matt lifted his head, and then turning it sideways to look at Jimmy, and with sincerity showing on his face, he said, " How do I go about getting a boy?" He then shrugged his shoulders again. Jimmy rapidly pulled his arm from around Matt's shoulder.

"Fuck me!" I gasped in astonishment at his statement. "I don't mean that literally," I explained, after I realized just what I had said. The man who wanted a boy was now looking with pure puzzlement from Jimmy's face to mine as we stared at him with grimaced expressions. Then the penny dropped for him. "No, not that ye pair of fucking eejits. You know what I'm on about, Jim, don't ye?" said Matt, now waiting on a confirmative from Jimmy. Much to my relief Jimmy started to laugh, which made me glad to think that there was more to Matt's predicated sentence that would explain all.

Jimmy replaced his arm back around Matt's shoulder, and said to him, "I think I know, Matt, is it the girl thing? Is that it?"

"What else, Jim?" said a disconsolate Matt. The whole conversation had me in puzzlement and was flying over my head until Jimmy explained Matt's predicament to me. Matt had a family of eight daughters that were born in succession over the last decade. His wife and he have been trying for a boy ever since the first girl was born, but alas to no avail. By his own account, he would not have such a big family if it were not for his desire to father a baby son. In complete contrast to Matt, Jimmy had five sons and one daughter. Matt was surely at his wit's end, because the next words to come from his mouth were stupidity in the extreme. "Now Jim, I want ye to tell me how to go about getting a baby boy, and please don't give me any of that crap that some of the lads say—-about putting on my battledress when I'm having sex, or leaving my combat boots under the bed while I'm doing it. I just want a straight answer as how my wife can have a baby boy. With you been blessed in that way, I was hoping that ye could steer me in the right way. For fuck's sake, could ye Jim?" said a pleading Matt.

Jimmy, putting his pint on the counter turned to Matt, "Are ye going home shortly, Matthew?"

"I'm off home after I get another one or two," Matt answered Jimmy.

"Good, now listen Matthew, I'm not going to bullshit ye or tell ye shit like wear your fucking combat trousers while you're doing it. No, none of that shit. I'm going to tell ye how to get a baby boy for sure," said Jimmy to the attentive, sonless father of girls. "What I want ye to do when ye get home," Jimmy continued, "take your darling wife up to the bathroom, and give her a good wash in the bath. Then while she is soaking in the bath I want you to get a crisp clean sheet, just the one, mind ye, and put it on the bed. Have nothing else on the bed bar the sheet and pillow. When ye have that done I want ye to go back to the bathroom, and take your wife from the bath and dry her off thoroughly, then take her to the bedroom, and lay her on top of the sheet naked—" Jimmy stopped abruptly as he reached for his pint on the counter.

"Yeah! Go on, Jim, go on for fucks sake," enthused Matt as he pushed his glasses back up along his inquisitive nose. After Jimmy took a swig from his pint, he said, "Now, where was I? Ah yes, after laying her naked on the bed I want ye to put an empty glass, and a full glass of water along with a baby bottle of Jameson whiskey on the top of the bedside locker. When ye have all that done I want ye to go downstairs, go out the front door, and get into your car and come back up and get me." Jimmy now burst into laughter. I started to go into the kinks. Matt then seen the funny side, and he started to laugh.

"You're some fucking arse wipe, McGrane." he chuckled.

"Well Matthew, ye ask a stupid question.....?" Jimmy laughingly replied. Then the first row of the day was about to break out. Kenny Larkin was standing directly behind me at the bar. Larkin was given the nick-name "piggy" by the lads, and rightly so. He was a greasy headed slob of a human being with small beady pig like eyes. The majority of the time that he would open his mouth was either to abuse people, or spew out derisive sarcasm. It was a complete mystery as to how he got N.C.O. status of Corporal. Piggy must have been listening in on what had been said between Jimmy and Matt.

He put his piggy face over my shoulder, and speaking to Matt, said, "So what if the next one is a girl, and see if I have this right that will be nine you'll have? Ok! So think about it; it does not work out too bad, ye see. Because another nine holes, and you'll have your own fucking golf course." He started to laugh. Matt, Jimmy and I did not see the funny side of it, but fat Paddy the barman did. He was laughing his head off behind the bar. Just as I turned to tell fat Paddy to shut up, Matt came over my shoulder, and hit Larkin in the mouth with a punch. I tried to get in the way to stop them but Larkin pushed me forward, and at the same time caught Matt with his fist on the side of the head, sending him flying into Jimmy. The Sgt. Major and a couple of lads put a stop to it all. Jimmy explained to the Major what had taken place, and what Larkin had said about Matt's family. On hearing this, the Sgt Major had Larkin escorted from the Mess.

As the pig was being led to the door, he had to have one last repelling snide remark towards Matt, and at the top of his voice he shouted, "Kinsella is married to the old woman in the shoe, and if she has one more kid—-her fanny will fall out." Then he was gone. Some of the lads were laughing at what Larkin said, but most of them were disgusted with his words. Everyone knew that Larkin had been drinking heavily since early that morning, and by the time the break up session started he was a loose cannon. The Major told Matt that he would deal with Larkin good and proper after the Christmas break. Everything went back to normal (if it could be called that) with the merriment and the drink flowing again. Matt had a few more drinks before heading home to his long suffering wife. Maybe he will give the dream of having an heir to his ginger kingdom another shot, and turn it in to reality, or maybe it is just an idle hope. After a while Jimmy and myself sat down with the lads from the Unit, to get down to some serious drinking, and maybe a Christmas singsong or a few ballads later on. Going to the bar for a refill, I met "Gypsy" Cummings who was also heading that direction to get another pint for himself. Waiting for our pints of Guinness to settle we got talking about this, that and the other. Gypsy, real name Eddie, got his nick-name from his natural dark curly and shining hair, and almost carbon black eyes that gave him an outward aspect of a Romany gypsy. He had a great inner belief in himself, and took nothing or nobody with seriousness, except Trooper Eddie Cummings. Taking a mouthful from his pint, and at the same time nudging me with his elbow, and making a head gesture in the direction of two young officers who were perched at the bar alongside him. The two young lieutenant's had only been in the Unit since the summer, and in so being were still unwise to rogues like Gypsy.

With the pint in his hand Gypsy turned to the naïve pair, "Excuse me Sir, but my friend and I were just talking about the films that will be on the telly over Christmas for the kids, ye know with elf's, dragons, and all that Lord of the rings shit in them. Well, we've hit a blank, and cannot remember what a horse with a horn is called, and we were wondering if one of you could enlighten us?" requested Gypsy.

In an educating tone, the officer nearest to us said, "Simple, Unicorn!" he smiled with his eyes opened wide with delight.

"No—no that's not it at all," said Gypsy, as I shook my head in agreement with him, and not knowing why.

"Listen, believe me, it is a Unicorn; I'm telling you, Unicorn." the second officer expressed to us with enthusiasm.

"That's just not it," said Gypsy. "No matter, Sir, forget about it. One of us will think of it eventually," he said, turning away from the two bewildered officers. No sooner had he turned away from them when he swiveled around to face the two young officers again. With a broad smile on his face, he clicked his fingers. Then placing his index finger to the side of his head, and with a smug look towards the young officer's, he exclaimed, "I've got it!" as he jumped in the air.

"Well in that case if it is not a Unicorn, then what is a horse with a horn called, in your opinion?" asked one of the two objectionable young officers.

Gypsy looked at me and smiled, then turning to the officers he put one hand on his groin, and the other hand on his hip, and with a sudden significant trusting motion to and fro of his groin area towards them, and in a sharp gravelly voice said, "A stallion, babies—a fucking stallion, that's what it's called." He now stopped trusting his hips, and started to laugh. Barely able to make out the officers faces from the tears in my eyes from laughing, I could see just about enough to realize that they had seen the funny side of it. They were mostly laughing at each other, than at Gypsy. Each was blaming the other for not catching on to the amusing ruse. "Welcome to the Unit, lads." said Gypsy as he bowed to them. He then took his pint, and giving me a smile and a wink, he turned and walked into the throng in the Mess. Sitting back down with the troops I was telling them about what had taken place up at the bar between Gypsy and the young officers, when I was interrupted by a stern and gruff voice. The whole group around the tables went quite, and as a result of this interruption the second argument of the day entailed.

"Well Braddock, that pint must taste very bitter going down your cheating fat neck, after your immature aggressive behavior this morning," rebuked Captain Coulter with tension in his voice, as he stood with a scowl on his bruised face across the tables from Sid. "Well, no Sir, not at all, as a matter of fact it tastes like victory going down my fat fucking neck, Sir!" replied Sid with a smile that was bordering on a sneer. Coulter stood there with his arms folded, and then moving his head to one side, and shifting his weight from one foot to the other, said, " I'll tell you what I want, Braddock, I want you to apologize to me. I want your fat mouth to say sorry, and I want it said in front of all your fucking drunken cronies here, ok Braddock?"

"Ok Sir, I'll say I'm sorry." said Sid, leaning forward in his seat. "I'm sorry, Sir. I'm sorry, that my foot wasn't in the fucking boot when it hit you right between your tapered fucking eyes," he said fumingly, and then stood up quickly and stuck his chest out in an arousing, provocative manner towards Coulter. Some of the lads started to cheer, which brought Jimmy McGrane to his feet.

"Right! Cut all that shit now," Jimmy demanded of the lads. "And you, sit fucking down now; do ye hear me, now!" he said pointing at Sid. With Sid now sitting down, Coulter stated to Jimmy that he wanted Sid placed under arrest. "Although Trooper Braddock should not have talked to you in that manner, Sir," said Jimmy, addressing Coulter, "I think that it was plain for all to see that it was you that caused this situation by using derogative comment's about Trooper Braddock's character and weight. Now Sir, this been the season to be jolly and all, I don't think that the C.O. would want his Christmas spoiled by hearing about this small change shit, what do you think, Sir?" proposed the now, harmonising Sergeant. Coulter stared at Sid for a few moments, and then walked off in a huff towards the bar, with Jimmy following on after him. Sid might have won the battle, but I had a feeling Coulter will win the war sometime in the new year. The rest of the day went well, it was a little loud in the main, but not obstreperous by any means. Some of the lads sitting near the Christmas tree further up the Mess were singing "The Fairy Tale of New York" with intensity. While in complete contrast, one of the nurses at the bar end of the Mess had kindly lost her inhibition of diffidence, through alcohol, and was emotionally belting out Patsy Cline's "Crazy." Each drunken group oblivious to the others melodic sounds. About an hour to go before closing time saw the Mess almost empty. Just a few stragglers sitting along the bar talking in hushed tones. At the far end of the bar, sitting on a stool with his head resting on the bar, fast asleep, was the Hook. He had three quarters of a pint and two small brandies (probably bought by Pebbles) beside his head on the bar.

There was an air of sereneness about the place, until a podgy grey haired priest with a high pitched voice walked in. "Hello, God bless all here; I'm the new priest in the area, and would like to wish ye all a joyous and holy Christmas," said the padre somewhat insistently in a squeaky voice. He worked his way along the bar, and one by one he shook our hands as we introduced ourselves. Then he came upon the Hook who had just woken up, and was wiping his mouth with the back of his hand. The priest was taking in the Hook's face as he greeted him. "Ye must have had a good day, son," said the priest.

"I did, father; I didn't think I was going to get my head off the canvas there for a moment. I'm O' Neal, father; I'm the cook. I feed the boys." said the Hook, a bit unsteady as he got down off the stool. As the priest was shaking hands with him, the Hook asked, "Do ye take a drink father?"

"Well to tell ye the truth, son; I do take a drink," replied the father with a look of elevated pleasure and expectancy on his religious face.

"Well I'm off to the toilet," said the Hook, "if ye take mine I'll break your fucking back." He then staggered off in the direction of the toilets, leaving the bemused chaplain standing there not knowing whether to take the Hook serious or not. Fat Paddy immediately asked him what was he having, as I got off my stool and walked quickly to the far end of the Mess before I broke down laughing in front of the collared shriller, who walked into that one with his eyes wide open. The Hook returned from the toilet to the bar, and with a smile on his gothic face he bought the now less priggish padre a drink.

"Here's to the Christmas spirit." said the priest, as he lifted and showed his glass to fat Paddy, and the rest of us along the bar. Lifting my glass, and thinking of the previous altercations made me wonder if the Christmas spirit was somehow the causative force behind the perverse activities in the Mess that day.

"Cheers," I said, cautiously.

GLAD RAGS

Talk about coincidences, it was just my misfortune that several of the other lads going on the C.O.'s inspection were in the same boat as myself, they had no uniform for the inspection. The commanding officer held an inspection once a month on the barrack square. One month he would inspect the troops in their number one uniform, and the next month in their battledress uniform. This month it was number one uniform, which I had mine in the tailor's shop for mending, worst luck for me because of the now pending occurrence which was to befall me very soon. On the morning of the C.O.'s inspection at eight thirty sharp there is always a secondary inspection parade which was taken by the Squadron Sergeant. When the Squadron Sgt's scrutiny was finished, and everything was satisfactory, the parade would then be marched onto the square and await the C.O.'s arrival with his entourage. Walking towards the area where the secondary parade takes place I could see that the troops were standing around, some having a smoke, and others helping one another with last minute alterations. Just in front of the troops, and to my horror, was a line of lads fell in, six of them exactly. The Orderly Sgt. was taking their names. They did not look a contented bunch, and to make matters worse, they were dressed the same as myself. Without waiting on the Orderly Sgt. to tell me, I fell in along side the other six of my own accord.

"I'd say the Squadron Sergeant will have something to say to you lot when he comes over," said the Orderly Sgt. with a smug grin on his face, while adding my name to the other six he had in his defaulter's roll. We looked and felt uncomfortably conspicuous from the rest of the troops who were dressed in formal uniform, as we were dressed in informal uniform of working dress fatigues. After standing there for almost fifteen minutes, and still no sign of the Squadron Sgt. we were told to fall out until he arrived. Now that he was late I just knew that matters were going to deteriorate more. While I was standing there having a smoke, Rusty Williams, one of my fellow defaulters, who was standing beside me said, "It's a lovely summers morning, isn't it?"

"Besides the weather, what's lovely about it?" I replied.

Taking a drag from his cigarette, and a little spit to the ground, he said, "Oh I see, you're afraid of what's going to happen when the big fucker turns up, and see's the cut of us. Don't worry; it'll be alright, it'll be alright." It was his answer for everything. Williams was a dark red headed Dubliner who was one of the most laid back and luckiest blokes I had come across. The roof could fall in on him, and he would come out without a scratch.

Rusty put his foot on the butt, and stamped it out, and with head down and eyes staring pass me said, "I don't like this fucking arse hole bastard of a Quartermaster, a real prick." He gave an upward motion of his head, signalizing for me to look behind myself. Turning my head around, I could see Quartermaster Feeney heading in the direction of the forthcoming parade. Rusty hit the nail on the head, Feeney was a weasel of a man, sly in every way. He was a thin man with a pigeon chest, with a concealed affection for strong alcohol. Unbeknownst to himself, he was the master of innuendos, which were most of the time, abrasively comical to all except the recipient. He walked straight pass us, and ignoring the parade, headed for the N.C.O.'s mess to get either tea or a quick one from the barman before the parade began. Rusty's eyes followed the Quartermaster until he was out of sight.

He then turned around and took his hat off, and running his fingers through his thick dark red hair said, "Do ye know what that sleazebag Feeney said to me on the last inspection? Do ye?" he did not wait on my reply. "He comes up behind me on the parade, and says to me, am I hurting ye, Williams, because I'm standing on your fucking hair back here. Then he tells me that the color of my hair is a disgrace, and I should get it dyed because it was like strands of shite growing from my head. I'll tell ye, I'll knock the living bollix out of him one of these days, that's if he has a bollix, the fucking oul one. Do you think my hair looks like shite?"

"No," I answered, lying. I don't know about Rusty's hair, but I think that Feeney Quartermaster should come under shit head in the dictionary. We got a shout from the Orderly Sgt. to fall back in, as the Squadron Sgt. was on his way over. We were now standing behind the main body of the C.O.'s parade, who were now fell in and waiting for the Squadron Sgt. to inspect them. Dressed in his number one attire the Squadron Sgt. breezed onto the scene, prompting the Orderly Sgt to hand over the parade to him for the preliminary inspection.

On finishing his inspection of the troops the Squadron Sgt. turned to the Orderly Sgt. "What's this?" he said, pointing in our direction. The Orderly Sgt. sprang to attention with his legs so tight together I thought that one cheek of his arse must have overlapped the other. With clarity in his voice he said, "These men came on parade with no number one uniform. Their names have been taken, and they will be charged accordingly, Squadron Sgt." His eyes now staring at nothing in the distance. The Squadron Sgt. told the rigid

Orderly Sgt. to stand at ease, and then speaking with contempt in his voice said, "Put this lot on parade with the rest of troops, and let them explain to the Commanding Officer why they have no uniforms, and why they look like one half of the dirty dozen." He then turned and walked away to take charge of the parade. We could not believe what we just heard, and by the look on the Orderly Sgt's face either could he. This had to be the first time that there was working dress mixed with good uniform on a C.O.'s inspection. I just knew that this was going to be a weird one. We were fell in according to height, and then formed into three ranks, which had the seven of us randomly spread out among the spic-and-span uniforms. The parade was marched onto the square and was given the order to open ranks. This maneuver was carried out as to let the C.O. inspect each rank separately. After about five minutes the C.O. came out from the Orderly room, and his uniform looking splendidly. Commandant Hugh "Hooker" O' Neill was the man with the authority, the Commanding Officer of the Squadron. He was a tall man who carried a bit of weight on the stomach, but still had the physical structure from the muscles left over from his rugby days. He was a gem of an officer, a soldier's soldier, the patriarch of the Squadron who knew how to play as well as work. But he was also known to lob of heads when crossed, a man to be loved and feared. He walked to the front of the parade where the Squadron Sgt. brought the parade to attention and handed over to the senior officer, who in turn handed over to the C.O., and the dreaded inspection began. After inspecting the three young officers at the front of the parade he then moved to the main body of troops. When the first man was about to be inspected, the Squadron Sgt. and Quartermaster fell in line behind the Captain and the C.O., to answer any questions that needed to be ascertained. The C.O. was quite contented as he went along the front rank until he got to the fifth man in line, Danny "Dopey" Doyle. Now Danny was not one bit dopy at all, it was just that his white as a sheet face was fast asleep, and had large drooping eyelids which gave the impression of lacking intelligence. The C.O. was taken aback when he seen the state of Danny standing there in his working dress. Not only was he standing there in his working dress, but Danny's face had an impact of making even a three piece suit look scruffy.

"Why are you not dressed properly?" inquired the boss, as he waved his index finger in an up and downward motion in front of Danny's informal attire. "My good uniform is in the dry cleaners, Sir, and I had no money to get it out." said Danny.

"And what of your wages?" quizzically asked the C.O.

"I bought something for the house, Sir, and then I lost the rest," replied Danny. The C.O. looked at him for a moment, and then said, "When the parade is over, go to the Adjutant's office and get a loan from the Unit fund until you get paid next week, it should tide your family over."

"Thank you kindly, Sir." said Danny, as the C.O. moved on to the next man in line. Dopey, my arse, it was more than likely that Danny bought a drink for the house, and lost his money to the bookies. When the C.O. was further down the line, Quartermaster Feeney made his way back to Danny.

He stood in front of Danny eyeball to eyeball, so to speak, and with a lingering hostile voice said, "You don't fool me, Doyle, ye scruff head. Look at the state of ye, when ye get the uniform out from the cleaners, ye can leave yourself in, ye muck bird. If I was you, Doyle, I would invest in a sunlamp and do something with that face, because ye look like a fucking seasick albino. I'm going to be keeping my eyes on you Doyle, and if ye as much as fart in slow motion I will come down on ye like a ton of bricks, ye gangrenous lump of shit." He then heard a giggle from someone in the middle rank. He looked over Danny's right shoulder at the middle rank but said nothing. With his pigeon chest stuck out and his hands behind his back, he walked away on the balls of his feet to follow the C.O. on his inspection. Everyone knew the reason for the verbal abuse on Danny. Feeney caught Danny calling him "a drunken weasel," a couple of weeks back, but could not prove it was him that Danny was talking about. He was out to get Danny ever since.

Down along the front rank I could hear the C.O. saying, "Ah, what have we got here? Another one is it?" He was talking about Bimbo Scott, the second culprit out of uniform to be inspected by the C.O., and most probably be crucified by Feeney. Bimbo was a loner who never mixed much, mostly owning to his heavy drinking and gambling. He had broken veins running across a red blood pressured face, from his over indulging lifestyle that would not normally be seen on a young man in his early twenties. He was a man not long for the Army, or life for that matter, if he did not alter the characterizations of his depravities. "I suppose you left your glad rags in the dry cleaners too?" inquired the C.O. of Bimbo.

Looking a little shaken, Bimbo replied, "No, Sir, I didn't."

"Well, where is your good uniform then?" said the boss, bewildered.

"The Lebanon." Bimbo blurted out.

"The Lebanon?" said the C.O. "The fucking Lebanon?" Feeney could be heard murmuring. "How in the love of God are your glad rags in the Lebanon, Scott?" asked the C.O., intently.

Looking a little shaken now, Bimbo said, "The Slant Burn took my uniform, Sir. The night before he went to the Lebanon we were having a drink above in the billet Sir, and I think he slipped me a Mickey, Sir." He then went quite as he seen the look of horror on the C.O.'s face.

The C.O. turned to the Squadron Sgt., and scrunching his face with revulsion said, "Will someone please explain to me exactly what this bloody man is going on about? I can't believe what I am fucking hearing." He threw his two arms in the air.

Bimbo, realizing what he had just said, finished what he wanted to say, very quickly, and before the Squadron Sgt. could say anything, said "The Slant slipped a Mickey Finn into my drink. I think he drugged me, Sir. When I woke up the next morning, Sir, my uniform was gone. I think Burn must have taken it, Sir. He told me the night before that he had no uniform for the trip overseas, Sir." He then, at last, shut up. The Squadron Sgt. walked behind the C.O., and whispered something into his ear. Everyone on the parade knew the whisper was about Bimbo's drinking problem. The boss now seemed more relaxed after coming to terms with the initial shock.

"So Trooper Scott, I am to believe that Trooper Burn drugged you so he could steal your glad rags?" said the C.O., to Bimbo. Bimbo did not get a chance to answer. "Now listen to me, Scott, did you sincerely think that I was going to swallow that tripe? Scott, I would not believe a word from your mouth, maybe I would have believed you if you had told me that he drugged you, and stole the shroud of Turin that you had hanging up in your fucking locker, you fucking imbecile. Get this man out of my sight, Squadron Sergeant, put him under arrest, and I will deal with him in the afternoon." said the C. O. with a gruff and stern voice. Bimbo was quickly handed over to a Sergeant from the parade, to be swiftly marched away. I did not know whether to laugh or cry, as my turn was coming shortly. The middle rank was now being inspected, and I was sixth in line.

Just before me and fourth in line to get it in the neck was Williams, who I could hear whispering, "It will be alright, it will be alright." I just hoped he was right. Somehow I took comfort in his words, as the jammy bastard was always right. To make matters worse, Shay Clancy was standing next to me shining like the north fucking star pissing rainbows. On coming down the line the C.O. caught sight of Williams, and bypassed two lads without inspecting them. He now stood in front of Williams, looking him up and down.

With his right hand caressing the back of his neck, and the index finger of his left hand pointing at Williams, the C.O. very cautiously said, " I want you to take great care with your answer Williams, and more so with your words. I know that you don't want to stay in the Army, and want out, but I want the truth as to the whereabouts of your good uniform?" There was complete silence. It was that silent I could hear Williams swallowing hard, and his breathing getting much heavier.

Not only was the C.O. stunned, but the whole parade was shocked when Williams said, " I burnt the thing."

Before the C.O. could say anything, Feeney barged passed him, and placed his face within an inch from the face of Williams, and with spit flying from his mouth like a volcanic eruption, he screamed, "Ye burnt the fucking uniform? Ye burnt the fucking thing? Ye crazy bastard. What did ye do? Did ye put it in the potbellied fire, or did ye put it in a corner, poured petrol over it and set it alight?" His eyes were now bulging from their sockets.

Williams calmly stretched his neck, and then wiping the Quartermaster's venom from his face with his cuff, and in a reasonable voice said, "I burnt my uniform with the iron while I was pressing it for the Commanding Officer's inspection, Quarter."

I was biting my tongue to keep from laughing, because Rusty caught Feeney hook, line, and sinker. Everybody knew that Feeney had grotesquely embarrassed himself, and the C.O., by his over the top rant.

"Quartermaster!" snapped the Squadron Sgt., "fall back in line. Quartermaster, Commandant O' Neill is more than capable of handling the matter without the assistance of yourself," said the Squadron Sgt. with a general quality of authority. The C.O. stepped back in front of Rusty, and stared at him for a moment. He then turned to his left and beckoned the Quartermaster to him. With the red faced Feeney standing to attention in front of him, the C.O. directed him to retrieve the damaged uniform, and issue Williams with a new one. He also told the Quarter to get a report from Williams explaining what happened the old uniform.

"I could do with an oul jumper too, Sir." said Williams speaking to the C.O., but staring at Feeney with a glint of menace in his eyes. Rusty Williams was now going for the jugular of the Quartermaster.

Feeney replied instantly, "I told ye the other day, Trooper Williams, when ye came to me looking for a sweater, that I have none. Now do ye understand that, Trooper Williams? Do ye?"

"Well I need a jumper, Quarter."

"There's no jumpers to be got, Trooper," answered a defined Feeney.

Feeney was now at boiling point, which Williams could see, and he went in for the kill. "Well I demand a jumper, and that's all there is to it," said Rusty, pushing for Feeney to go ape shit before the C.O., or the Squadron Sgt. could step in and stop it all.

It worked; Feeney let rip, "Look, sonny I don't knit the fucking things, when I get them, you'll get them. I'll tell ye what, sonny Jim; I'll buy the wool, and ye can get your oul one, or your fucking granny to knit ye one; how does that suit ye? If ye took the spuds that are growing in your fucking ears out, ye might understand me, ye little bollix ye," he spewed. He did not get a chance to say anything else, because the C.O. himself grabbed him and pulled him away, and told him to go and wait outside his office, and he would have words with him shortly. The boss then walked back to the parade. He told the Squadron Sgt. to dismiss the parade as it was a disgrace, and a shambles. In his own words, "a fucking mockery." He then walked away with the Captain, and the young officers. We were marched off the square into the lines, where all of us in working dress were informed by a fuming Squadron Sgt. to keep our working dress handy, as we would be making great use of it for the whole weekend. When the Squadron Sgt. fell us out, and when he left the scene we all had a smile on our face. It was worth getting confined to barracks for the weekend just to see Feeney get it in the neck for once, and none more so than Williams, who had the biggest and most satisfied smile of all.

As we were standing there talking about what had happened, Feeney came walking towards us with a bull thick head on him. He walked passed us without a word, got in his car and drove off.

"That's odd?" said Rusty.

"What's odd? Him walking by us, and not saying a word?" I asked.

"No, what's odd is, he went in to the C.O.'s office with his glad rags on, and came out with his sad rags on." Laughter was all round.

MESS AMUCK

The orderly sergeant stood the parade to attention on the square, and then handed over to the Squadron Sgt. for inspection. This was the nine o clock morning detail parade, and it was cold and raining. All the lads just wanted to get their work details for the day, and get out of the cold and rain. On the morning parade the Squadron Sgt. would first inspect us and then signal out different lads for various jobs around the barrack area. The cushiest job of the lot was room orderly. The room orderly's job was to look after and clean the room, toilets and wash area of the billets. He would be nice and snug for the day. As I was waiting for my place of employment for the day, I knew it was not going to be room orderly, as on the previous morning I had been late for the parade, and knowing the Squadron Sgt., being true to his nature, I would get a shitty job. Shitty was not the word when I saw who had appeared onto the square, it was Sgt. Sean Knight, aka "Body Snatcher". Sgt. Knight was the Mess Sergeant over the Officers Mess. He is the manager of the mess from top to bottom, and rules with efficiency and dedication next to none. On seeing Sgt. Knight the lads on the parade got a lot colder. Every few days Sgt. Knight would turn up at the morning parade when there was a lot of work to be done in the mess, and ask the Squadron Sgt. if it would be all right to grab a few bodies to work in the mess for the day, hence the nickname. He was a turbulent kind of a man who never seemed to relax, always on the go. Although the hair on his head was grey he had big black bushy eyebrows, and had a robust build. Behind the strictness that he might show, he was non coercive, but not too soft as to push him too far. He would often make a reference of himself as being like a part of the male anatomy, soft when left alone but fierce fucking hard when pushed.

Three lads and I were indicated out to go with Sgt. Knight to work in the mess for the day.

When we stood out to go with Sgt. Knight, he was not too pleased at all. He waved us away, and at the same time saying to Squadron Sgt. Wall, "There is no way on this earth that I am going to let them four into my mess, Gerry." He called the Squadron Sgt. by his first name.

"Well, Sean, if you don't take them, I will give you no one, and that's the be all and end all of it," said the Squadron Sgt. as he waved Sgt. Knight and us away. So off we headed to the Officer's Mess with a not so happy Sergeant. All in all I could not blame Sgt. Knight for not wanting us, as each one of us had giving him torment in the past, mostly Trooper Jock Knight, (no relation of the Sergeant) who was a fearful skit and an aggravating individual when he wanted to be, but also a great crack to have around. He was a short stocky guy with the protection of big brown sympathetic eyes that saved him from detention more times than he would like to think about. Then there was the two tall lads, Trooper's Pap Coffee and Jonny Wilson, the former being the tallest of the two, who was very giddy and never took anything seriously. Jonny was a Jack the lad, who always wore his Glengarry on the back of his head; that is when he was out of sight of the hierarchy. When we got over to the Mess, the Body Snatcher gave us our duties for the day. Pap and Jonny were given the task of fire orderlies, which consisted of stocking up of the fuel room at the back of the anteroom with turf and logs. They would be responsible for keeping the fires blazing in the Mess until four fifteen. Before leaving they would make sure that the fuel room was well stocked up for the rest of the night. Jock Knight was appointed Mess waiter for the day, which was the worst job of the lot. The Mess waiter had to be there during lunch when the rest of us were off. He would also be there late in the evening until the last officer had finished his meal, and sometimes that could be very late indeed. In between waiting on the meals he would have to serve the morning coffee in the anteroom. It looked like the good Sergeant was really sticking it to his unfavorable Trooper. I was sent upstairs to the kitchen to the cooks, as general dog's body, but it was far better than waiting on the officers. When I got to the kitchen the cook Sergeant and two old sweats from the barracks were sitting down talking. The two old boys knew the cook Sergeant, Dermot Hennessy for years, as they joined the Army together. They would come up to the kitchen in the mornings and have a chat and a cup of tea and reflect on old times, there was not that many of them left. Dermot looked forward to their little kitchen confluences. Dermot was more of a chef than a cook, as he had represented Ireland in competitions, and was highly thought of, hence being the cook Sergeant in the Officer's Mess. Dermot was a tall heavy set man who did not physically possess a potbellied abdomen like most of the cook Sergeants that were over the age of fifty. His head was a black mass of curls, not a grey hair to be seen. Although he would be laughing and joking most of the time, he had a profound tendency to anger when things went wrong.

On seeing me entering the kitchen Dermot said, "The hard and the wise, there's a bit of breakfast in the hotplate there if you want it, help yourself." I got on well with Dermot, and that was the reason why I was sent to the kitchen. "Did ye catch sight of Mrs. Blackwell on your way up? The woman was sent down to the serving area for cups ages ago, and did not come back yet; what in the hell is keeping her?" inquired Dermot as he looked beyond me to the kitchen door, hoping that she was following behind. Mrs. Blackwell was a short bowlegged middle fifties cleaning woman who had a deep hoarse voice, no doubt from the cigarettes, I have never seen her without a fag in her mouth, always stuck in the side of her mouth with one eye half closed from the drifting smoke. Dermot was not very happy when I told him that I had not seen hide nor hair of her. "I'll make a fresh pot of tea, because that one will be like fucking tar before that oul Blackwell one appears," said Dermot as he poured the stewed tea into the strainer in the sink. Tommy and Timmy, Dermot's two old friends, were beginning to get apprehensive about their morning tea and chitchat as they started to try and get the better of one another, which they were well known for. Tommy and Timmy never got married, although there were a lot of girlfriends over the years; they just seemed to be fond of the single life, or maybe one did not want to leave the other, as they were childhood friends and joined the Army together. Where there was one, you would always see the other. If I did not know them I would take them for brothers, as they had a lot in common physically. The two of them were small in height and had receding hairlines, but the unusual characteristic was that they both possessed a boxer's nose, which gave the impression that they could look after themselves. The only indifference they had between them was they had a mission in life for one to best the other, if one said big the other would say bigger.

Timmy was the first to speak, "Did you know, Dermot, that the British have a smart bomb now that would kill everybody in Ireland; did you know that, Dermot? Yep a smart bomb that would kill everybody in Ireland," he said to Dermot but meant for the ears of Tommy.

"Is that so; well, that's some smart bomb," said Dermot as he winked at me. There was a kind of victorious air to Timmy as he watched Tommy in complete silence with head down and winding his watch back and forth.

After what seemed like an eternity Tommy broke the silence, "That's fuck all; Ireland has a smarter bomb, and it kills no one, Dermot."

"Kills no one, so what does this smarter bomb do, Tommy?" said Dermot, knowing that Tommy was indirectly getting at Timmy.

"It kills nobody, it rounds everyone up and brings them in for questioning," chirped Tommy as he got to his feet and slapped Timmy on the back. I was having a good laugh as I thought it was a good comeback, but Dermot was splitting his sides and wiping the tears from his eyes, even Timmy was in titters. Tommy was standing in the middle of the kitchen with his hands on his hips, and with a straight face said, "Someone should round that oul Blackwell one up and bring in for questioning about her disappearance with the teacups, in the name of jasus where can she be?" He did not see Mrs Blackwell standing behind him.

"I'm sorry, Dermot." she said, and at the same time giving Tommy a dirty look. "Ye see, Dermot, I was coming back up with the cups when I had to rush to the toilet, very rapid like. It was kind of an emergency, if ye follow me drift like," she said, as she walked towards us with the fag hanging from the side of her mouth. It was only then that we all noticed that she was not carrying the cups by their handles, but was holding them the same way a barman would collect pint tumblers with the hands spread out and the thumbs and fingers grasping the inside of the cups, four in each hand. We were all staring at the cups in total silence, when what she said next made grown men weak at the knees. "I would have been here a lot sooner only for the oul haemorrhoids; they have me killed so they have," she said, putting the cups down on the table.

Tommy shook his shoulders as if someone had just walked over his grave, and then dragged out the words from his mouth, "Sweet loving, lamping, divine fuck." His chin and head going deeper into his chest with each word. He then walked quickly to the kitchen door and out of sight.

Timmy jumped to his feet, " His right, Dermot, we were supposed to be down in the stores ten minutes ago, that's why Tommy was in so much of a hurry; I better get down there myself. I'll see you later, Dermot," said Timmy as he headed for the door. Mrs. Blackwell started to pour the tea into the cups, on seeing this Dermot made a beeline out of the kitchen, and without turning around he said, " I have to go down to the ration stores; the Quartermaster wants me to sign for rations." I ran after Dermot and caught him halfway down the stairs.

"What will I do, Dermot?" I said in wonder.

Dermot looked up at me and said, "I'll tell ye what ye can do, get rid of them cups before I get back. I never want to see them again. Throw them into the incinerator at the back of the Mess, and while you're at it, fuck that oul one in along with them." He gave himself a shake and was gone.

Thank heaven for small mercies, because as I was going back into the kitchen, Mrs. Preparation H came running past me, and without stopping she said, "I have to rush, I forgot that I had to do a job for Sargent Knight, will ye tell Dermot. Oh, and there's a cup of tea on the table for ye."

"Ye can fucking ram it," I half mumbled.

She came to a standstill. "What did ye say?" she inquired.

Thinking fast for what my life was worth I said,

"I said damn it; I was to do something for Dermot, and I can't remember, so I said damn it."

"Ah, sure don't worry, son, it will come back to ye," she assured me, and then she disappeared down the stairs, thanks be to fuck. I put the cups onto the dumbwaiter and lowered them down to the serving area.

After I had disposed of the cups I was passing the anteroom when I heard a scream. When I went into the anteroom I saw Mrs. Ditch hunched over in fits of laughter, and Pap standing in the middle of the room with a load of turf in his arms. Mrs. Ditch's face was as red as beetroot as she pointed at Pap, and said, "Ye dirty little so and so ye," as she fanned her blushing face with her hand. Mrs. Ditch was a gentle natured woman who always had a smile on her face when you met her, and always seen the funny side of life. She was a small slender woman of about fifty with high cheek bones that made her look a lot younger. The way she had a bun in her hair, and the glasses she wore would not make her seem out of place teaching in a classroom. Pap walked over and threw the pile of turf that was in his hands into the fuel bin. Rubbing one hand of the other to remove the turf particles, he winked at me with a smile on his face. Composing herself, Mrs. Ditch went on to explain the nature of her scream, and pointing at Pap she said, "He was busy bringing in the fuel, so I asked him would I light the anteroom fire for him? and he said yes. I then asked him for a match, and he said they were in his trouser pocket, and I would have to reach in and get them as his hands were full of turf, so I put my hand into his pocket." She started to laugh again. After a few moments of tittering she continued, "When I put my hand into his pocket, there was not a lining to it, and he is not wearing any underwear, the dirty little rascal." She began to blush again.

Through the laughing I inquired from Pap the reason for doing that, and with a smug grin on his face, and his eyebrows arched, he replied, "She went into the wrong pocket; the matches are in the other one. The pocket she put her hand into is the one I keep my cigar in." Then he began to cackle. Mrs. Ditch, with her legs crossed and a hand holding her side, was in the kinks laughing, and with the other hand pointing at Pap gesturing him to stop.

The three of us were all having a right giggle when Sgt. Knight burst into the room. "What's all the commotion about? I was up the far end of the mess, and I thought I heard a scream coming from down here; now someone better tell me what's going on? Come on, start talking," he said, placing his hands on his hips.

Pap put up his hand, "It was me Sarge; I came into the anteroom and seen that the wallpaper and carpet clashed. So the feminine side of me came to the fore, and I let out a sharp shrill. I don't know what came over me," said Pap, as he turned his head sideways and placed the back of his hand on his forehead.

Half laughing, Sgt. Knight said, "Ye will be doing some shrilling in a minute when I choke the fucking life out of ye if ye don't tell me what the fuck happened." He then started to break out laughing. After we all finished laughing I told him that the real reason for the scream was that Mrs. Ditch had seen a mouse crossing the anteroom. Just then we could hear Mrs. Blackwell shouting Sgt. Knight's name over and over, as she was coming down the staircase that led down from the bedrooms. We all went out into the hall, and there at the end of the stairs, and holding on to the banister, was a breathless Mrs. Blackwell, with Jonny in tow.

"Right, Wilson, what in the name of shit did ye do now? If ye done anything to this woman I'll fucking swing for ye, swing for ye," said Sgt Knight, threateningly.

Mrs Blackwell waved her hand in front of Sgt. Knight's face, and said, "The young lad didn't do a thing, he was giving me a hand to clean the upstairs rooms. When we got to Lieutenant Harry Nugent's room, I asked young Wilson if he would clean up the room and also make up the bed, and he obliged me. I went on and done the next room. After a few minutes the young lad came and got me and brought me into Nugent's room, and what I saw was a shameful disgrace." At this stage she stopped and arched her hand, and placed it at the corner of her mouth, and continued in a very loud whisper, "The sheets on his bed were sopping wet, if ye follow me drift, like. I can tell ye here and now that me and that young fella are not going anywhere near that bed or room until this is sorted out by your good self, Sargent Knight, so there." She then clasped her hands together and threw her eyes up to the heavens.

Sergeant Knight's face was now red with rage, and in a growling voice said, "The dirty little bollix, and him being the only officer that does not make up his bed in the mornings. Well I can tell ye here and now that he will make it up from here on in, the little shit head. I'm going to hunt him down and drag him in front of the C.O. to let him deal with the matter." He then stormed off muttering to himself. The two women went into the service area for a cup of tea, leaving Pap, Jonny and I together in the main entrance hall. In the middle of the hall Jonny started to pivot with his hands in his pockets.

When he stopped pivoting he had a smile, and a look of satisfaction on his face, and as he began to rock back and forward on his heels and toes, he said, "It's amazing the shit that can happen over a little drop of H2O, a fucking amazing."

"Ye didn't, ye fucking didn't?" I inquired of him.

Taking a hand from his pocket and simultaneously clicking his fingers, and lifting his leg said, "I did, and I'm glad I did. That asshole had it coming to him for a long time; fuck him!" once again clicking his fingers. The asshole he was talking about was Lieutenant Harry Nugent, a right dick head, who had the nick-name around the barracks as, 'the final frontier' (from Star Trek) because there is nothing inside his head but fucking space. He was as thin as a lath, and lanky to suit. The baby face and fair curly hair, together with a little turned up nose bore true to the air of aloofness for which he possessed.

We were silent for a few seconds, and then I queried, "How did you do it?"

"Mrs. Blackwell was in cleaning the next officer's room, so I simply walked down the hall to the toilet and got a mouthful of water which I kept in my mouth until I got back to his room. I repeated this over and over again until I compiled enough water to complete the job. Then I went and asked Mrs. Blackwell, was I to make the bed or flush it, and she took it from there, so let the show begin," Jonny said, as he took a bow. We were all elated. When the two women returned we all went back to our place of employment with the knowledge of knowing that Nugent was going to get a right rollicking. Later on that morning I was sent down from the kitchen to give Trooper Jock Knight a hand with the morning coffee. I was to make pots of coffee and tea in the serving kitchen and bring them into the anteroom for Jock to serve out. The officers would come into the mess at ten to eleven for their morning coffee break. They would go to the anteroom, where the beverages would be served to them. Everything was going fine until I went back into the anteroom with a refill of coffee. The first thing I saw on entering was a bunch of officers gathered around mad Martin, who was sitting on the floor screaming a string of expletives in the direction of Jock Knight, who was cutting a lonely figure standing by the table of coffee pots, cups and saucers. Mad Martin, or to give him his right name, Captain Martin Behan, was a tall lean man with hair on the sides of his head, but there was only a few strands crossing over the top. He had been in a car accident a few years back and nearly lost his life. An operation on his head had saved his life, but he was never one hundred percent right in the head department after that, and of course out of his earshot, he was known with soldier affection around the barracks as mad Martin. Even though he was a little bit touched in the head, the Army gave him a cushy job to let him work out the couple of years to his pension.

I walked over to Jock, and without asking him what had happened, he said, "The crazy bastard just went mental and took a fucking mad fit right in front of me as I was pouring him a cup of tea."

Waking towards us at this stage was Lt. Colonel Kelly, and he did not seemed too pleased. He walked up to us and looked us up and down, and then said, "Would the two of you please leave now; we will look after ourselves. One of you can find Sargent Knight and inform him that I wish to speak with him at once, tell him that I will be here, good men." He then began to pour himself a cup of coffee. We did not have to look for Sgt. Knight because as we walked out into the long hall, there was Sgt. Knight down the far end of the hall coming toward us. Between the two of us we told him what had happened, and that the Lt. Colonel wanted to see him in the anteroom at once. He told us to go into the service area and wait there until he came back.

While we were sitting down in the service kitchen having a cup of tea, Jock explained in greater detail what had happened, he began, " I was standing there giving out the tea and coffee when I notice mad Martin coming towards me with his pipe in his mouth, and his glasses on the end of his nose. He just stood there staring at me, and I can tell ye, he was freaking me out. I kept asking him does he want tea or coffee, but he just stood there staring and saying nothing. He then picked up a cup and held it out and muttered something that sounded like tea. I picked up the large teapot and began to pour. I had only started to pour when he opened his lips and started to bite down on his pipe. Then he began to squeal like a pig, and started to shake. I got nervous, as I thought he was having a mental fit, so I poured faster and faster. Then he let this unmerciful screech and spit out the pipe, and at the same time fucking the cup of tea up into the air. Still screaming he staggered backwards and fell on to the floor. I shouted that someone should put a spoon in his mouth to stop him swallowing his tongue, because it was more than likely an epileptic fit, but no one seemed to mind me. The mad fucker then sat up on the floor and started to shout and swear at me in tongues. I'm telling ye he was fucking possessed. It's not a psychiatrist that fucker wants; it's a specialist from Rome. Ye think it was my fault that he had a mental breakdown, for fuck's sake." Dejected, he lit up a cigarette.

Bursting out laughing I said, "I'm sorry Jock, but it's so funny, come on, think about it." Then I waited on his response. At last he began to see the funny side of it and started to laugh. The two of us were in knots, and were standing there mimicking mad Martin when Sgt. Knight came into the room. We ceased immediately.

"Don't let me stop ye, carry on, ye pair of claw hammers." said the Sergeant. "I don't know how ye do it, Trooper Knight, but you seem to have it down to a fine art. You're definitely going to hell, Knight, because God won't take ye, and do ye know why, Knight? Because ye would have heaven fucked up within one hour flat." He then just stood there in silence staring at Jock.

Jock looked at me and then at Sgt. Knight with disbelief on his face. Raising his voice he said, "Hold on a minute here; it's not my fault that the good Captain out there turned into Mr. fucking Bean on acid. I'm not having that, no way am I," said Jock with alarm shown on his face.

"As a matter of fact, Trooper Knight, ye are responsible for turning the good Captain into a nervous wreck. Ye see he was not taking a mad fit; it was just you pouring the tea from the teapot. What ye failed to notice was that the bottom of the spout on the teapot was leaking like the fucking Titanic, and the faster that ye poured the more scalding tea was cascading on to the good captain's hand and thumb. That's why he was screaming, ye dozy little bollix ye. Now the two of ye get into that anteroom and get them teapots out of there, and change them all with the Quartermaster. Oh, and while you're with the Quarter, ye can ask him can he issue ye with a government health warning that ye can wear for the rest of your time in service, not that ye will last that long anyway," said the Sergeant as he placed one hand on his forehead, and gently squeezed each side of his head with forefinger and thumb.

Jock quickly retorted, "I don't think I will be in service as long as those teapots. Collins and Dev must have got coffee and tea served to them out of those, and even then, they were more than likely passed down by the Brits on the handover. Leaking, it's no wonder the arses are not gone out of them, they are that old." He was now waiting on a reply from the Sergeant, which he got.

"The Brits handed over something else, Trooper Knight, the guardroom, where I will send ye if ye don't shut the fuck up. Now go very rapid and do the job I asked ye to do, now, move it," he said, walking away down the back hall in the direction of the main kitchen. We went back to the anteroom which was by now devoid off all officers and we had a really good laugh, and crack about the sequence of events which had occurred earlier. Later on I was back up in the kitchen, and went into the back room of the kitchen which was the preparation area, as I had to peel potatoes for the dinner that evening. I had just left Sgt. Knight in the kitchen warming himself at the range, and drinking a mug of soup, when I heard a familiar nauseating voice addressing Sgt. Knight, it was Lt. Nugent.

"Ah! Sergeant Knight, the very man. One of the people downstairs told me that you would be up here. I have just come from the Commanding Officer's office where I spent ten minutes apologizing and groveling to him.

I don't mind that so much as he is of a superior rank, and sometimes to get along in your career one has to be a yes man, do you follow me Sergeant Knight?" he said in an aggressive manner.

"No, Sir, I don't follow anybody as I am not into stalking. Now, if you're trying to get at me for reporting ye to the C.O., I suggest that ye think long and hard about that. With all due respect to your rank, Sir, you're not talking to one of the young lads over in the barracks now. If ye try to start that kind of intimidating behavior with me I will have ye back in front of the C.O. before your feet can touch the ground. Now I don't think you're a stalker, so I won't say, do ye follow me, okay, Sir. Oh, and ye know that ye will be making your own bed up from now on in, Sir," said Sgt. Knight.

At that moment there was a silent air of agitation hanging over the kitchen until Nugent said, "I apologize, Sergeant, for this morning, and of now, and I hope that you will accept that, and that will be the end of the matter."

"Look Sir, should ye not be apologizing to Mrs. Blackwell and Trooper Wilson? I mean they were the ones at the side of the bed, not me."

"Listen, Sergeant, I was at a stag party last night, and I was pissed out of my mind. I don't know if I done the deed or some of the other officers were playing a trick on me. Well I will tell you here and now that I will not lower myself by apologizing to a pretentious demigoddess or even worst, a lowly Trooper. End of matter," said Nugent, who never fails to carry out his usual ignominies. After he had left I went back into the kitchen, and saw Sgt. Knight looking at the floor, shaking his head from side to side. Dermot returned back to the kitchen from the orderly room, and the Sarge told him all about Nugent.

Dermot was cutting up a load of mushrooms on the table when he stopped, and said to me, "What have a young Lieutenant's pips and Mrs. Blackwell's hemorrhoids got in common?"

"I don't know, what?"

Dermot was laughing as he said, "Only assholes get them." He got back to the mushrooms. We all cheered up after that. After lunch I went downstairs and told the lads what Nugent had said, and they were not too pleased, especially Jonny.

"His in the anteroom having a cup of coffee after his lunch, the scummy bastard," said Jock who was serving the coffee out and was making a fresh pot for the officers in the anteroom.

"Right!" said Jonny. "Come with me." He then led Pap and me to the fuel room. Jonny went into the anteroom, and after a few moments came back, and gathering turf in his arms said, "Everything is grand; the fire is low, and Nugent is sitting beside it having a cup of coffee and reading the paper. Grab some fuel and follow me, and I'll do all the talking." Then he entered the anteroom. Pap and I followed; as we got in the door I could see Nugent sitting beside the fire with his cup of coffee on a saucer resting on an antique table beside him.

We were loading the logs and turf into the great fireplace when Jonny, making sure Nugent could hear him, and speaking to Pap and myself, said,

"Do ye know lads I was in France a while back, and the way they speak is weird. I mean when they say wee-wee, well over there it means yes. Now here, when we say wee-wee it means piss." He now placed another sod of turf on the fire.

Nugent, dropping his newspaper down from his face said, "Don't be so vulgar Wilson, and hurry up and get the fuck out." He then shook the paper, and went on reading.

Nothing was going to stop Jonny; he spoke fast, "I mean, Sir, if yourself were in the French Army and ye had to grovel and apologize to a superior officer, well over there ye would not be called a yes man, no, Sir; ye would be called a wee-wee man for the rest of your life," said Jonny with a sneering expression.

Nugent, with hatred in his eyes, snarled, "Get the fuck out of my mess now or I will put you three swine's under arrest." He then sat and watched the smoldering turf. As we were leaving, Jock was coming in with a pot of coffee. With his head and eyes, he gestured to the teapot he was carrying. It was the same leaking teapot that scalded mad Martin that morning. He walked by us and headed straight for Lt Nugent.

"A refill Sir?" said Jock. Picking up, and holding out his cup the Lieutenant still in a pissed off mood demandingly said, "Yes, and be quick about it."

"Oh yes, Sir, I'll be real quick about it," said Jock, standing up straight, and ready to pour. The three of us made a bolt for the anteroom door. We were halfway down the long hall when we heard the scream coming from the anteroom.

"Where did that scream come from?" inquired Sgt. Knight as he emerged from the snooker room.

In bits laughing Pap said, "That's just Jock, Sergeant, taking the piss out of a right piss pot.

MIND YOU MIND OUT

The officer's mess bar was a place I did not wish to be, but being detailed for it, I could not refuse. Working as bartender in the mess was a good number, a week of serving the officers, and their guests. When I was finished my week working I would get a week's leave and extra money in my pocket from the customers, in a roundabout way. All in all it was a cushy job that usually had the lads queuing up to volunteer to go into the bar for six months, but not of late. There are two barmen that work the officers mess bar on a week on, week off basis. Trooper Fergie Morris, the barman I was taking over from, and Trooper Barry Ryan, the other barman, were down money after their individual stock checks for the last two and half months. Fergie told me that he was glad to get out as it was costing him money to work in the bar. Word of the two lads' plight had been heard on the troop grapevine, thus no volunteers. So here I stood in the bar with Fergie, and the mess officer Captain Laverty, as we completed the stock check. Laverty had a condescending nature, who patronized above and below his rank, all for below, optional for above. The characteristic of his face was that of a minor, almost infantile, with squinting blue eyes, a button nose, and shallow lips that looked like they were drew on to his face with a eyebrow pencil. He now stood at the bar humming a tune as he totted up the last of the stock sheets. Every now and again he would stop humming to inform Fergie that the stock check was not faring well at all.

"Finish!" he rapped, with a look of satisfaction on his face as though he had just put the final touches to a work of art. With the stock sheets in one hand, and taking a small bottle of orange from the shelf with the other hand, and opening it off the bar opener, he said to Fergie, "You are down a lot of money in the stock check. So you will have to pay it back to......him." He was pointing the stock sheets at me. He took a swig of orange from the neck of the bottle. Wiping his mouth with the back of his bottle hand, and giving a small belch, he said, " I will take what Trooper Morris owes the bar from your float, and therefore the good Trooper here will owe you the money, which he can pay you every week until he has his debt to you finished. So I think that is a satisfactory and acceptable way out of the whole mess."

In a quite sincere voice I said, "No, Sir, the way out of this mess is through that fucking door right there, which I am about to use." I walked out. As I got out the door I could hear Laverty saying to Fergie,

"Where the fuck is he going?" he asked stunned; he followed me out into the long hall. I was half way down the long hall when he caught up to me. He told me to stop walking, and when I did, he queried, "Where are you off to, Trooper."

"Look, Sir, Trooper Morris does not owe me any money. He owes the mess that money, not me. I suggest, Sir, that you work something out with Trooper Morris, or I am out of here. I didn't want to be here in the first place, so sort it, Sir, or I walk. It's as simple as that," I said, knowing I had him over a barrel. He knew that if I went back to the Unit with a genuine excuse, the Squadron Sgt. would not send anyone else over.

"Ok, ok, I suppose you do need your float, so I will leave it with you and sort something out with Trooper Morris. But I will not tolerate any bad language like that which was used back there in the bar. Do you understand me?" he said, saving face. We went back down the hall to the bar where Fergie was waiting outside. The Captain told me to wait inside the bar until he got back from the Mess office, as he had to sort the money problem out with Fergie, so off they went. The social side of the bar was very luxurious with plush red carpet flecked with pearl grey. There was a large column which was central, and about six feet from the bar which could not be classified as an integral subsidiary of the building as it was erected there for decoration, and not support. Inside a glass wooden frame, hanging on the column was a small piece of brown paper. Drawn on this piece of paper with pencil was a battle strategy, supposedly made by Field Marshal Rommel during the desert campaign of World War Two, it was held in high esteem by many of the officers. Hanging from the ceiling in the center of the room was an elegant chandelier, which when turned on would shed light onto the elaborate and finely carved tables and chairs of the Mess. For all its elegance, the Mess was eerie, and lacking atmosphere; it was like a champagne chapel of rest that sold ports and porter to inanimate clientele. The ladies and gents toilets were outside the room, just across the long hall. The working side of the bar was like any other bar except it had mirrors with the Cavalry Corp crest etched into them. There was a backroom, or actually it was more of a laneway; it was that long and narrow. Inside the backroom there was the beer kegs, sinks and fridges, two of each, and a small television for myself to watch. The barman's television being the concept of the Mess body for the barman's entertainment as he was not allowed to stay in the bar area once he had served the Mess clientele, he had to retreat into the backroom until he was summoned to serve again. The concept also had an undercurrent of underplay to it, whereas the noise from the television would drown out the conservations from the bar, therefore preventing any shop or loose talk getting to the barman's ears. It stated in the barman's orders that when the barman was on the premises, he would insure that the television would be turned on, and the volume turned up at all times. I, for one, was elated with that order, as I would not have to listen to a nonsensical drunken lecture from some asshole who wanted to invade the Isle of Man, or some other head melting bollixogly that will be spoken with loud slurring.

The Captain returned. "You are now the barman of the Officers' Mess bar, so how do you feel about the position?" he said to me as though he had just promoted me to Sgt. Major.

Looking at him with a big insincere smile on my face, and with a sarcastic tone, I said, "Well, Sir, I'm so delighted that I think I will have to restrain myself from doing a lap of honor around the barracks." I think he got the message, as he left without saying a word. The job itself was cushy enough as there was very little to do. I opened the bar at lunch time from half twelve to half one, and was nearly killed by the rush. In the whole hour, four young officers that were on a training course in the barracks came in and bought a bar of chocolate each. After I gave them the chocolate I continued on with what I was doing before they came in, stacking pint tumblers. I could not help notice that the four of them were opening the wrappers of the chocolate bars, not only in the same way, but in unison. I stood there in a bewildering curiosity watching them undo the wrappers. They took the bar in both hands, and then running the thumb of the right hand along the paper seam at the back of the bar, undone the outer paper wrapper perfectly, without a tear. Then they took the gold wrapper, and opened it very slowly to reveal the bar of chocolate, complete, and intact. Their eyes devouring before their mouths touched. It was really weird, and before I could think I blurted out, "Hard luck, lads, the last golden ticket was found about a half hour ago by an officer from the Engineers." I threw a little smile and waited for the fallout.

To my surprise three of the officers started to laugh, but one just stood there, and as he placed a square of chocolate in his mouth, said, "What golden ticket?" as he stuck another square in his mouth. Fuck that, I was gone like a shot into the back room, and left the other three to tell him that he should not have watched so many fucking war films at Christmas, I turned up the telly.

I had only opened up that night at eight o clock when the bar door opened, and in walked the Willie Wonka quartet with a few more friends. They had finished a six week course they were on in the barracks, today, and were out to celebrate. The usual crack was to have a few drinks here, and then head further a field into a bar in the town, and then on to a nightclub. They were in great form and high spirits. They were not only happy about finishing the course, but were happier about returning to their parent units. After I served them I went into the backroom and placed my chair just inside the opening of the door with my back to the bar. The reason for putting my chair there was the noise from the television, and the boisterous young officers, would make it easier for me to hear if someone is asking for service. I had only sat down when I heard the creak of the bar door opening. I got up from my chair and saw the O.C. of the barracks, Lt Colonel Clarence Cleary approaching the bar.

"Ah, I see that we have a new barman," said the O.C. as he eyed up the young officers at the other end of the bar.

"Yes, Sir, I just took over today," I said.

Without taking his eyes off the young officers, he said, "Welcome aboard, my boy." He was talking to me but walking towards the young officers. He shook hands with them all, and congratulated them on finishing the course. With his left arm extended, and his hand opened, palm up, and pointing it at the nervous young officers, and with his right hand waving at me, he said, "My boy, give these fine young men whatever they're drinking, and put it down to me; thank you, my boy." Rubbing his hands together, he took a seat at the bar. The young officers over thanked him to the point of embellishing a simple gesture. What the young officers did not know was that the good Lt. Colonel was of a caprice nature, and could turn on them at the drop of a hat. He was touching sixty, but his demeanor made him look a lot older. He was small and scraggy with overgrown eyebrows, and when walking he had a limp as though he had a hip operation at some stage. Being an old bachelor he resided in the Mess during the week, and at the weekends he would depart the Mess for a house that he owned on the outskirts of Dublin that was left to him by a late sister. After he took a mouthful from his pint of Guinness, and wiping his mouth with the back of his hand, he informed me, "Now, my boy, as you may know, I am the C.O. of the barracks, and there are just two things for you to know, and we will get on fine together. One, I come in here every night from Monday to Friday, and I expect you to be here. Two, and most important, that while you're here, you will let no one, and I mean no one, fool around with that over there," he was pointing at the Rommel tactical plan that was hanging on the column, "because I have a great affection for it. Now if you can get those two things right, we will get along fine. Well, my boy, is that all right?" he asked, taking a swig from his pint, waiting for my response. I did not get a chance to answer, as the bar door flung opened with a force that was dramatic enough to make it an area of concern for everyone in the bar. Entering through the doorway was the towering, and, disordered figure of Big Tim Breslin. Tim noticing the young officers staring at him, and he scurried to the opposite corner of the bar from the young officers. Nobody could blame the officers for staring at him. Tim was wearing a three quarter length coat that gave the impression that it was too small for him, maybe because of his six foot three frame that was bear like in resemblance. The knot of the tie he was wearing with the white shirt was flat, and to one side as though he had pulled on the front strip instead of the back strip. His hair was thick and tossed, and although Big Tim always had five o' clock shadow, because of his dark complexion, and heavy growth; he now wore dirty stubble. His big black Cookie Monster fucking eyebrows didn't help either, I thought to myself. What the young officers did not know was that Tim Breslin was a Commandant up till a month ago, and was destined for a glittering career.

There was even talk that he would make the youngest Chief of Staff one day, but it was not to be. He was medically discharge from the Army for reasons of mental health. Before the mental health issue, he was a military genius, and had an exceptional intellectual ability for almost anything, but he just stepped over the fine line.

"Hello, Clar, will you have a drink?" Tim asked the C.O.

"I won't, Tim," was the reply from the C.O. as he got off his stool. The C.O. then told me he was going to the anteroom and to pull him a pint, and to bring it down to him there. As the Lt. Col. limped toward the door, he wished the officers a good night.

"He didn't wish me goodnight, the little leg dragging whingeing fuck. No! But he wished them fucking arse splinters over there goodnight, the little bollix," growled Big Tim, as he banged his fist on the counter. The young officers went quite for a few seconds, and then one of them quietly motioned with his head for me to come down the bar to him. He asked me what the story was, and who was Tim. To save all arguments I told him Tim was a Commandant here in the barracks, with a bad temper, and should not be annoyed, especially by young officers who want to go on the town for the night, and not be confined to barracks.

That seemed to do the trick, because the young officer called down the bar, "Will you have a drink, Sir?"

"I'll buy my own drink, scutter arse," replied Tim in his own inimical way. He then looked at me with those glazed eyes, and said, "Same again." pointing at the counter in front of him.

"I don't know what the same again is, Sir, as you did not order your first drink yet." I informed him.

"Same again, same again," he repeated.

He could be here until the end of the night saying this, I thought to myself, so I said to him, "I can't remember, Sir, what your last drink was; was it whiskey and water?" I waited for his reply. The reply came only after he took a small box made from plywood from his pocket, and placed it on the bar.

The box contained small cigars, from which he took one, placed it in his mouth, and lighting it said, "Gin and tonic," as he blew smoke from the side of his mouth. After I finished serving him I went into the backroom, and sat down to watch some telly. I was sitting with my back to the door, and directly behind me sitting at the other side of the bar, was Tim. I was only sitting down a few minutes when there was a rap on the counter. I looked around, and Tim was holding his empty glass, and mumbling, "Double," as he handed the glass to me. I no sooner gave him the double gin and tonic, and it disappeared down his neck. "Same again, same again," he demanded. I gave him the same again, and went back to watching telly. I had only sat down again when one of the young officers called me. When I went out to the bar the young officer thanked me, and told me they were off into town. I was just about to wish them all the best when a bar stool was thrown to the floor by Big Tim. Then another, and another, and then he just sat back on his stool at the bar. "Same again, same again," he said, as though he was oblivious to what he had just done. Most of the young officers vacated the Mess very rapid like, except for a few who stood at the doorway for a few seconds staring back at Tim and myself, and then the door shut and they were gone, leaving me and Pierre the mad fucking trapper alone together. I went out my door and down the hall and into the bar. First I collected the young officers' empty glasses and put them on the counter. Then I picked up the stools, and placed them back at the front of the bar.

I felt a bit nervous being so close to Tim without the safety of the bar between us, but plucking up the courage, I said to him, "Listen, Sir, you can't be throwing bar stools around the Mess just to get my attention for a drink; there's other ways to get my attention without doing that." But I was walking away as I said so. I don't think he was listening, as he just stared into the bar with a blank expression on his face, he probably thought I was still in there. I went back behind the bar, and gave him the 'same again' to keep him quite. I was just about to sit down when there was a knock on my door from the long hall. There in front of me when I opened the door was Captain Laverty. In a whispered voice he told me to bring a pint for the C.O. down to the anteroom. He was doing the Lt. Colonel's dirty work, as he also was apprehensive around Big Tim, and that was the reason he did not come into the bar, but used the barman's door instead. So, to see what he would do, I said, "Commandant Breslin is in the bar, Sir; I think he is looking for a bit of company. Will I tell him that you're here?"

"No!" he yelped, as he grasped my arm with a look of terror on his face. After he composed himself, he said in a soft whisper, "There is no need to tell him; I'll just pop in and surprise him." He was pointing down the hall to the bar door.

I leaned a little backwards, and looked into the bar, then turning my head to Laverty, I said, "Sure there's no need to surprise him, Sir; he's just got off his stool, and it looks like he is heading for the toilet, sure you'll meet him in the hall in a few seconds."

"Oh...my....jasus." he said, as he took flight. I never seen him move so fast, pass the bar door, and down the long hall into the anteroom. I thought the fucker was on steroids. I closed the door, and went back into the bar, and said, "The same again Sir," as I lifted Big Tim's empty glass of the counter. Big Tim had not gone anywhere. I thought to myself, you're some fucking messer. On returning from my forced delivery of the pint to the anteroom I could see that Big Tim was at it again. He had thrown four stools onto the floor and was now sitting doodling with his finger with some gin and tonic he had spilt on the counter. He was mumbling something to himself which I could not make out, and he was breathing very heavy. Looking at him I thought best not to say anything about the stools. One thing I knew for sure was that I definitely was not going around into the bar to pick them up; they could stay where they lay until he left. Leaving him to his heavy breathing, and doodling, I sat down to watch some film that had just started on the television. I had been watching the film for about five minutes when this excruciating fucking pain came through the back of my head that made me jump to my feet, and squeeze the cheeks of my arse together. The first thought that came to me, was that Big Tim had a gun, and the mad bastard had shot me through the back of my head, because I wouldn't pick up the stools for him. I was in a frantic state rubbing my head, and slowly releasing the cheeks of my arse to ease the pain out when I noticed Big Tim's wooden cigar box on the floor at the back of my chair. Then I realized that the crazy mad bastard had thrown the wooden cigar box at the back of my head. As it was made of plywood, it must have been thrown with great force. The pointed corner of the box must have hit the back of my head, because when I picked the box up, one of the pointed corners was missing. Probably impaled in the back of my head somewhere.

Still rubbing my head I looked at the big swine, and with one big black hairy eyebrow cocked up, and the other one down, and with a little shake of his head, he said, "Did that get your fucking attention?" Then dropping the eyebrow, and tapping one finger on his glass, he said, "Same again, same again."

"You can call me for a drink; you don't have to throw a fucking cigar box at me. I'll give you this drink, but it is your last, to be honest with you I have a pain in my bollix with you all night, not to mention my fucking head," I said, as I gave him his gin and tonic. I went inside, and took the chair away from the door, and closed it. If anyone came in for a drink they could call, or knock. After a few minutes standing there, still rubbing my head, there was a knock on my door from outside in the long hall. Good, I thought to myself, it's Laverty ordering another pint for the Lt. Col. I'll tell him what went on, and that I want Big Tim out of here. When I opened the door I nearly shit a brick, for standing there, and filling up the whole frame of the door, was Big Tim. His shadow alone covered half the backroom. He just stood there with his head down, with his chin on his chest, and these great big bulging eyes staring down at me. Then I nearly had a nervous breakdown when I got this overwhelming fear, as I noticed that his big hairy right hand was caressing his groin area. Visions came rushing into my sore head of him strangling me with one fucking hand, and someone finding me in the morning lying there with my trousers and skivvies around my ankles, dead, and with a cigar box rammed down my fucking neck.

"What's wrong with you, Sir?" I nervously inquired, with my knees knocking together, and my testicles gone up into my stomach. He just kept staring at me. He was now drooling from the mouth, and licking his top lip. I thought to myself, please God don't let that be about me.

Then he spoke, "I'm bursting to relieve myself, but I can't go into the toilet because Clar, and his friends are in there talking about me. I can't relieve myself with them on the walls of the toilet talking about me," he moaned in a voice that was full of misery. He may not be able to relieve himself, but I was fucking relieved that that was the reason why he was rubbing his groin. Looking up, and turning his attention to the ceiling, he blabbered, "The flies are the worst. They hate me; they're not my friends."

I have no friends left, none." He then dropped his head. This guy needed a mega amount of psychiatric treatment, and medication, and so would I, if I did not get him the fuck out of here, I thought to myself.

I plucked up the courage, and moved towards him. I placed my hand on his arm. "Well Sir, I'm your friend, and I'll tell you what, Sir, if you go back into the bar I will buy you a drink, and we can talk about what's going on in the toilet," I lied. He just stood there staring at me with a blank expression on his face. Then after a few seconds he staggered backwards a small bit before turning, and walking back towards the bar door. I waited until he went into the bar, and when I heard the bar door close I had it away on my toes as fast as I could move. I think I broke Laverty's record for getting from the bar to the anteroom by a couple of seconds. Opening the anteroom door I saw Captain Laverty sitting beside the fire looking at the telly. Getting his attention, I beckoned to him to come outside. When he came out I told him all about what had happened in the bar, and backroom. When I was telling him what went on with Big Tim, I thought to myself that he had no interest in what I was saying.

He proved me right when he said, "Don't worry about it; Tim is just acting the gobshite. Just go back to the bar, and talk some sense into him, good man; what do you think?"

"I really don't think that I can talk sense into this man, who at the present moment has the brains of a Curly-Wurly. I mean, his head at the moment is like Old Mother Hubbard's cupboard, fucking bare, there's nothing inside. Now Sir, I suggest that you go down to the bar, and sort this out." I pleaded, throwing my arms in the air, and taken a few steps away from him.

"Look, Trooper," he barked. "I am giving you a direct order to go back to that bar, and continue to serve Ex Commandant Breslin, and don't come back near me. Do you understand?"

"I understand,Sir; I understand perfectly, Sir, that because Commandant Breslin thinks that the Lord of the fucking flies is in the toilet becoming best friends with the C.O., he is not going to use it. So if he decides to go the toilet on the carpet in the bar, well, Sir, you will be responsible, and I can tell you Sir, he is bursting at the moment," I said, stressing the point. He stood there deep in thought, running his finger back and forward along his chin.

"He's bursting?" he inquired.

"Well, Sir, forgive me for being so forward, but he was bursting when I left the bar, so right now I would say his balls are floating around in his sack, and if he leaves it any longer it will rise up into his lungs, and fucking drown him," I said, smiling.

Giving me a mocking grin, he said, "Less of the fucking dry wit. Right! I will have to get the boss to deal with this." And he entered the anteroom. After a short time he returned with the Lt. Col,, and without saying a word to me they proceeded down the long hall towards the bar, I followed behind. When we got into the bar, Big Tim was sitting on his stool, as quite as a mouse. The C.O. pointed at the stools lying on the floor, and told me to pick them up. "Come on now, Tim, time to go home, good man now. Let's go," said the Lt Col from a safety distance of six feet from Tim. I could see Laverty's eyes scanning the floor for evidence of any bowel movement on behalf of Big Tim. As Tim stood up, his stool fell over onto the floor. He did not notice the stool falling, as his eyes were fixed on the Lt. Col. He pleaded with the C.O. to have a drink with him, but the C.O. refused, and told him he would have one with him during the week. I left the room, and went down the hall to go back behind the bar. When I got in behind the bar I could see Laverty and the C.O. leading Tim out into the hall.

"Peace at last, I can relax now," I said, speaking out loud to myself, as I washed a few pint glasses out the back. I spoke to soon, because there was a knock on the bar counter. When I walked out into the bar, Laverty was standing there with his face rigid, eyebrows raised, and his lips slightly opened and stretched across his face. I just knew by his facial expression that there was a big entreaty on the way to me.

"We need a very big favor from you, if you would. We would be grateful if you would drive Tim home in his car," he pleaded.

"Yeah, right, you have two hopes, Sir, Bob Hope and no hope; why don't you drive him home yourself, Sir?" I retorted. He told me that he was Orderly Officer for the night, and that he could not leave the barracks. He also told me that the Orderly Sgt, would follow me in a land rover, and bring me back to the barracks from Tim's house. I again told him no, as it was too dangerous driving with Big Tim beside me in the car. He left the bar, and went out into the hall.

He must have had a discussion with the C.O., because he came back into me and said, "I was talking to the boss, and he said that you can have the weekend off from the bar if you will do this."

"Right, I'll do it," I said, "but if he starts any rough stuff on the way in, I will leave him high and dry, and come back with the Orderly Sergeant." I warned him. He told me fair enough, so I closed the bar, and went up to the main entrance hall of the Mess, to where they were waiting on me. For the first time that night I pitied Big Tim.

He was standing in the middle of the hall, with the front of his shirt hanging out of his slacks, and with tears streaming down his face he asked the C.O. with emotion, "Will you get me back into the Army? For fuck's sake, Clar, please, Clar, will you?"

There was no emotion in the voice of the C.O., only gruffness as he said, "Would you get a grip of yourself man, and cop fucking on. There's no getting back into the Army. Now, if you don't go home right now, you will be banned in the future from entering the barracks, and I will see to that. Now this man (pointing at me) will be driving you home, so give him the keys, and stick your shirt in, my boy."

Standing next to the grandfather clock in the hall, Big Tim fumbled in his pocket for a few seconds, and then producing his car keys, he said, "I'm not your fucking 'boy' Clar, and I never was; that's always been your problem with me. Because I never licked your arse, not like Laverty over there, the baby faced arse clinker, who's been up your arse so much that he forgets what his own shite smells like." He then turned to me saying, "Will you please inform gimpy that nobody drives my car unless I say so, and tell him that if he can get Laverty away from his arsehole long enough, that he can shove his fucking barracks up there. Now, goodnight." Then he staggered towards the door. The three of us were standing there dumbfounded when he surprised us by turning around, and winking at me, threw me the keys of his car.

"Drive the prick away, get him out of my sight," the Lt. Col said to me, as he toddled towards the door of the anteroom with Laverty in tow. After I steered Big Tim to the car, and got him into it, I drove off to bring him home, with the Orderly Sgt. following behind.

As I was driving up to his house, Tim whispered, "Mind you mind out."

"Mind out for what?" I asked.

Turning his head to me, and still whispering, he said, "Mind you, that's you, as you still have your mind, and mind out sadly to say, well that's......me. I have gone from a military intellectual to an idiotic spectacle; fuck it." He then got out of the car. When I got out of the car I told him that what is lost can be found again. I don't know if he heard me as he walked up the path to his wife, who had heard the car, and came out to meet him. I gave his wife the keys, and told her that he was just a bit tipsy, and everything was all right. Tim stood there with his coat opened, and his shirt hanging out like a big school boy as he told her that Clar had banned him from the barracks. She told Tim not to mind Clar, and to come inside, and that she would do him a big fry up. Putting her arm around his waist, and his arm around her shoulder she led him to the front door. Going into the bar the next morning I saw a perturbed C.O, staring up at Rommel's battle plan. Someone had colored it in with crayons, and at the bottom, inscribed with a pen, was, "Mind Out."

THE PEEPING TOM

The sweat was pouring from me as I stood leaning on the spade, taking a rest from scuffing grass and weeds. The reason for the scuffing was the forthcoming inspection of the barracks and surrounding areas by the General Officer Commanding (G.O.C.) of the entire command. This inspection was carried out annually, and for two weeks every year there was blood, sweat, and tears shed to ensure that in no way would the G.O.C. be disappointed. Being a Corporal in the Transport office, I was given the task of carrying out the necessary action to ensure that there was not a weed or unwanted blade of grass left in sight, surrounding the transport buildings and area. In order to execute this odious, repetitive, and unvaried task, the Squadron Sergeant had allotted two Troopers, who were placed under my control until the work assignment was fulfilled. Hughie McHugh and Richie Rivers were the Troopers assigned to help with the workload.

Hughie and Richie were of the same personality, in that they both possessed a whimsical nature of the mischievous kind. They were both of average height, but Richie's slender body frame had the effect of him being taller, while Hughie was in no way fat but was a lot sturdier in his appearance. Richie possessed the Scandinavian characteristics of blond hair and blue eyes, though for a young man of twenty-four, the hair was thinning on top, a feature about which he was somewhat very conscience and an inner embarrassment of. Hughie, being the same age as Richie, was the complete opposite in the hair department, as his hair was brown and thick with no great fear of alopecia ever becoming a problem for him.

So here we were on Friday afternoon, coming to the finishing line after a hard three-day scuffing. Looking at the large orderly piles of weeds, grass, and clay that had accumulated from our hard work and the general cleanliness of the whole transport area, we could now see at long last the immense difference that our toiling had produced. We had a small bit more to do outside the front door of the forage barn, and then we were finished. The forage barn was a very old large building that was built somewhere around the end of the nineteenth century by the British, who in that period of time were occupying Ireland, and therefore commanded the Curragh Camp. The British first used it as stables and later in years as a forage barn to store straw and hay for their horses, and nowadays it is used for the purpose of a parking building for the parking of the Unit vehicles. The British also left the cobblestones that were directly outside the door of the barn and were somewhat of a nuisance. The moss and weeds were imbedded between the cobblestones, and the blade thickness of the spades could not scrape in between the narrow spaces of the cobblestones.

"We'll be here for a month of fucking Sundays," said Hughie, as he chipped off a splinter of cobble, trying to uproot some weeds with his spade.

"Listen," I said, "go across to the Quartermaster's store, Richie, and ask them for a couple of knives so we can scrape the shit from between these fucking things, and hurry up because the inspection is at four."

The Quartermaster's store was just across the road and up a little way from us, so it should not take Richie that long to get there and back. With the time now twenty-five to four, it did not leave us much time to get this lot scraped and cleaned up before the inspection at four o'clock.

While Richie was gone to get the knives, Hughie and I went around to check the back of the forage barn and around the transport office to make sure that everything was in order for the inspection. When we got back to the front of the barn, Richie was already scraping between the cobblestones with a knife, and he was mumbling to himself quietly.

"What's wrong, Rich?" inquired Hughie.

"That stupid big bastard of a Squadron Sergeant, the big melon-headed bollix, calling me a peeping fucking tom," said a perturbed Richie.

Picking up a knife and starting to scrape, I asked him what had happened.

"Well, the store's door was locked when I got there, so I stood on the top step and leaned over to the side to look in the window to see if anyone was in there. I was looking in the window when I was grabbed from behind by that asshole Gerry Wall. I told him what I was doing, about the knives and all, but he just called me a peeping tom and walked on shaking that big pumped-up fucking head of his. His ancestors must have posed for them statues on Easter Fucking Island," said a fuming Richie, as he dug his knife in between the cobbles that little bit harder.

Just as Richie calmed down, Hughie went off on one. Casually pointing and waving his knife in the direction of the barracks, and with a tone of disappointment in his voice, Hughie said, "I joined the Army to get a trade, a fucking trade like a driver or an electrician or something, and what have they got me doing? Cleaning fucking cobblestones." He then went quiet. The silence was only momentary, as he then threw his arms into the air and, in a contemptuous vocal spewing, said, "Yeah, I see it now, yeah! When I'm finished in the Army, I will receive my trade certificate, and stated on it will be that I am a fully qualified cobblestone-cleansing technician. Sure, who knows? Maybe I'll get a job on fucking Coronation Street cleaning their cobbles."

"Well," said Richie, "ye never know. One day ye could go all the way to the top and end up cleaning the fucking Giants Causeway, ye big sappy bastard ye."

The mood turned jovial again.

We had finished the work, and as we were gathering up the spades and brushes together to hand back to the stores, I seen Squadron Sergeant Wall heading toward us for his inspection of the area. I sent Richie around to the transport office to have a last-minute check and make sure that everything was in order.

"Come with me," said the Squadron Sergeant, addressing myself to go on walkabout with him of the transport area.

Squadron Sergeant Gerry Wall, or otherwise mockingly nicknamed "Mallet" by the troops in relation to his oversized head, was a middle-aged man of a tall stature and of a limited sense of humour. He possessed a facial countenance of a permanent moderate smile, which was not befitting of his rigorous nature. It has been said that if he did not enlist in the Army, he would have made the perfect barman.

"That's a fine job," said Wall, as we finished the inspection outside the forage barn.

Then in the same breath as he had made the compliment, he informed me that nobody was going anywhere until all the piles of scuffing were picked up and got rid of to the dump. I tried to explain to him that I tried a couple of times during the afternoon to get the piles picked up, but the Sergeant who was in charge of the Land Rover and trailer, and whose job it was to pick up the piles, was nowhere to be found, and that all the work parties around the barracks were in the same boat with their piles of scuffing.

"He fucked off on the drink, him and them two fucking dopes his with," blurted out Hughie.

Wall told Hughie to shut up and then, turning to me, he annoyingly said, "I don't care if the good Sergeant is gone to the Munich fucking beer festival. I want those piles picked up and gone before you leave here this evening, Corporal, and I don't give a flying shit as to how you achieve the task."

Between thinking of the hard toiling of the last three days and the arrogant manner in which he spoke to me, a red mist descended over me. Impulsively and without thinking, I said, "Maybe if you gave me a lend of your hat, Squadron Sergeant, we could put all the piles of shit into it—as a matter of fact, we could put the rest of the barracks piles into it and get rid of the whole fucking lot at one go. How about that?"

There was no time for him to take any action against me, for Hughie started to crack up laughing. He was in convulsions down on his knees, and then, pointing at Gerry Wall, he squealed, "Wheelie bin head—oh! Sweet loving Jasus—wheelie bin fucking head—oh sweet fuck."

"Tell him to shut the fuck up, Corporal, or I will lock the two of you up," said a boiling-over Squadron Sergeant.

I told Hughie to give it over, but to no avail. I don't think that he could hear me from the noise of laughter and his eyes firmly fixed on Mallet's unusually large head.

Richie appeared on the scene and wanted to know what all the commotion was about. It was just then that Hughie stopped laughing, and I began. I went into the kinks of laughter, which started Hughie off laughing again, and the laughing went to hysterics when Richie, pointing at Wall, said, "Is he making a laugh of me about the peeping fucking tom thing? Is that why you're all laughing? You're a load of fucking assholes."

"What the fuck are you on about, Trooper?" snapped Wall. "You're a load of fucking head cases, that's what ye are, and you! Rivers, you paranoid fuck, and shit for brains, if I thought for one moment that you called me an asshole in that verbal shit that you came out with, I would lock you up so quickly that I would be in front of the C.O. for speeding."

Wall then looked at his watch and walked off at a fast pace, heading in the direction of the Orderly room, without saying a word.

"He must have a more important place to be," I said to the lads.

"Or bursting for a fucking shite," quipped Hughie.

Either way, a meeting or a shit, it got us out of the shit.

I thought there for a moment that we were all going to be locked up. Thank God for small mercies.

The following Monday, Richie and I were assigned the task of painting the inside walls of the transport office. It was a cushy enough job, as we were able to listen to the radio and could make tea every now and then. We had only finished laying the protective covering on the floor and did not lift a paintbrush yet when Richie decided it was time for tea.

"This is more like it, better than that scuffing shite we were doing last week. I hope I'm back in here tomorrow," he said, switching on the kettle.

Taking two cups from the press and, with a heavy sigh, I said, "That pig of a cash escort is on tomorrow, Richie, and I have got a depressing feeling that I'm going to be sent on the bullshit fucking thing."

The function of a cash escort is to provide armed security for cash in transit to and from banks and post offices to cities and towns in allotted counties. This particular escort Richie and I were talking about was one of the worst of its kind. The escort kicked off at five in the morning and did not finish until eight o'clock that night. It was by all accounts a tiresome, repetitious, energy-sapping humdrum from start to finish, and it was not the one to be on.

Sipping his tea, and his eyes looking over the top of the cup at the rain belting off the window and moving backward to the heater to warm his arse, Richie said, "I'll tell ye something for nothing. If that fucker Wall has me on that escort in the morning, I will crack up. I done the last two in a row, and I'll be fucked if I am going to do this one. I swear to Jasus if he puts me on it to get his own back on me for last Friday, I'll get a chisel from the workshop and let daylight through that big fucking head of his."

"Where do you bury your fucking dead?" I said to him, laughing.

"I don't. I let them rot where I drop them. How about that?" he said with a childish giggle.

Returning to the painting after we had finished our tea, we were still having a confab about the cash escort. Richie told me that he was going to go up to Wall's office in the afternoon and sneak into his office to see the morning detail sheet to see if he was on the cash escort the next morning. He said he would sneak in when Mallet went for his three-o'clock cup of tea in the N.C.O.'s mess and asked if I would keep a watch out while he went in to have a look. Immediately I said I would, because when Richie does something it usually turns into a foul-up, and a hilarious fuck-up at that, and I wouldn't miss this for anything.

In the afternoon at about five to three, Richie and I left down the paint brushes and headed for the administration block. Knowing Richie was going to somehow make a complete and utter debacle of sneaking into the Squadron Sergeant's office gave me a small distressing feeling, so I stopped him as we were nearing the administration block and advised him not to proceed with the whole notion and to just wait like everyone else until Wall put up the escort detail at half-four.

He was having none of it. "It will be too late if I wait until half-four for Gator Face to put up the detail, because the minute he puts up that detail he's gone home in a flash, and I won't get the time to argue my case. Besides, you're the one who said I could fuck off early," said an unreflecting Richie.

I did tell him that he could skive off early, but I only said that in order to take his mind off going into Wall's office.

Once more we started to walk toward the block, and after a couple of steps, Richie stopped suddenly. "What will I say if he comes in and catches me?" he asked with a blank expression on his face.

"If he catches you, just say that the Barrack Quartermaster sent you to take measurements of his office to see if he had enough headroom for himself in there," I joked.

"Stop acting the bollix," he said. "That's a stupid excuse to come out with, and me standing there with no fucking measuring tape in my hands."

Looking at him in disbelief, I was just about to walk off to distance myself from a total idiot when he started to laugh.

"Fucking caught ye, didn't I?" he said. "Fuck Wall. If he catches me, he catches me."

The administration block was a one-story building that stood side on at the top of the barrack square. It was yet another British-built, aged, red-bricked, wall-roofed structure that was converted into office cubicles to provide space for the distinct employments within the administration staff. Three steps led up to the entrance, which in turn led into a long, narrow hallway with office cubicles on both sides. Facing the inside of the entrance and at the opposite end of the hall is the Commanding officer's office.

The Squadron Sergeant's office was the first on the left when entering the building, and directly across from his office was the Orderly room. Next door to the Squadron Sergeant's office was the Adjutant's office, and on the same side down the hall was the Intelligent office and across the hall from that a record of training office. The last office on the right-hand side was that of the second-in-command.

Passing through the entrance door into the long hall, we noticed that the Squadron Sergeant's office door was closed. On seeing this, we immediately turned and pretended that we were looking at the photo gallery board that was hanging on the wall just outside the Orderly room. The gallery board was placed there for the troops to pin their preferred and amusing photographs. Without saying a word, Richie stepped over to Wall's office door and then, bending down on one knee, he began to peer through the keyhole. I was standing there, keeping my eye on the entrance door, thinking to myself that this whole thing was crazy. But crazy was not the word for what happened next.

Turning to look at Richie, I got the shock of my life, for there, walking out from the Intelligent office and carrying a sheet of paper in his hands, was Squadron Sergeant Wall, and I could not say a word to warn Richie. It was at this moment that Richie started to vulgarise the keyhole.

"I don't think the big swine of a fucking mutton head is in there," rasped Richie.

Wall just stood there in stunned silence with his big head to one side, staring at Richie in total amazement.

"No! It looks like the big fucking mallet-headed brainless bastard is not in there. I'm going in there," snarled the soon-to-be ill-fated Richie.

Standing there, I was numb on the outside, but I was screaming on the inside for Richie to please shut the fuck up.

Before Richie could get to his feet, Wall said, in a very calm voice, "Are you going kinky, Rivers? Up to your peeping tom tricks again, I see."

Rickie looked up and went into pure shock. As he stood up, there was a small sound that indicated he had broken wind. Between shock and acute self-consciousness, he walked straight into the wall of the Orderly room. He then turned and walked into me, then turning again, he walked bang into Gerry Wall's chest. "Measure-fucking-ment, measure-fucking-measure," he mumbled incoherently.

Wall smiled. It was one of the few times that I had seen him with a real smile on his face other than that insignificant wax smile he was born with.

"Get out, Rivers, ye weasel-faced fucking peeping tom. Get out of my sight before I thump ye one," said a still-smiling Wall, as he pushed Richie aside and went into the Orderly room.

When Richie turned to leave, I noticed that his eyes were glazed, and he had two small dry white spots of saliva, one on each side of his mouth, which depicted to me that his mouth must have dried up from the fright he got. The poor bastard did not know where he was, and a few seconds later it was proven right.

On leaving the building, he missed the three steps leading down, and with his arms outstretched to protect himself, he looked like he was diving into a swimming pool. He hit the ground with all the grace of an emergency landing of a plane that could not get its landing gear down. The fall must have brought him to his senses, because he was up as quickly as he went down. Not saying a word, he walked off at a fast pace. I shouted after him to ask if he was all right.

"Fuck off," he barked.

I began to go into a fit of laughing, thinking about what had happened, and I could not resist it. "I'll see ye in the morning, Tom!" I shouted after him.

He did not reply. There was not a *peep* from him.

THE DRIVING TAILOR

It was Friday morning, the day of the driving test, and being an instructor on the driving course for the last six weeks, I was elated that it was coming to an end today. My inner pleasure of the course finishing was that I somehow survived the mental anguish and the physical intactness of my bones, from which both had been severely tried on umpteen occasions throughout the course by the four incompetent and intellectually impaired students who were assigned to me for the endurable task of developing them into drivers. After the daily morning parade, the Sergeant in charge of the driving course told Neil Reynolds, who was the other driving instructor, and me to take our students and vehicles to the front of the Orderly room at the top of the square in readiness for the technical and practical driving test, which would be carried out by Captain Donald Hatcher. On hearing that Captain Hatcher would be testing them, it brought a collective look of horror to the faces of the would-be drivers. They knew Capt. Donny Hatcher was not a man to be trifled with, and most certainly not to be crossed. He was a complex man with a roaring temper, which did not reflect his tall, dark, and calming Mediterranean features. He also possessed a disgusting behavioural tendency to showily scratch his testicles through the inside lining of his trouser pocket in view of all in sundry who were unfortunate to be in proximity to him as the mood took—thus, he was known throughout the Command as "Scratcher Hatcher," which was only ever used in a personal health sheltered utterance.

Prior to the daily morning parade, Cpl. Reynolds and I collected two cars from the Unit transport garage, drove them to the top edge of the square at the side of the guardroom, and parked them there. After the Sergeant had gone to report to the Captain that all was ready for the test, I handed the keys of the jeep to one of the students, Trooper Bart Conlon, to move the car from the side of the guardroom and park it outside the Orderly room. For no reason other than to rid myself of his senseless questions, I sent Trooper Gerry

"Ghost" Connors to accompany Conlon. Ghost was aptly nicknamed because of his sickly ashen face, dark-circled eyes with high cheekbones underlining them, and a skeleton-like body to boot. He was not well up in the intelligence department, or as Neil Reynolds said to me, "He has the brains of a melting iceberg," with which I gladly agreed. The two groups of four students each now stood in front of their designated car for the technical test to be carried out by Hatcher. The Captain came out of the Orderly room, and as usual he had one hand stuck in his pocket, working away. My four students were the first of the two groups to go under itchy members' inquisition.

Hatcher placed two students on each side of him, so as to leave himself central as they all stared at the engine under the lifted bonnet of the jeep. He began by pointing out components under the hood and then selecting an individual to name the part.

Hatcher pointed at a component. "What's this called?" he asked, directing his question to Trooper Toby Breen.

Moving his plump body closer to the car, Breen pointed a fat stumpy finger at the part in question. "This one here, sir—this one?"

"Yes, son, that one—can you name it for me?" quietly replied the officer, with a favourite uncle-like quality to his tone.

"Jasus, sir, I know the name all right—I know it all right," said the freckled-faced Breen, as he bowed and shook his head while squeezing his eyes shut and all the time clicking his fingers and repeating himself.

"Well, Breen, are you going to answer the question, or are you just going to stand there giving me a fucking Elvis impersonation?" snippily asked Hatcher.

Breen now stood with his lips puckered and, waving his index finger at the engine in general, said, "It's on the tip of my tongue, sir. Jasus, it's on the tip and I just can't...what's it called? What's its name? Jasus, sir, it's just there, it's...."

"It's the carburetor," interjected the officer, cutting Breen off in mid-sentence.

With a relieved look on his face, and with an affirmative nod of his head, Breen concurred, "That's it, sir, that's what was on the tip of my tongue—the carburetor—that's what it is, sir, the carburetor. How could I not think of that?"

"It isn't its bollocks! It isn't its bollocks!" roared the exasperated Captain, moving slightly back from the car. "It's the fucking radiator—the fucking radiator—ye bluffing little bastard ye!" shouted Hatcher, at the shocked and crimson-faced Breen.

The Captain then went quiet and began pacing back and forward directly in front of the students. He then suddenly stopped pacing and, leaning slightly over to his right side, he shoved his right hand deep into his pocket and began to fidget franticly at his disordered nether region, much to the discomfort of the cringing students. When he had a good scratch and had calmed down, Hatcher instructed me to take Breen away from the test area, out of his sight. The long frame of Neil Reynolds followed me as I marched the depleted Breen off the square and into the lines.

"Did ye see the bastard rooting himself?" said Neil, finely folding his somewhat oriental-faced trait in disgust, as I fell Breen out in the lines. "There is no fucking way there is a lining left in that fucking pocket. I mean, he must have gone to the fucking knuckles in that sack of his. He was tearing himself a-fucking-sunder," expressed a perturbed Neil, who then pointed his finger at Breen. "And you! Fucking radiator head—what were you thinking?" Neil asked the plump bluffer, who was standing looking at us, shaking his globelike head.

"I was thinking the way he ferociously pokes himself that he must have lost one of his balls somewhere up in his stomach to carry on in that fashion, Corporal—what do you think?"

"What do I think? The fuck do I think...I wasn't talking about...look! Get the fuck out of my sight, ye nancy fuck. Get up to the billet and scrub the toilets before I fucking throttle ye!" screamed Neil, at the already fleeing trooper. "How did that asshole slip under the net?" Neil asked me.

Looking back to where the rest of the lads were being tested, I told Neil with all true graveness that Breen was not the only one on the course to have slipped the net. When Neil and I returned to the cars, we could see Hatcher had finished the test, and he was now talking to the Sergeant, who was looking over the Captain's head; he was embarrassingly averting his eyes the farthest he could away from Hatcher's one-handed self-mutilation.

We soon got the word from the Sergeant that all had passed the technical test with the exception of Breen, who had got a reprieve and would be retested in the afternoon. When he had finished his cup of coffee in the Orderly room, Hatcher took Neil and his students out in the jeep for the driving test. In the meantime, while waiting for the Captain and the lads to return, I sent Conlon over to the billet to get Breen so I could go over the engine parts to try and ready him for the afternoon. Standing at the front of the car waiting on Breen to arrive, I noticed one of the students, Trooper Benny "Stitch." Kenny had his two hands against the guardroom wall and looked like he was dry-retching.

"Are the nerves getting to you, Stitch?" I asked, as I patted the stooped trooper on his back on reaching him.

With no response from him, I advised him to take his time and deep breaths, telling him that I would speak to him when he was ready. Trooper Benny Kenny was the Unit tailor, hence the humorously invented name "Stitch," given to him by the lads of the Unit. With the age of the other students averaging from eighteen to twenty, Stitch was the oldest on the course at twenty-six years of age, as he had been very elusive in participating in courses since he was crowbarred into going on the tailoring programme. Now standing in front of me with his cap off, and running his fingers through his thick and brown wavy hair, Stitch, with his pencil moustache, dimpled chin, and large gleaming front choppers that were bordering on bucktooth, induced a mental image in my mind of the 1940s.

"Sorry about that—but the thoughts of driving any officer let alone that fucking headcase makes me as nervous as fuck," expressed Stitch to me, as he wiped away the last of the heaving caused water from his eyes.

"Well, I would normally tell nervous students to relax and picture their driving examiner in their underwear sitting beside them, but with scolded scrotum testing...well, I don't want any of you driving into oncoming traffic...deliberately—wash that thought from your mind. You will just have to bite the bullet, wont you?" I said to Stitch, as he shrugged his shoulders and walked to the back of the car.

Ghost Connors was the first of my students to undertake the driving test. The other students and I got into the back of the jeep, with myself sitting directly behind the Captain. Ghost adjusted the driver's seat and then fastened his seatbelt. He then visually checked the side and rearview mirrors before fixing his dark eyes on the officer for the word to start the car and proceed.

"Right, off you go, Trooper," instructed Hatcher.

"Oh! I nearly forgot," said Ghost, unbuckling his seatbelt. He then turned his body slightly left and placed his left hand onto the knob of the gear stick. Then covering his left hand with his right hand, he began to shake the gear stick from side to side in the neutral position, with great force and rapidity.

Conlon, who was sitting beside me, had gone blue in the face, in keeping from laughing. Ghost continued to shake the gear stick with hectic enthusiasm until Hatcher roared, "What in the name of fuck are you doing, Connors? Are you having some kind of fucking fit?"

"Not at all, sir," answered Ghost. Then with one shake of his head, and a wink of the eye, Ghost released his hands from the gear stick. "Just taking the heavy skin off the top of the petrol, sir," explained Ghost, who then gave the gear stick one last flick with his hand.

Hatcher removed both of his hands from the comfort of his pockets and covered his face with them. With his thumbs imbedded at each side of his lower jaw, and with the back of his hands arched outwards from his face, he slowly dragged his fingertips downward from his forehead to his thumbs, with mouth agape, as though he were yawning.

Taking his hands down from his face and slapping them forcefully onto his knees, the Captain calmly turned toward Ghost. "I know I should not ask this—but I have to. Who in the fuck told you that by shaking the gear stick...what was it again? Ah, yes! That it would remove the heavy skin from the top of the petrol? And please don't tell me that it was one of the instructors; I just couldn't handle that," said Hatcher with a look of concern, as he removed one hand from his knee and returned it back to work in his trouser pocket.

Just as I was about to voice my concern to Hatcher about his snide innuendo toward the instructors, Ghost hastily answered the officer in a childlike voice. "Conlon—it was Conlon—he made me do it, sir, it was—"

"I didn't me arse, sir, don't mind that lying Casper-faced graveyard fucker," retorted Conlon, buffering Ghost's accusation.

In a hostile manner, Hatcher growled at Conlon to shut up. With a solemn face, he nodded his head toward Ghost in silent indication to continue. Ghost began by telling Hatcher that I sent Conlon and him to move the car from the side of the guardroom to the front of the Orderly room. He said Conlon was in the driver's seat, and he was in the passenger seat.

Conlon opened his window to talk to Trooper Cody, who was standing outside the car. As Conlon was talking to Cody, he had his hand on the top of the gear stick, shaking it from side to side.

"When Conlon had finished talking to Cody, I asked him why the shaking of the gear stick, and he told me that he was taking the heavy skin off the top of the petrol, sir. And then he said that the instructor must have forgotten to tell me and that I should make sure that I should carry it out before starting the car—on the test," explained the unperceiving Ghost to the depleted-looking officer.

Through the whole of Ghost's explanation, Conlon was pinching the nostrils of his flat boxer's nose to aid him from bursting out laughing.

"Is this true, Trooper Conlon?" ask Hatcher, not bothering to turn his head to face the accused.

"He's an eejit—a dopy bastard of an eejit if there was ever one, sir," blurted Conlon, with sounds of laughter. Conlon covered his mouth with his hand and sat back in his seat when I gave him a slight warning nudge with my elbow into his ribs.

"Sir—I swear, sir, I'm telling the truth, sir,'" gasped Ghost. "On your wife and kids' lives, sir, he told me to—"

"On my fucking wife and children's lives!" Hatcher interrupted Ghost's self-saving oath. "On my fucking wife and…get out of the fucking car before I—Corporal, get this piece of shit out of the car before I embed his head into the gear stick, and take that laughing hyena Conlon with you—they'll never be drivers in this Unit as long as I'm breathing," roared an infuriated Hatcher.

Just as I closed the passenger door of the car, and luckily out of the Captain's earshot, Conlon quipped, "Did he say breathing or scratching? Because if it's breathing, we have some chance." He smiled in mock amusement as I told him to shut up and report over to Corporal Reynolds with Ghost and explain to him as to what had happened.

Getting back into the car and apologising to Hatcher for the behaviour of the two lads, I could not help feeling a little bit apprehensive when I saw a trembling Benny Kenny sitting in the driver's seat. To my surprise, the rest of the day could not have gone better, as the tailor and my other student Trooper Maher passed with flying colours, with the exception of Breen, who was retested in the afternoon and again failed the technical exam. Parking the cars that evening, a wonderful feeling of elation swept over me when the thought of starting my two weeks' leave from Monday came rushing into my head when Neil began to moan about the continuation of the driving course on Monday, instruction of the trucks for two weeks.

Monday morning four weeks later, I found myself in the role of Orderly Sergeant, a twenty-four-hour duty that consisted of carrying out an attendance check on morning and afternoon parades, and mainly, be available throughout the twenty-four hours to rally troops in case of any unforeseen event occurring.

The Orderly Sergeant also had to be at the Squadron Sergeant's beck and call throughout the day to carry out various tasks for him. One of these tasks would be carried out shortly, as I walked through the lines, heading for the tailor shop to detail Benny "Stitch" Kenny, the tailor, for the duty of driver to the Commanding Officer (C.O.) of the Unit. Monday to Friday, from nine in the morning, there would be a driver designated with a jeep to wait at the Orderly room, should the C.O. need to travel. This duty ended at four-thirty in the evening, if otherwise not required. The thought of telling Stitch that he was to be C.O. driver for the day bothered me; it was only four weeks ago that the thought of driving Captain Hatcher on the driving test had him dry-retching, through nervousness.

"Jasus! Ye scared the loving shit out of me. I thought there was nobody left in the Unit—with them all gone on manoeuvres, for a second there I thought ye were an officer," said the startled tailor to me on entering the shop, as he had been sitting down drinking tea and reading the racing form from the morning paper. The colour drained from his face, and the cup of tea that he had picked up from the table was visibly shaking in his hand when I told him that he was to be the driver for the C.O. for the day; as he pointed out there was nobody left in the Unit, and as he was the only trooper left, the task fell to him.

"Listen!" I said. "Don't ye know yourself that the C.O. rarely goes any-where? Just sit in the Orderly room, and say nothing, and if the C.O. should decide that he wants to go somewhere...well, just get into the car and drive him. I mean, what's the worst that could happen? He can't shoot you—can he?"

"No—but he can ground me from driving, and there's me only after get-ting me driving licence, and all of a sudden it's gone, and even if he doesn't ground me for nervous driving—he will surely ground me for the smell in the car, because let me tell ye, I will fucking shite in my trousers, and that's not a word of a lie," yapped the agitated tailor, as he paced around the shop.

Telling him that he would be fine and that I did not think that the C.O. was that inclined as to ground him for being a little nervous, he raised one eyebrow and gave me a hesitant look before saying, "That's a load of bollocks! You of all people should know that. Weren't you with Bones Phelan when he got grounded by that drunken fucking head case of an officer? Commandant—what's his name?"

"Duncan—Commandant Duncan," I inserted knowingly.

Commandant Duncan was and still is a diverged character of the officer status: He was a law onto himself, and I remember only too well the incident that Stitch was talking about. One morning almost three months ago, I was detailed to accompany Commandant Duncan to the military heavy firing range that was situated in the Wicklow Mountains. Duncan's mission was to contact and liaise with the Range Warden and sheepherders in order to have all livestock cleared from the range site and surrounding area before the morning of the shoot. My own task up there was to acquaint myself with the locations where the range sentinels were to be placed before and when the range was active, as I would be in charge of sentinels on the day of the fire practice. Duncan was old school, and an alcoholic, who being in his early fifties would have been at the rank of Lt. Colonel, but for his constant thirst. He was a well-fleshed man of middling height who had procured over the years a definable feature of a dense and overly developed moustache that hooked upward at both ends onto his reddish cheeks, which were littered with broken capillaries. When speaking, he spoke with a drawl; he would pronounce his words with slow inflection. The driver of the car for the expedition to the mountains was Trooper Donald "Bones" Phelan, who on that morning was a sight to behold. His long, thin frame could not stay easy, as he nervously walked around in circles at the thought of driving Duncan.

When I first approached the car that morning, Bones told me that he had only just got his military driving licence two days previous, and that he did not think that he was ready to drive any officer just yet, especially a hard and sarcastic case like Duncan, who was not shy on the matter of grounding drivers. "Drunken Duncan—drunken fucking Duncan, I would have to get the most cantankerous bollocks in the barracks to drive—wouldn't I?" said Bones, who was nothing short of sending a flow of tears from his bulbous eyes, down his freckled-nosed face.

Moments later, Bones and I felt a little disconcerted when we heard the familiar drawling voice of Commandant Duncan coming from outside the front of the car, which left us dreading (more so Bones than me) if he had overheard what had been said.

"Are we ready to go—are we?" Duncan asked, as he walked to the front passenger door and opened it.

Bones clambered into the driver's seat as I made myself comfortable in the passenger seat directly behind him.

"Right, driver! Drive me to this heather strewn and mountainous fucking Hades—drive...driver...drive," slowly rasped the seedy-looking Commandant, which sounded like he was talking through a funnel.

Bones' anxiety went into overdrive when this loud grating noise filled the car when he turned the key in the ignition; he had already started the car moments earlier. Now full of panic, he meant to turn on the indicator to move off, but he mistakenly turned on the windscreen wipers, which in turn made an exasperating dragging sound as the rubber blades ran across the dry glass.

"Drive on, for fuck's sake, driver...before you do something with the gear stick that will remind me of another part of my anatomy...drive on," expressed the hung over officer, staring straight ahead while gently massaging his throat with an unsteady hand.

Looking at my watch that morning, I could see that we had been travelling for approximately half an hour and were now approaching from a side road toward a crossroad in the middle of a small village, which had a main road running through it. In order to cross the main road to continue our journey, we had to negotiate traffic lights. Bones was taken the driving handy as we neared the lights, which were green. Our car must have been almost twenty yards from the lights when they changed from green to amber.

Suddenly, a sense of dread came over me; I could see Bones moving forward in his seat and going rigid with anxiety on seeing the glow of the amber light. Back where I was sitting, I could hear him stamping his foot down hard on the accelerator, and in so doing the car raced toward and against the amber light. Too late—for just as the car got to the lights, the amber light went out and the red light came on. Instead of dropping the anchor, Bones accelerated again, and through sheer panic he drove the car at speed through the red light, and across the main road, and all the time jerking the top part of his body as though this action would make the car go faster. After running the red light and getting to the far side of the main road and onto our route, there was no sign of Bones slowing down the car; if anything he was going faster.

Moving along the seat to get my balance, I could now see out the front of the car. I could see a bend in the road ahead. Then to my horror, I caught sight of a ramp stretching across the road just ahead of us, and as it was too late to warn Bones, I grabbed my seat and held on for dear life. A split second later, the front of the car was in the air as the front wheels hit the ramp. From my clinging position on the backseat, I could see Duncan's head hitting the roof. He had only landed back on his seat when the back wheels struck the ramp, sending him upward with his head hitting the ceiling once more. The rear of the car came back down to the ground with a shudder and sent the car swerving into the bend in the road, which was now upon us. The car was shaking and leaning to one side with the tyres screeching as Bones tried to hold the road and bring the car under control. Coming out of the bend with one last shimmy of the vehicle, Bones, who was now perspiring like a pig, took control and slowed the car down.

"Stop the car! Stop the fucking car! Stop the fucking car, now! Trooper!" ordered the rattled Commandant sternly, without losing the drawl.

When Bones pulled the vehicle over to the side of the road and stopped, Duncan and I open our doors and got out. Duncan walked forward to the front of the car and stood solemnly staring at it. With his bottom lip covering his top lip, the depleted-looking driver sat behind the steering wheel with a hangdog look on his face as his large lifeless eyes were firmly fixed on the Commandant. From the front of the motor, the Commandant pointed his finger and beckoned to Bones, who was still looking out from behind the windscreen.

"Step this way—Trooper...step this fucking way," cried out the Commandant abruptly.

With Bones now standing in front of him, Duncan pointed down at the registration plate. "What does that say, Trooper—what does that say?" the officer asked puzzlingly.

The bewildered Trooper looked down at the registration plate and said, "931—GZE, sir."

"Yes!" snapped Duncan. "Yes, Trooper, it says 931—GZE...it does not say Boeing 7-0-fucking-7...you're fucking grounded. What's more...you can walk back to the barracks....The Corporal will drive from here on in, until we return. By the way, Trooper, I suggest that when you return to barracks that you immediately put in for your discharge from the Army and go and join Aer fucking Lingus and tell them "Drunken Fucking Duncan sent you," the contemptuous officer drawlingly said.

The Commandant and I motored on, and Bones walked all the way back to the barracks and has never got his licence back since, so on that evidence I think the tailor has a case for not wanting to drive an officer until he gained more driving experience. Alas, unfortunately for him, he was the only Trooper left in the barracks, so I told him to report to the Orderly room and went on my way. For the whole morning, Stitch remained in the Orderly room and was chuffed when lunchtime came without any officer looking for the car to travel.

Later on in the afternoon, I walked into the Orderly room to find Stitch almost trying to conceal himself to the side of a filing cabinet at the back of the room. Smiling, I asked him as to how he was faring out, to which he told me everything was fine, and with only a short time remaining for finishing his role as C.O. driver, it was looking good that he would not be driving any officer today.

Just as he had the words out of his mouth, Lieutenant Mason walked hastily in through the Orderly room door and approached the counter. "Have we got a driver, Corporal? I need to get to Command H.Q. as quickly as possible," said the young and resolute Lieutenant, addressing me.

"We do, sir, Trooper Kenny, sir," I said, pointing at the wide-eyed, open-mouthed, and unenthusiastic tailor.

Stitch mumbled some words that were inaudible, which prompted the officer to ask him if he had a problem, and if so, he was to speak up.

"Look, sir, I've only passed my driving course recently and have little experience behind the—"

"Shut up, Kenny, and get out and drive the jeep," interrupted the tall, sturdy officer. "It's hardly the bloody space shuttle I'm asking you to drive, is it?" he questioned Stitch sarcastically.

Stitch was about to say something but thought better about it and walked past the officer and out of the room, murmuring under his breath, and an appearance of resentment on his face, which brought an air of discord between officer and trooper.

Having to see the Manpower Officer up in Command H.Q., I asked Lt. Mason if it would be all right if I got a lift with him, to which he okayed and told me to go to the jeep as he had to go back to his office to get his cap. Stitch never noticed me getting into the back of the car, as he was having trouble getting the gear stick into first gear. He kept forcefully pushing at the gear stick, but to no avail; it just would not slot into first gear. He was starting to get himself worked up, as he lifted his foot up and down off the clutch, all the time trying to force the stick into gear.

Just as the Lieutenant opened the door of the jeep, Stitch simultaneously and, speaking of the gear stick, shouted, "Get in, ye fucking bastard ye—get in."

"Don't call me a fucking bastard—fuck face!" shouted Mason, thinking Stitch was talking to him.

" I—I—wasn't talking to you, sir," cried the flustered tailor, to the now-fuming officer.

"Just shut up, Trooper, and drive!"

"But sir, I was not talking to you—it was the gear stick I was talking to—not you, sir," embarrassingly, Stitch tried to explain.

Quickly I had to take the smile from my face, as Mason turned around to me and made small imaginary circles with his finger to the side of his head, indicating that Stitch was demented.

"Right! Let's forget about going to Command and head straight for the psychiatric ward at the hospital. Because you will be telling me next that the gear stick is answering you back—well, is it? Fuck face," spewed the liverish officer.

Disengaging the gear and returning the gear stick to the neutral position, and then applying the handbrake, Stitch turned in his seat to face Mason. "I don't think so, sir. In the first place, sir, I don't talk to the gear stick, and it does not talk to me, and even if it did talk…it's a Nissan jeep, sir, and I don't talk or understand—fucking Japanese! So quite frankly, Sir, and with no disrespect, I think you're talking through your—"

"Not another fucking word—Trooper," rattled off the officer, intercepting preventably the last and most dangerous part of the tailor's sarcastic sentence and condemnation of the Lieutenant.

Having had enough of both their "crapanese," I departed the jeep silently and unnoticed and walked toward the sanctuary of the Orderly room, away from the tailor-made calamity.

TWO TIMES TWICE

There was a feeling of great contentment among the crew of the car, of which I was a part of. The justification for this elation was due to the early finish of the escort duty that we had just carried out. The escort had left the ammunition depot in the Curragh Camp, Co. Kildare early that morning, with the task of guarding a consignment of explosives in transit to Aiken barracks, Dundalk Co. Louth. With the explosives being of a small quantity, and being transported in the back of an ordnance van, the security only required an escort of one Nissan jeep with an armed crew of three. The crew consisted of a driver, with one riflemen and I, commander of the escort party. With the mission completed and having left Aiken barracks, we were now driving through the streets of Dundalk heading back to base in the knowledge of knowing that when we got back to barracks we would be free for the rest of the day, and it being Friday made it all the more rewarding.

"That was a handy one, Willie," I said hesitantly, not knowing what response I would get from the driver, owing to his complicated nature.

"It will be once were finished, because I'm fed up listening to that stuttering bastard in the back since we left this morning. If the escort was any longer I would end up shooting the repetitious fucker," replied Willie in a gruff and agitated voice, without taking his grey piercing eyes off the road. The repetitious one that Willie was making reference to was the rifleman in the back of the car, Pat Rush. Willie and Pat were both of the rank of Trooper, though equal in rank Willie had a higher status over Pat in height and muscles, being a very burly and tall individual with a short fuse, and a predisposition to strike out if someone antagonized him. Pat, on the other hand, had a nature of docility about him, and would not harm a fly, which often made me wonder why he joined up in the first place. Willie had a couple of years on Pat, who in his mid-twenties looked a lot younger due to his brown complexion, and faint freckles that seemed to be pebble dashed onto his face. He also had a fierce stammer which at times could be very comical, and in been so made him a favorite to some of the hierarchy.

"Yo, yo you can't tell..tell me to stay qui..quiet, Trooper co-cor..Corish, I'll t...talk if I wan... want to," said Pat, who had moved and leaned forward in his seat when he had addressed Willie.

Moving his head slightly sideways to the left, and with eyes at an angle Willie looked at Pat for a moment, and then turning his eyes back to the road in front of him, he said, "But that's the whole point, ye cant fucking talk because your mouth is fucked up; it's broke, and if I was you I would not say another word until I got it fixed. Because when you speak you're murdering the words that come out of your mouth, and ye use the same method every time, and to my ear's that makes you a fucking serial killer of the English language. Now shut the fuck up, ye ear fucker before I stop this car and rip your fucking word trapping tonsils from your scrawny neck." There was complete silence in the car as Pat inched his body back into his seat, looking bewildered. Noticing that Willie was getting red in the gills, and was opening his window to let some air in I told him to take it easy, and that Pat had the same right to speak as he and I had.

To get my point across to Willie, and also try to restore some confidence back into Pat, I said, "Well. Pat, did you enjoy the twenty first birthday party ye went to last Saturday night?" I was sorry I opened my mouth.

"It—it was fuc—fuc, great," he said, as he sucked in air. "De-a- de-a- the night was brilliant, a-a-and I got-got locked drunk., he said, smiling.

"Locked? I'd say the conversation must have been fucking mind altering?" muttered Willie under his breath.

Paying no attention to Willie, I turned to Pat. "Well, you must have had a great time then?" I asked him.

Pat's head started to jerk back and forward violently, and then in a staggered gasp he answered, "Yeah!" He then smiled again.

I knew that Pat had gone to a twenty first birthday party, but did not know who's party it was, so I asked, "Whose birthday was it, Pat?"

"It-it was Tim-Tim- Timmy, oh wh..what's—what's his name, Timmy—oh-oh what's he-he-his fucking name, ye-ye know the far-father—Skippy O-O-O'Leary from the engin..eers, Timmy—Tim—Timmy...."

"Would it be Timmy O' fucking Leary? O'Leary, ye stupid bastard ye," roared Willie, looking through his rear view mirror at Pat.

Leaning forward in his seat Pat tapped Willie on the shoulder, and with a puzzled look on his face, said, "How-how the fuck d-do you no-no-know, were you a-at d-d-the party a-a-as well?" He looked away from Willie towards me, and then glanced at Willie waiting for an answer. The whole conversation hit home to Pat when he saw me bent over laughing. "Oh fuck, yeah, na-na-now I know, I-I made a bol... bollix of de-that, did..didn't I?" stammered Pat, and then his speech condition ceased, to make way for a roar of laughter, and at the same time he gave Willie a friendly slap on the shoulder as he let out another roar of laughter. "That—that was a-a good one Wi..Will, wasn't it?" he expressed to Willie in between small breaks in his laughter.

To my surprise, Willie started to laugh, and shaking his head, he exclaimed, "Only you, Rush—only fucking you!" He looked at Pat and gave a small chuckle. Pat, through his speech impediment would be forever getting flustered because of his hastiness when vocalizing. Because of this hastiness he did not always have the continuum of mind and communicating utterances, and because of this failing his complete thought that he wished to express would sometimes emerge orally disrupted, which could be confusing, or, comical entertainment for the listening party. There was one such time that I remember when there was confusion and laughter to a Pat anecdote to the Squadron Sergeant and myself of his visit to the General Military Hospital on the Curragh, for the morning sick parade. It happened one morning as the Squadron Sgt. and I were returning to the Administration block after the morning coffee break. As we approached the Admin block both the Squadron Sgt. and I noticed Pat laboring to negotiate the three steps down from the block, and he looked to be in some pain.

"Well, Trooper Rush, how did you get on with the morning sick parade?" inquired the Squadron Sgt,. who along with myself was now standing in front of Pat, as he came down off the last step with his sick book tucked under his arm.

" I have t-t-to go in-into ho..hospital, Squadron Sergeant, they..they have admit—admitted—me," explained Pat, with beads of perspiration emerging from his forehead.

"What ails ye?" asked the Squadron Sgt.

"There—there go..going to take my—my test..testicles out, Si—Sir," stammered Pat, wiping the sweat from his brow. I could not believe what he had just said, and started to break out laughing,

"Your fucking testicles, Pat?" I asked him.

He started to go in to a rage because I was laughing, and then with his bottom lip covering his top lip, and his head shaking to extract a word from his mouth, that was now making repeated supping sounds that made him look like a fish drowning, finally blurted out, "Fuck...fucking sure! I have a-a-a temperature of a hun—hundred and thre-three, ye—ye laughing fu-fucking jack-jack-ja—donkey ye."

"I think ye mean your tonsils, Pat, not your fucking testicles," I said, as I went into another fit of laughing. The Squadron Sgt. just stood there wearing a solemn expression on his face taking everything in. Pat, realizing his clanger, dropped his sick book to the ground, and placed his head into his hand's with embarrassment. With a muffled voice from behind his hands, he apologized.

The Squadron Sgt. pushed Pat to one side with the back of his hand, and at the same time said, " I had a feeling it was not your testicles, Trooper Rush, because I know for a fact that they don't do brain surgery in that hospital. Now get out of my way, and get your arse down to hospital." He then brushed by Pat. That little episode explained to me Pat Rush's dilemma in a nut shell, I thought it funny whereas the Squadron Sgt. thought it un-perceptively irritating. We were cruising along the N.7 motorway on the Co. Kildare stretch of it, when an ambulance with its siren on full blast, and all lights flashing sped pass on the other side of the motorway heading in the direction of Dublin.

"There's a poor girl heading to Dublin from Naas hospital to have her baby," I said on a passing impulse.

"Not necessarily," contradicted Willie, "could be there is a big accident in Dublin, and they're going to help out," he said, as he looked into his wing mirror at the now fading ambulance.

"No, it's more than likely a bird going to have a baby, as the main maternity hospitals are in Dublin," I insisted. Within seconds of saying this, another ambulance, going in the same direction as the first one, whizzed by.

"There! I rest my fucking case, that's two ambulances, so it has to be an accident in Dublin, and they're going to help out." said Willie, with a smug grin on his face.

I had just conceded to Willie, when Pat, who had been listening to everything, tapped Willie on the shoulder. "I a-a-agree with t..the cor-cor-Corporal, Trooper Corish, could—could—couldn't it be twins?" said a slightly excited and intrusive Pat. An atmosphere of library quietness descended inside the car, as both Willie and I turned to look at Pat, incredulously, in that he had just made such an absurdly ridiculous remark, and therefore convincing me that Pat, was the possessor of an insentient brain. I looked over at Willie, who had now made a fist with his right hand, and was biting down on the first knuckle. His other hand had a grip on the steering wheel, that was so tight his knuckles were showing white.

Willie released his knuckle from between his teeth, and then opening his hand he placed his index finger across his top lip, thumb at his jaw, and the other fingers resting on his chin, and with his eye's on the road, said, "Well tell me this, Rush? What if it had been five ambulances that passed by? Would that mean that they were fucking quins, would it?" Now he was looking in his rear view mirror at Pat, with anticipation of a stupid answer.

Pat did not disappoint. " It wo…wouldn't put—put it pass me—b..b..because that Quinn fel—fella is a—a—a horny bastard, he..he would tip..tip a fucking cat so—so he would, I..I wouldn't let Quinn near—near my fuck…ing—wife," enthused Pat. Quinn being Trooper Joey Quinn from the Unit. I turned around to Pat in disbelief, and was relieved to see him winking at me and sneakily pointing his finger to the back of Willie's head, and then burst out laughing.

"I'll tell ye what," said Willie, not seeing the funny side of it, as Pat and myself were in knots laughing. "The next ambulance that we see, ye stuttering bastard, will be for you, because if ye don't shut the fuck up I will hospitalize ye, and while you're in there ye can ask them to remove that fucking elastic that holds in your words, ye stupid bastard ye," snarled Willie, as he took both hands off the steering wheel and tried to turn around in his seat to punch Pat. The laughing ceased very quickly as I grabbed the steering wheel with one hand, and pushed Willie back into position with my other hand. Willie took control of the car again as I told him to calm down. Pat sat in the back, silent and very distressed looking. " Twins, I'll give ye fucking twins when we've fin- ished this escort; I'll give ye two black fucking eyes, one identical to the fucking other, how's that for twin—twins, ye distorted piece of shit," proclaimed Willie. Lucky for Pat that Willie had to rush off when we got back, as he got word that his wife had gone in to have her baby, or maybe twins?

WET GEAR

M id January, pouring rain and strong winds, typical weather for the range, and that's exactly where I was heading this morning. There were sixteen of us from the Unit that was to fire our annual range practice. Looking at the troops huddled inside the doorway of the Ordnance stores waiting to sign out their weapons, I could see by their blank faces that were staring out the door at the swirling rain, that all interest in shooting had gone astray, including myself. The range officer for the day was Captain Noel "Manky" Maher, who had just come through the stores door shaking the rain from his already drenched and oversized waterproofs. The term "Manky" was humorously ascribed to him by fellow officers, owning to his shabby dress sense, and disheveled appearance. He was a small wiry man who sported a purposely unkempt moustache in order to conceal a cleft lip that he had sustained from a bad motorcycle accident, in his youth. Manky was not overbearing, he was more of a common sense man, but this fine characteristic was deeply overshadowed by his ill nature that could explosively present itself at the drop of a hat. The Captain made his way through the throng of lads in the store, and entered the counter door to sign for the ammunition for the shoot. After signing the ammo book, Manky, for whatever reason, started to ask each individual that was signing and drawing their weapon at the hatch, questions in relation to the rifle. He asked off the cuff questions, such as; how many rounds does the magazine hold? What is the range of the rifle? So on and so forth to the dismay of everyone in the store. He carried on like this until a senior Trooper, Joey Hayes approached the hatch.

"Can you tell me how the gun is operated, Trooper Hayes?" asked the officer. Holding the rifle horizontally, and chest high to himself, Joey, before answering the Captain, ran his grey steely eye's over the gun from barrel to butt before raising them, and his brow's, to stare fixedly at Capt. Maher.

"Water cooled, Sir." answered Joey, in his normal gruff voice, after some deliberation. There followed a pin drop silence in the store as Manky's neck had a small muscle contraction which in turn sent his head slightly backwards showing a look of astonishment on his face.

"How in the name of fuck did you come to that conclusion, Hayes?" queried the mystified Captain.

"Well, Sir," began Joey, not bothering to look at Maher, but instead he once again ran his eyes over the length of the rifle, as he continued, " it seems to me, Sir, that every time I fire this weapon on the ranges....well it's always pouring down fucking rain from the heavens, so I was thinking that it must be water cooled in order to fire it, Sir," explained Joey, as he lifted his head with a broad smile on his face, to look at the officer. The whole of the store erupted in laughter, which included Manky, who, between the laughter told Joey to go out and get on the truck for the ranges, or he would lock him up. Coming out of the armory I could see that the rain had eased off somewhat, but the dark skies to the left could only mean a conclusion to the easing occurrence of the bad weather, and therefore the skies would be spilling again by the time the truck got to the ranges. Just across from the stores and to the rear of the truck, and manically trying to organize everything, was, Bill Beasley, the Sergeant in charge of the troops on the range. Anyone acquainted with the Sergeant be it officer or man (when not in his presence) would refer to him as "Wild Bill," most with affection, but there were some that would utter it with animosity, through pass dealings with Bill. People that had heard of the nickname "Wild Bill " were taken aback when first setting eyes on him; they were expecting Bill to resemble the character " Wild Bill Hickok " from wild west folklore, with that of a giant of a man with long flowing locks, and a great untamed moustache. What they got was more like Alfred Hitchcock than Bill Hickok, as the Sergeant was a podgy middle aged man with an almost bald head, but for a comb over of some flimsy strands of hair. When in all fact the chosen name "Wild " was bestowed on him for the sheer reason of a quick temper, decidedly more so for his quicker fists.

"Come on, lads, up on the truck. The sooner we get down and shoot the quicker we get off the ranges," enthused Bill, as he herded the lads coming out from the stores, towards the truck. Walking over to get on the truck I could see Bill lifting his eyes to the heavens before he lowered his head into his opened hands, and from behind them he muffled, "Good jasus—that's all I need now." He then lifted his head from his hands to give a cheek swelling sigh. Thinking it was me that he was perturbed with I pointed my finger at my chest while at the same time giving him a wide eyed quizzical "me?" look. He shook his head at me, and then again with his head he gave a sharp upward motion that silently indicated to me that the distracting thing was behind me. On turning around and looking, I could tell right away that Bill's disconcertment was in the form of the monstrosity that was Trooper Wally Coulthard, who, for a tall and overweight man in his early twenties has a tendency to contagiously irritate people through his infantile speaking ability. On seeing the

Sergeant standing at the rear of the truck Wally formed a contented smile with his thin lips, and walked by me, making a beeline for a now listless looking Bill. Lifting his arm up in the air, before bringing it down lifelessly and uncontrolled to let his hand fall, slap, and rest heavily on Bill's shoulder, to which the Sergeant quickly shrugged off before stepping to one side, and with an uncharacteristic demeanor calmly told Wally to mount the truck.

"Sarge....darge, you're my best friend in the whole army, Sarge......Sarge—I would gladly take a bullet in the balls for ye—I would darge, honest I would Sarge." said Wally, in a voice that sounded like kindergarten grammar, and which was why he was so feverish to all that came into contact with him.

"Good man, Wally!" Bill's voice went up decibels. "Now get up on the truck before I give you an unmerciful root into those courageous balls of yours," said the now threatening and intolerant Sergeant.

This threat did not seem to faze Wally, as he leaned his head to one side with eyes half closed and fluttering, and a big smile on his enormous childlike face, he began speaking over Bill's head. "You're some joker, Sarge, all right Sarge—I'll get on the truck, but will ye help me with my disengaged eye when we get to the ranges, will ye darge?"

"I will, Wally; now for fucks sake get your arse on the truck—go on, good man," said Bill, as he bowed his head, and rubbed his forehead with his hand. At that moment a hand was placed on my shoulder, it was Captain Maher's hand. Maher told me to stay where I was for a minute as he had a job for me to do, but first he wanted to talk to the Sergeant, he beckoned Bill over to him.

"I was listening to all that, Billy," said the Captain, with a look of disgust on his face. "That man Coulthard gives simpletons a bad fucking name."

"Ye can fucking sing it, Sir," replied Bill. "The inside of the dopy bastard's head must be like a big empty fucking warehouse. How in the name of jasus did an overgrown cabbage patch kid ever get onto the army, Sir?" Bill queried the Captain.

"Simple—a bit like himself, his father is well off, and a first cousin to the Minister for Defence, and seemingly this fucking eejit wanted to play soldiers, and no officer wants to ruffle the Minster's feather's, so that's the be all and end all of the matter....oh for fuck's sake!" shouted Maher, as the heavens opened up again which made him scramble back towards the shelter of the stores with myself in tow. The job Maher had for me was carrying out the live ammunition to his jeep. When I had completed this task we headed for the ranges, with the truck already departing five minutes before us. On getting to the range I was informed that I was on firing detail number two. Being only two details to fire, and with our detail to shoot our fire practice second, we were assigned to the butts to erect and operate the targets. The rain had eased somewhat, but the wind was picking up, and to make matters worse when I got to the target shed, which was adjacent to the butts, all the lads were standing outside the shed which was locked as someone had forgotten to collect the keys from the range warden. Some of the lads took shelter in the butts while Mick Holmes, the Corporal in charge of the butts went to get the keys from the range warden whose hut was a fair walk away at the other side of range number one. With the hoods of our wet jackets up, a group of us did not bother to take shelter in the butts, but instead stood around in a small circle, chin wagging. We all stood there outside the shed in the wind and rain talking about this, that and the other.

That was until Trooper Bart Nesbitt opened his mouth, and put his foot in it. "Listen, boys," he began, as a single rain drop lingered from the tip of his button nose, and matted to his forehead from the rain was a coil of hair that had dangled from his fair headed growth. His blue eyes seemed to sparkle with the anticipation of telling us the story, as he continued, "I was in a jeep last week, and I was giving it loads—I mean I was ripping it. I was doing wheelies all round the back of the barracks, and having a right fucking crack until Mucky Maher comes on the scene. He stops me and takes me out of the jeep and tells me that if he ever sees me doing that again that he would take a radio aerial to my arse," he spewed. Oh—oh lamp lighting divine, please—for jasus sake Bart shut the fuck up, I thought to myself. The rest of the lads and myself could see Manky looking down embarrassingly at the ground, and moving a small stone to and fro with his foot, standing next to Bart. The lads around me must have been thinking the same thing, as Bart carried on. " Who does that scruffy, Manky little fucking bastard thinks he is?—the mank......." he stopped talking abruptly, as he had turned slightly left, and at last seen Maher standing beside him with head still bowed. Anyone with a cigarette could have lit it off Bart's face, it was glowing red. We all thought (including Bart) that the Captain was going to punch Bart to a pulp, but to everyone's surprise, and Bart's relief, he just turned, and simply walked away in the direction of the firing point, and as he did Bart strongly grasped my shoulder as his knees began to buckle. Leading him over to the target shed wall I was just about to tell him to lean on the wall when he let go of his grip on me, and hunched down with his back to the exterior of the shed, with the laughter of the lads ringing in his ears. "Oh for fucks sake lads, I feel like someone has just kicked me in the bollocks wearing a miner's hobnail boot. I feel like I want to shite—piss, and vomit all at the one time—there's a fucking wind going up me mickey, and me stomach is dropping—like that feeling ye get when ye go over a sudden hill in a car." delicately explained, Bart, with hood down, and the crimson in his face now substituted by ashen.

Trooper Domo Black stopped laughing and walked across to Bart, and stood over him. "Don't worry, Bart; the reason Manky said nothing to ye was because he was wearing his rubber ear-plugs. I could see them in his ears—he couldn't hear a fucking thing," said Domo, with a serious expression on his face. Bart, though still on his hunches, his upper part of his body went rigid with what Domo revealed.

"Maher had his ear-plugs in? He had his ear-plugs in—did he? Did he, Domo?"

"No! Ye fucking eejit ye, your fucking life is not worth living, because you're fucked. I'll tell ye one thing though, I thought I would never see a man on death row, so ye see—wonders never cease," jeered Domo, who then went into a fit of laughter which set the rest of us off laughing again. Bart now got to his feet, and told Domo that he would get him back one way or the other.

"Wait and see if I don't, Black, ye pot bellied sarcastic little old fucker ye," shouted Bart, with a healthy color now returned to his face. Being twenty something made me wonder why he called Domo old, as Bart was only a few years younger that Domo. Mick Holmes returned with the keys of the target shed, and we went about our business of taking the targets from the shed and placing them into the target cradles. There were two cradles for each firer, one behind the other, which each held a target in place. When one target cradle was hoisted up, the other came down with wheels, chains and gravity coming into play, and while one target was up and being fired at, the one that was down would have small adhesive patches applied to the bullet holes that were presenting on the target canvas. It was not that long before the shooting began, and the ball ammunition was hitting and piercing the canvas targets, and thumping into the enormous mound of earth that was directly behind them—the butts. Domo got very annoyed when Corporal Holmes told him that he would have to operate the radio that communicated with the firing point as well as looking after his own set of targets. All the time that the shoot was in progress, Domo became more uncooperative, especially when it came to using the radio. Mick Holmes had to rebuke him a number of times for not using proper voice procedure when he would be speaking on the radio to the firing point.

"You're a fucking monkey, Black, and if ye keep carrying on the way ye are....well ye will see what happens—slowly—slowly catch a fucking monkey—ye monkey fuck," blasted Mick Holmes, with a look of sincerity on his face.

"What's all this monkey fucking shit?... I mean what's with the monkey—are ye related to fucking Tarzan or what? There's only one fucking ape around here, and that's fucking....." The monkey could not finish his sentence, as his air supply was now shut off. Mick, who must be six foot two, or thereabouts, and strongly constructed, had Domo pinned against the wall of the concrete butt shelter with one hand firmly fixed around his throat, and squeezing, not that hard as to cause damage but to have Black gasping for air.

"Throttle the fucking bastard, Mick—will ye use both hands for fucks sake, Mick?" shouted Bart Nesbitt, who was watching it unfold from down the butt shelter. Just then the radio crackled into life with the firing point wanting to know what the delay was with the targets being hoisted. The Corporal released his grip on Domo's neck, and picking up the handset from the radio he relayed to the firing point that the targets were going up now. He then gave the order "targets up" to the rest of us, and at the same time bent down and gripped Black's target cradle at the bottom and brought it up to be viewed by the firers on the range. He did not say a word to Domo, he just walked away, down along the butt shelter with the cracking sound of bullets passing through the targets, and into the butts.

After hoisting his target on Mick Holmes command, Wally Coulthard, whose target cradle was next to Domo's, turned to him, and said, "Deeten diten though don't ye know, ye were very naughty to Corporal Holmes, and ye should not talk to him like that—don't ye know that—Trooper Black?" He then leaned against the running rail of the cradle.

Domo, who was now caressing the front of his neck with his index finger and thumb of his left hand, while rubbing the back of his neck with his other hand, gave Wally a look of disgust. "What in the name of jasus is that baby shite coming out of your mouth ye big baby featured pumped up headed fucker? Are ye taking some kind of childish drug or what? I mean are ye injecting yourself with a dosage of Calpol, or smoking fucking Liga? Are ye in some way related to Barney? Because it looks like ye just stepped out of his pink fucking suit," ranted a disgruntled, Domo.

"The only big spoilt kid around here is you, Trooper Black." rapped Wally.

Domo, looked at me, as I had the targets to the left of his, and said, "Did ye hear that, and this is coming from a shite bag that wears fucking pampers instead of underpants. I'll tell ye—I don't normally punch kids to a pulp as a rule…but I'll gladly make an exception in your case ye big moon faced fucker," threatened Domo, with hostilely towards Wally, as he moved closer to him.

Just in time, Mick Holmes interceded on behalf of Wally. "Touch him, Black, and I'll punch you to a fucking pulp, do ye hear me?" snarled the Corporal. Not a word from Domo, as he turned and walked towards the radio, as the firing point was trying to make contact.

Domo picked up the handset. "What fucking ails ye?" he replied to the firing point radio operator, who he knew would be a fellow Trooper, and therefore he would be devoid of trouble. "Wrong!" shouted Domo, into the handset with rapidity, on seeing Mick looking at him contemptuously. "Firing point—this is butts—you are ok—have you got a message for me—over?" said Domo, into the handset with proper voice procedure, and a shade of military diplomacy, while all the time averting his eyes from the Corporal. The firing point's message was that we were to take down the targets and patch them up, as the first detail of firers were about to begin their last practice, which was the "the run up" practice. This practice started off at the three hundred yard marker where the firers would discharge five rounds of ammunition at their targets that would be displayed for thirty seconds. When finished at the three hundred they would walk towards the two hundred marker until their target's would appear again, and in so doing the firers would run to the two hundred marker and fire another five rounds, and then the same procedure at the one hundred, which would complete their annual fire practice. We had the targets all set to shove up, as the firers were now walking towards the one hundred, and we were just waiting on the command from Corporal Holmes to display them to the firing detail.

"Targets up!" barked Mick. Bending down I gripped the bottom of the front target cradle, and hoisted it above the butt shelter to be seen by the troops running towards the one hundred yard marker.

"Me fucking back! Me bastaring back has fucking locked on me, oh I can't fucking move—the pain—I can't move....I'm not able to straighten up—oh for the love of jasus help me I'm paralyzed—for the love of fuck will somebody call an ambulance?" screamed Domo, bent over and face downwards with spit flying from his mouth. From what I could see, and from what he was screaming, it seemed to me that his back had somehow locked as he bent over to hoist his target cradle. First things first, I bent down and lifted his target up, or else Manky would have being roaring down the handset from the firing point.

"What fucking ails ye, Black? Did ye lose something?" asked Mick Holmes, sarcastically, as he approached to see what all the commotion was about.

Domo turned his head to the side to look up at Mick. "Yeah! Holmes, -a photo of your missus in the nip...hello! My fucking back—are ye going to get an ambulance or what?" cried a red faced and pain stricken Domo. Before Mick Holmes could say anything, Bart Nesbitt pushed his way to the front of the melee with a huge smile on his face, and rubbing his hands together, and told Domo that he would give it a right go at straightening him up, which brought a look of sheer terror to the face of Domo. "Don't come next nor fucking near...." Domo began but did not get a chance to complete his sentence, as it was curtailed by the Corporal.

"Shut the fuck up, Black! It's a crying shame that it was not your cesspit shit ejector mouth that got fucking locked instead of your back," snapped Mick, who then told Nesbitt to stop play acting, and that he was to take Trooper Daly and go to the target shed and fetch a stretcher that he had seen there earlier on when bringing out the targets. While the lads went to get the stretcher Mick Holmes walked along the targets, taking down the final scores. Before doing this he told me to send a radio message to the firing point that an ambulance was required, to which I carried out, and explained what had occurred to Trooper Black.

The pain to Domo's back seemed to be very severe, as he was now moaning with long plaintive high-pitched sounds. "Will....aah...aah...one of you open the belt and button on my combat trousers, and loosen them on me?....ah...for fuck's sake....they're too tight—they're fucking killing me," cried Domo, with a grimaced expression on his face.

"I'll do that!" volunteered, Bart Nesbitt, with a somewhat air of excitement in his voice, as Daly and himself returned with the stretcher. Bart told Domo, that he would undo his belt and button after he was placed onto the stretcher, to which Domo, uncharacteristically thanked him for coming to his aid. "It's all my pleasure, yes—my pleasure indeed," declared Bart, with an ironic tone, and a insolent smile forming on his face. Domo was placed on all fours, kneeling, while holding onto two poles that ran through a coarse canvas on each side to form a somewhat crude stretcher, so as not to cause him any more discomfort and pain. Bart Nesbitt then proceeded to lower Domo's waterproof slacks down to his knees. After this he opened the belt and button on Black's trousers but did not stop there. After opening the flies of the combat trousers, Bart struggled but then succeeded to wriggle the trousers down to join Domo's waterproof slacks, and in so doing, revealed a snug fitting pair of red underpants for all the troops to gaze upon as an object of contempt and ridicule. Domo's cries of exasperation were drown out by the loud laughter, wolf whistles and witty remarks from the lads.

"Right, that's enough—grab your gear, and move to the firing point to fire your own practice, and two of you pick up that stretcher, and remove that scruffy looking article up the range for the ambulance to collect," ordered the Corporal. Two of the lads, lifted the stretcher in quick motion, which put a sudden stop to Domo's moaning, as he grasped the two poles to regain his balance, as he almost went over the side of the stretcher.

"Hold it!" rasped Bart, to the two stretcher-bearers. "Do ye know what, Black? Your sister's red knickers look disgusting on ye. Let's see if I can hide them a small bit—what do ye think?"

"I swear, Nesbitt I'm going to—oh! Ah! What in the name of jasus have ye done, Nesbitt—ye dirty swine?" wailed Domo, as he felt the full force with which Bart had violently yanked his red underwear upwards and into his crevasse, and therefore leaving the two cheeks exposed. Because of the severe pain in his back, Domo could not reach around to cover his humiliation and vulgar display of windswept flesh, which had him crying out to Mick Holmes to order someone to cover him, but to no avail. Mick told him that it was himself who had asked for the comfort from the pain, by loosening and relaxing the clothing around the back area. Mick then gave Bart a wink of his eye, and walked from the butts shelter towards the firing point, much to Domo's dismay. Suddenly, and almost simultaneously there was the sounds of a sharp lively smack, closely ensued by a lingering and retarding howl. Turning around I could see Wally Coulthard standing over the stretcher with a satisfied smile on his large oval face, as he stared down on the clear, pinkish red imprint of his hand mark on Domo's benumbed right buttock. Turner and Redmond, the two stretcher-bearers were laughing that much, that they almost had Domo over the side, once more.

"By right I should give ye six of the best, Black, for your naughtiness to the Corporal and myself," said, Wally, with his childlike pronunciation.

"Oooooh—ye big simp fucker—I am going to....as soon as my back is normal again—I'm going to punch...no—no, I'm going to knuckle you into a coma—I'm going to take my boots and socks off so I can really feel every bit of kicking your ball's to death—I'm going to give ye a fucking physical handicap to match your mental one—do ye hear me ye mutton headed bastard?" babbled Domo to Wally, who was now lifting his hand to administer another stinger to the rambler's mounds of flesh. Intervening before Wally's hand could strike for a second time, I told him to cut it out, and at the same time hastily motioning Turner and Redmond to move the stretcher to the firing point, to which they readily complied. The torment for Domo was far from over; as the stretcher passed by the one hundred marker, the first detail of firers who were picking up their empty cartridge casings, readily observed Domo, in his unconcealed and embarrassing posture being carried on the stretcher. Some of them promptly made their way over to the casualty, and commenced to playfully tease Domo about his cheeky predicament, while all the time propelling empty casings at his clenching posteriors. Through gritted teeth, Domo snarled various threats of vulgar violence towards his tormentors, which did not seem to alter their pestering of him, as after Domo's threat's, some of them made their way forward, and inserted empty casings into the crevasse of his rump.

"Jasus, Black, if ye leaned over on your side—that hole of yours would look like fucking Pac-Man," quipped one of the firers.

"Yeah!" said another.

"The size of that crack, did someone fucking plough it? I mean—ye could grow fucking vegetables in there—it's that big and fucking mucky." He then joined in the laughter with the rest of the pestilent troops. Much to Domo's relief, a loud shout came from the firing point, from a boisterous Wild Bill, calling for the lads to get a move on with picking up the empties, and return to the firing point. Domo had enough; he told Turner and Redmond that if they did not cover him up that he would throw himself from the stretcher onto the ground. The two of them came to a halt with the stretcher, and looked at one another with quizzical looks on their faces in wonderment as of what to do. Making their minds up for them, I reminded them that the tea and sandwiches were at the firing point, and that the lads would scoff the lot if they did not cover up Domo, and get him down there, rapid like. They looked at me, and then at each other, I misjudged them completely; they placed the stretcher on the ground, and walked away hurriedly in the direction of the sandwiches and tea, with Domo shouting abuse after them. There was only Wally coming behind, so I asked him if he would give me a hand to carry the stretcher, and to my surprise he did not object, but instead obliged. As I was just about to re-arrange his trousers, Domo asked me if I would first bring his underpants into place, to which I sternly told him not to push it. After the trousers and wet slacks were risen to restore his dignity, Wally and myself proceeded to carry Domo on the stretcher to the firing point, to wait on the ambulance.

"Well, Black, how is the back? Very-very sore—I hope." said Captain Maher, with cold dispassion, as we placed the stretcher on the ground to the rear of the firing point. Domo started to babble on at Maher, with his grievances about his treatment at the hands of the lads and Corporal Holmes, and asked him what he intended to do about it. Maher, leaned his head slightly back to gaze at the sky, and placed his index finger to his bottom lip, to form a pondering stance.

"Now, let me see now, ah yes! Black—Black…with the fucked up back…now! That seems to rhyme. Do I look like I give two fucks about you Black—do I?" calmly said, the Captain, in a soft spoken voice, who then turned and walked away. Wild Bill was shuffling among the lads as they were eating sandwiches and drinking tea, and all the while telling them to hurry up and finish, because as soon as the last detail had fired, everyone could get back to barracks, and in so doing he could keep an appointment he had to attend in the afternoon.

"I'm eating mine as quick as I can, Sarge." sputtered Wally, as he chomped on the whole of a sandwich that he had just placed into his mouth. Wild Bill gave Wally a fictive smile.

"Good man Trooper, Coulthard, but ye see it's not you I'm worried about, because you have a mouth like the back of a fucking bin lorry," maliciously voiced, Bill, who then walked on through the troops, harassing as he went along, and leaving Wally, none the wiser in his fatuous state. Wild Bill, in the end got his wish through badgering, as the second detail was now lined up to receive ammo for their firing practice, as the rain started to fall again. Corporal Holmes, who was now in charge of issuing out the ammunition to the firers called across to Captain Maher, who was still swigging tea, that he had found a snag with the amount of ammunition that was left to fire, there was not enough. After going through the ammunition book, and counting the remaining bullets, Maher came to the conclusion that there would be two less firers on the practice. He then started to loudly express his disgust at the incompetence of the store Sergeant giving the wrong amount of ammunition, but at the same time seemed to selfishly ignore his own imperfect functioning of not counting what he had signed for. Redmond and I were not to fire, as we were first in the queue, and therefore selected. We were to help Mick Holmes loading magazines for the firers, as the shoot progressed.

"Right lets be having ye, get your loaded magazine and go and stand behind your firing position," shouted Wild Bill, with an air of authority, with hands on hips.

"Sarge—Sarge, what about my disengaged eye—what will I do about it Sarge?" inquired Wally, of Wild Bill.

"Come'ere ye tormenting fucking eejit," said Bill, as he took a roll of gun cleaning flannel from his jacket pocket. He then rolled out the flannel in his hands until he was satisfied that he had the correct amount for his purpose. "Now, tie this around your head and cover your disengaged eye—problem solved....do ye totally understand that—do ye?" reasoned Wild Bill, as he handed Wally, the long piece of torn away flannel.

"But Sarge, what if it slips down when I'm firing?" anxiously asked Wally.

"Don't worry, because if it does slip, then I have the very cure for your fucking disengaged eye—have ye got that—have ye?" vowed Wild Bill, with a look of intention on his face, and an enduring nodding of his head. After the lads received their loaded magazine's they were brought into a listening group behind the three hundred marker to hear the Captain's spiel on range safety. Looking across to the three hundred marker I could see that Wild Bill was pacing back and forth along the firing positions with his hands behind his back looking very perturbed; he knew from old that Maher, somehow always dragged out his safety speech, while knowing that it should be superficial at most, and Bill was getting more irritated by the second.

" I can still hear that moaning swine, and after me putting him around the side so I wouldn't have to listen or look at him," whinged Mick Holmes, who had earlier dragged Domo on the stretcher to the sided end of a long narrow hill that stood between number two and number three range, to wait on the ambulance.

"At long fucking last!" shouted Bill as the lads made their way onto their firing position's to begin the shoot. Both the wind and rain started to pick up, which made our job of filling the magazines with rounds for the next part of the shoot, more annoying.

"Who's in charge here?" came a voice of authority from a tall burley figure dressed in wet gear, who was standing over us in our ammo filling kneeling position. All three of us knew by the grey steely eyes and stone face that were under his hood that it was Commandant Barr, from Command training office. Mick Holmes stood up, saluted and gave his rank, and then informed him that Captain Maher was in charge. "Corporal, could you please explain to me why there is a man at the end of that hill kneeling on a stretcher with his bare arse cocked in the air, and wearing a fucking red g-string while screaming like he has just been fucking gang probed? Don't bother Corporal—just get me the Captain," demanded the Commandant. Mick started to explain just why Domo was there, and what had befallen him, when the officer raised his hand, and told Mick with a certain amount of flippancy and impatience to shut up and go and fetch the Captain, at once. Mick informed Barr, that he could not leave the ammunition, so he dispatched me to give Maher the message. As I was walking across to the Captain, it became apparent to me that Nesbitt had once again placed Domo into a humiliating posture. Earlier, when I was filling ammo I noticed Nesbitt coming from the side of the hill where Domo was situated and thought no more of it, as I thought he had gone behind the hill to relieve himself, and it had never entered my mind (until now) he was returning from a mission of degradation. On reaching Maher, he stood with his back to me, and with the noise of the lads shooting I tugged on the sleeve of his waterproof jacket to get his attention. When he turned to face me I raised my voice, and began to tell him the message, but by placing his hand up in front of me and tapping and showing me one of his earplugs was an indication that I was to wait until the firing had finished. The firing finished, and the lads were still lying on the ground waiting for the order to unload when Maher removed his earplugs and moved forward to the position of the first firer in line, on the ground.

"Don't fucking skit or slag me off again, Nesbitt, ye little fucker ye," rasped Maher, who at the same time sent a ferocious kick into the side of the helmeted and waterproof hooded figure on the ground. The scream was ear piercing from the body on the ground.

"Sir! I promise I'll never slag ye off again. I swear to fuck, Sir, I'll never, Sir, as long as I fucking live—never," roared Nesbitt, who was lying next to the screaming Trooper Collins, who had unfortunately been mistaken for him, by Maher; he had forgotten about two less firers, and therefore the firing positions would move places. Collins was screaming that his ribs were broken, as Maher stood there in disbelief with the blood drained from his face. Wild Bill had his head in his hands and was also in disbelief over another delay. Quickly I informed the stunned Maher that his presence was required by Commandant Barr from Command. He looked across the twenty five yards with squinting eyes to where Barr was observing all from under his hood. Looking across I could see Mick Holmes waving and indicating to the two medics, who had just arrived with the ambulance and were heading towards Domo, that their assistance was needed on the firing point.

"Man down! Man down! Suspected heart attack! Medic—medic!" shouted Maher at the top of his voice, making sure that Barr could hear him. He then bent down over the now whimpering Collins and whispered to him to play along, and that he would get him onto the next N.C.O. course. Then Wally Coulthard, got up from the ground, and removing the strip of flannel from around his head and eye, started to walk towards where Wild Bill was standing.

" Sarge—Sarge, I still can't close my disengaged eye, Sarge. Will ye help me close my disengaged eye, Sarge…Will ye, Sarge?" pleaded Wally, as he moved closer to Bill. The expression on Wild Bill's face was one of contortion, as his top lip was raised up tightly over his upper deformed teeth. He moved quickly towards the oncoming Wally, and when reaching him, Wild Bill jumped upwards, and plunged his thumb into Wally's left eye, bringing an agonizing roaring cry from the now reeling Wally.

"Can ye close it now, ye big sappy bastard ye? Can ye?" shouted Bill, who then screamed at the lads still lying on the ground to shut up laughing and to stand up and unload. He then detailed two of the lads to help Collins over to the ambulance and then told me to show Wally and his closed disengaged eye the .way over. Captain Maher now made his way over to the Commandant, who had seen enough, and started to walk away. The training officer's car was parked beside the ambulance, and as he approached it he saw the two medics carrying Domo on the stretcher, who was loudly voicing very extreme expletives to one and all.

"And you Captain!" cried Domo, to Maher, who had rushed up to, and was now standing beside the bewildered looking Barr. "I want something done about Nesbitt and Corporal Holmes—oh me fucking back—the pain—and where were ye two fuckers?" He was now taking it out on the medics. "Where did ye come from with the ambulance—Cork fucking hospital? I think I got hypothermia of the sack and numbing of the bollocks waiting on you pair of fucking ball shavers," griped Domo, who seemed to have suddenly forgotten that it was the medics who had covered up his humiliation with a blanket. The medic to the rear of the stretcher gave it a small shake, and told Domo to shut up. "Teah—yeah! I get the message " Florence." Now for fucks sake will yourself and your pal "Clinger" there, get me into the back of the ambulance, and get me to fuck out of this shit-hole?" spewed Domo, sarcastically.

"Talking of shit-holes, Captain." said Barr, "I think that is where yourself and the Sergeant are about to be shortly."

"But, Sir…"

"Shut up, Captain; it's bad enough that I am being pissed down on from the heavens without you trying to shit on me too," expressed Barr. He then instructed the Captain to cancel the "debacle of a shoot" and to get the injured parties to the hospital at once. Wally and Collins were placed into the ambulance to join Domo, as Commandant Barr, without speaking another word hastily departed the range with his driver. Maher approached the ambulance just as the medic was closing the back doors.

"Well, medic, what is the extent of the injuries?" asked Maher.

"Eye—rib—and back," answered the medic. The Captain simultaneously closed his eyes and raised his arms in the air. He then brought his arms with speed inwards and slightly downwards to let his hand's rest on top of his head and at the same time opened his eyes to glare at the medic.

"I'm surrounded by fucking clowns." expressed Maher, to no one in particular. "Listen, Private!" he addressed the medic. "I asked you for the extent—the extent of the injuries—not the name of the fucking German center forward who played in the world cup. Now could you expand, explain in more detail the extent of the injuries?" he insisted, with wide eyes and a rapid nodding of his head that signaled an impatient gesture to the reticent medic to answer.

After a few stunned moments the medic's mouth went into action. "Well Sir, the locked back could be the muscles around the facet joint has gone into spasm. The ribs seemed to be broken, and the eye is heavily bloodshot, caused by ramfatdigititus."

"What in the name of fuck is ramfatdigititus?" queried Maher.

"Well, Sir, in layman term, and from the information that Trooper Coulthard gave me, it's caused when some halfwit rams his fat thumb into an eye socket," said the medic, smiling, and wrong thinking that Maher possessed a good sense of humor.

"Well, well, now let me tell you, medic, get into that ambulance and take those men to the hospital—quick, before I ram my fat fucking boot up your hole, and dislocate your pancreas. Move your fucking arse—move it!" shouted Maher, with disdain.

Without saying another word the medic walked quickly away. "A fucking dickhead if there was ever one," said Wild Bill of the medic to Maher. "It's pissing fucking rain, I mean—should he not be wearing a fucking condom over that stupid prick-head of his? I'll be seeing Mr. fucking medic again, and when I do he won't be calling me a halfwit again, in a hurry," proclaimed Bill. The Captain then told Wild Bill to take his jeep, and follow the lads to the hospital, and smooth things over, and that he would travel back in the truck.

"I just did not notice Barr standing there I mean with the wet gear…well, I thought he was one of the lads," said Maher, who was now talking to Mick Holmes, who was making his way to the truck.

"Now ye know how I feel, Sir," said Nesbitt, who was walking beside the Corporal, carrying the ammo box. "May I suggest, Sir, that ye put in a recommendation to the Quartermaster General, that all officers' waterproofs should be orange in color and visibility illumed gobshite proofed," advised Bart, with whimsicality.

The Captain's overgrown moustache was lifted by his upper lip rising to reveal clenched teeth, with his face contorted. "You little antagonistic bastard—fuck—face....." snarled Maher. "Yourself!" he roared at me,. "Get on that radio and contact that ambulance, tell them to return to this location as we have a black and blue half strangled casualty," ordered the seething officer. Bart dropped the ammo, and ran towards the back of the troop filled truck for an un-hospitalized witness seeking program from the lads. Maher stopped me walking to the radio with a gesture of his hand. "Don't bother the way my luck is going...I'll thump him another day....when he is not in wet gear." He then dropped his head and walked through the driving rain to the cab of the truck.

THE STRAIN FACTOR

As we moved in formation towards the hide, I knew that this would be my last chance to grab some sleep. I would need whatever sleep came my way because at four o' clock the next morning we would be on day two of a seventy two hour military exercise. There would be no sleep for the next forty eight hours as we would be performing mobile operations through areas of Co. Cork. The reason behind the maneuvers was a Troop Commanders course. Each officer would be tested on their skill and capabilities of leading a troop of men, and armored cars through various tactical and battle situations. I was the radio operator in the Troop officer's Nissan jeep. The commander of the troop, which was B. Troop, was a lady officer, Lt. Mullins. The troop itself consisted of one Nissan jeep, and four armored cars, two of which were armored personal carriers (A.P.C.), each of which had a crew of a Commander in the back hatch, a gunner in the turret, and a driver. The interior of the car held two anti-tank teams, which consisted of two men as a team. There were also four riflemen as part of the crew. Of the other two armored vehicles, one had a 60mm gun, while the other possessed a 90mm gun; both cars had a crew of three: Commander, gunner and driver. The troop also consisted of a recovery truck, in case of any breakdowns. The troop is part of a Squadron on the ground, which is broken down into three troops, A. Troop, B. Troop, and a reconnaissance troop (Recce Troop) and a mobile command unit, at the rear. Other than the Squadron, there is also a mock enemy that keeps the Troop Commanders on their toes with complex methods of warfare. The Troop Commander's car was the first into the hide, and was situated at the back of the wood. The hide itself was a small wood that had plenty of cover. The trees of the wood were well dispersed, giving plenty of room for the vehicles to be placed in strategic defense positions around the hide. The vehicles were also camouflaged as a stratagem to deceive the enemy. The hide is where we would replenish ourselves with food and rest, and in order to achieve this, we had to move into the hide one hour before dark to set up our makeshift tents, and cook some food. Once, we have entered the hide there is complete silence, and if someone had to communicate orally, it was done in whisper. We must leave the hide at dawn, and as this was the month of July there weren't a lot of hours to get some rest between dusk and dawn. Besides Lt. Mullins and me, the other crew member of our car was Trooper Jay 'Pip' Gilroy, the driver. I don't know where he got the nick-name 'Pip' from, because he was a block of a lad who was touching six feet in height. He was a real likeable bloke who as long as I knew him, I never seen him in bad humor, and something told me that I did not want to either. He was over protective with Lt. Mullins, as she had an unassuming nature. He would not let any of the lads get out of line with her, and if any did, they would have him to deal with, so she got a quiet enough time from the Troop. The Lieutenant and Pip went for a walk around the hide to check on the troops, and left me to mind our car at the back of the hide. As I was setting up a small propane burner to cook some grub on, I heard voices coming from the side of the hide that was not occupied by the Troop. Moving very slow and carefully, I made my way through the trees, and as I did so the voices became more audible and very familiar. It was then I realized that the recovery truck was parked on a small dirt road that ran along the side of the hide. The voices I heard were that of Sgt. 'Miser' Murray and Sgt. Wally Turner, who were the crew of the recovery truck. The recovery truck also carried drinking water for the Troop, and as it was only present for mechanical emergencies, and was not participating directly with the exercise, it did not enter the hide. I made my way back to the cooker, and carried on getting some grub ready. Stretching out and sleeping in the Nissan meant that I did not have to erect a bivvy, so I got on with the cooking. Now with three burners on the go, of which two had a mess tin each with stew in them, while the other one had a mess tin of water boiling for some tea. Standing in front of the Nissan, keeping a watch on the burners, I noticed Lt. Mullins and Pip coming back along a narrow clearing in the wood, when all of a sudden Pip pulled the officer down to the ground.

"It's the enemy, Mam." Pip said to Lt Mullins, as the two of them took up firing positions. It was obvious to me that Pip had heard the same voices that I had heard a little earlier, that of Miser Murray and Wally Turner, and mistook them for the enemy. Pip gestured for me to get down and take cover. They gave me a quizzical look as I stood there and lit up a smoke.

Taking a drag from the cigarette, I said to Pip, "It's Miser Murray, ye fucking eejit." I began to laugh. Just as the embarrassed duo stood up, there was a very loud shout from the direction of the recovery truck. "I'm no fucking eejit, de yis hear me? I'm no fucking eejit, yis load of shite bags, there will be blood spilt in that camp tonight, I'm no fucking eejit." It was the voice of Miser Murray. Now I know that sound travels in a quite wood, but the little fucker must have the hearing of a wildebeest, as I did not speak that loud.

"I wasn't calling you an eejit, ye fucking eejit," I roared back to him. Lt. Mullins jumped to her feet, and in an agitated voice called for silence.

Too late, Miser retorted in high volume, "I won't be giving out any water in that fucking camp tonight, ye load of fucking eejit's yis." His voice was drifting away. There was silence, but it was the silence before the storm, because all hell broke loose. All over the hide the lads started to hurl abuse at Miser.

"Don't waste the fucking thing ye jumped up little bastard, drown yourself in it," one of the lads shouted from the far end of the hide.

"Blow it out your arse ye head melting fuck," came another voice from the middle of the hide. It was like this all over the hide, and the lieutenant was on the verge of having a nervous breakdown, as she was now screaming for silence. Suddenly there was a coarse, amplified voice that drowned out all other voices in the hide.

"Shut the fuck up!" It was a voice that everyone in and out of the hide knew, and feared. "The next person I hear talking, I will place under arrest after I kick the living shit from them," said Commandant Danny Molloy. Molloy was a hard and strict disciplinarian who was the officer in charge of the Troop Commanders Course, and did not suffer fools, end of story. After he called for the Troop Commander and Troop Sergeant to come to him (for a rollicking) not a murmur was heard in the hide. On her return from a one sided debate on noise control the Lieutenant informed us that Commandant Molloy would be staying the night in the hide, and would be travelling in our car all day tomorrow, assessing her intelligence and competence to lead a troop in a problematic combating state of affairs. Calling Pip to one side and out of earshot of Lt. Mullins, I told him that I had better put the rest of the lads wise about Molloy staying for the night, in case any of them walk into trouble. As it was just about dark I would have to move fast around the tents to inform the lads. Side by side, and running along the middle of the hide were a row of five, two-man bivouacs that were camouflaged with small branches of tree. Right next to the bivvies stood what I can only describe as a walk in tent. The crew from the A.P.C. had joined their groundsheets together, and with some bungees they erected a well formed makeshift tent around four trees. Entering the ample well-built tent I was not surprised to find that the interior was snug and cozy, with a small lamp emitting light to the lads sitting on their sleeping bags, and eating the food from their mess tins. Moments after I told the lads that Molloy was staying in the hide, a voice presented itself from outside the tent, it was the voice of Trooper Eddie Fagan, who was Molloy's driver. Fagan was a lick arse bastard, and an officer groupie who always seemed to be there when an officer needed something. Even the sight of him would turn anyone's stomach, with his abundant content of abdomen, and a pumped up head with a long nose protruding from it that would never be beaten in a photo finish.

"Commandant Molloy, Sir, do ye need anything before I go to my shelter, Sir?" said Fagan in a whispered voice outside the tent. With his one track mind he must have thought that because of the size of the tent it could only belong to an officer and therefore thought that Molloy was inside. There wasn't a sound inside the tent; we looked at one another and knew we had the fucker.

Joey Donavan nudged me with his elbow, and then in a gruff, but low voice, said, "Is that you, Trooper Fagan?"

"Yes, Sir, it's me Trooper Fagan, Sir," answered the still soft voice of Fagan. I don't know how Joey kept so serious, as I had to put my hand over my mouth to stop myself from laughing.

"My pack ration has been stolen, Trooper Fagan; do you hear me? Trooper Fagan, fucking stolen. Sound the alarm, sound stand too, ye fucking idiot, move your fucking lardass, now!" snapped Joey, as he had Molloy's voice down to a fine art.

"Yes Sir…yes Sir, at once Sir," gasped Fagan, as he moved off. Pulling the flap back on the tent we could see him running down the hide, and screaming at the top of his voice, "Stand to…..stand to, the officer's rations have been stolen, stand to…..stand fucking to, call out the guard; the Commandant's vittles have been robbed."

He was like a raving bastard of a lunatic running around in circles banging at his mess tin with his knife and fork. The whole hide was in uproar with bodies running every direction to get to their defensive positions, with no one knowing what was going down. Molloy came sprinting by us, and made a beeline for Fagan.

Gripping Fagan around the throat with both hands, and lifting him up off his feet, Molloy snarled, " I will bite the fucking tongue from your head Fagan if you open that shit hole of a mouth again; do ye hear me? Just fucking nod Fagan." He must have nodded because Molloy threw him to the ground. Molloy then shouted for everyone to stand down. Once again Molloy sounded off for the Troop Commander and Sergeant to come to him. Lt. Mullins, who had been running around organizing the Troop during the turmoil was now passing, and stopped to ask us what had happened. Joey told her that Fagan had blown a fuse and was running around screaming something about Commandant Molloy stealing his rations. Back at the Nissan I was telling Pip about Fagan, and we were having a good giggle when Lt. Mullins returned from her second visit to Molloy. She told us that Fagan was relieved of the driving of Commandant Molloy and placed on sentry duty at the front of the hide for the rest of the night and would be sent back to the Curragh tomorrow.

"Fucking deadly, I'm over the moon for the lick arse bastard, A— fucking—yes," blurted a delighted Pip. On seeing the inquiring look that herself was giving him, Pip smiled, and with jovial empathy for Lt. Mullins said, "Did I just say that out loud. I'm sorry, Ma'am, I seem to be always doing that a lot lately." He waited on her response. She smiled, and walked away. After having something to eat, we settled down in the Nissan for the night without any further occurrence. Just before dawn I was awoken by the noise of Lt. Mullins leaving the car to go to the toilet deep among the trees. Pip and I got out of the car to go for a slash and proceeded to the opposite side from the Lieutenant. Who should walk by as we were having a whiz, but the king of the fucking eejits, Miser Murray, who was coming back from a water run into the hide.

"What was the story with ye last night, Sarge?" I inquired.

"Ah, I was just joshing about with yis all," said an embarrassed Miser as he hurried on by.

"Yeah, we know," I said, " ye fucking eejit."

"What did you say?" said Miser, as he stopped and turned.

"I said yeah we know, ye fucking tease ye," I replied. The flow of urine from Pip was nearly giving the game away as it was stopping and starting to splutter as he tried to keep in the laughing. Miser grunted something and walked on. The Troop Commander's car was the last in the queue of vehicles preparing to depart the hide. Pip and I were the only persons in the car, as Lt. Mullins had gone out onto the road to organize the Troop leaving the hide, with Molloy going along with her to observe. Pip was to pick them up out on the road. Moving slowly along at the rear we could see a tired and disheveled Fagan standing at the side of the exit from the hide, directing the traffic out. Pip stopped the car, got out, and fiddled with the bottom of the windscreen wiper, and then got back into the car.

"That's just about right." he said, winding down his window. I did not have to wonder for long as to what Pip was up to, as he drove the car to the exit of the hide, and stopped beside Fagan. With a pitiful expression he looked at Fagan, "Good Lord, man, ye look dirty and tired. Were ye up all night?" asked Pip.

"Yeah I was," moaned the rump kisser.

Pip smiled broadly. "What you need to do is throw a drop of water on your face; here, let me help ye, ye lick arse fucking muck pup ye," said Pip.

With the surprise of the jet of water from the windscreen washer hitting him in the face, Fagan stumbled backwards, over a stump of a tree, and landing on his back. Pip had turned the windscreen washer to the side so he could squirt Fagan in the face. We could hear Fagan shouting abuse at us as we motored out of the hide, and up the road having a right good laugh, as we joined the rest of the Troop. Lt. Mullins got into the car, and Molloy sat in the back beside me, and off we headed for another long exhausting day in the Cork countryside. By early afternoon the enemy had engaged us three times at various locations, and on the three incursions Lt. Mullins came through with flying colors. The lads in the Troop had come good for her on her tasks due to the overindulgent affection they held for her. Molloy was satisfied with her all round performance, and therefore informed me to send a message on the radio for another candidate to assume the role of Troop Commander, and report to this location. The Troop was now stationary at the side of the road on the outskirts of a small village. After finishing the transmission I walked down to where Lt. Mullins was stretching her legs beside an armored car and told her that a car would pick her up shortly and bring her to a location code named "Snack Box."

"Bloody great," she said, with a large smile on her face. She looked up at Sgt. Scrapper McDonald in the turret of the armored car and asked him if he would look up his slide chart for the location of "Snack Box," as she had left her slide chart back in the Nissan. The Scrapper looked down at her with tired squinting red eyes that looked like the sandman had just took a dump in them.

Then in a dazed state, he opened the chart which was resting on the armored plating in front of him and stared at it for a moment, and then in a slurred voice he muttered, "Snack box, let me see here, fucking snack box, yeah snack......box." Then there was silence. Lt. Mullins and I were looking up at him as he was dabbing the chart with his finger, and his head going slowly downwards until it came to rest on the chart.

"Are you all right, Sarge?" asked the concerned officer.

"I think he is asleep, Ma'am." I said, smiling. I couldn't believe the fucker done a Rip Van Winkle in front of the officer, unbelievable.

"Ah well, I guess we are all tired," she said, "some more than others." As she was walking away she passed the second armored car, and looking up at the Commander and Gunner in the turret she pointed at the Scrapper's car and without stopping she said, "See, the Sarge is asleep, lads." She then went back to her car. There was no acknowledgement from either the Commander or the Gunner to the officer's remark about the Scrapper, which I thought was odd, so I strolled down to the armored car, and on looking a little closer than the Lieutenant did, I could see that the two of them were fast asleep behind their sunglasses. I smiled to myself and walked back towards my car. Walking passed Scrapper's car I could see that he was awake again and looking all around, maybe thinking that the officer with the snack box was a dream.

Smiling up at him I quipped, "The two lads are having a short nap behind their sunglasses and would like you to order them two snack boxes, and to wake them up when they arrive."

Well, he let a roar out of him that must have shaken the little village. "Hey!" he bellowed. "Yis pair of snoozing fucking shit heads, there will be no sleeping when I'm in charge," and then turning to me, and pointing his finger, "and you ye little bollix can fuck off back to your car, and mind your own nose."

Talk about the pan calling the kettle 'black arse.' The toil of the exercise was starting to take effect, and the strain factor was now setting in, and I was wondering when it would present itself to me. I did not have to wait long for the exposure of the embarrassing effect it would take on me. We waited another ten minutes at the side of the road before Lt. Mullins replacement arrived to relieve her of her position as Troop Commander. She was replaced by Lt. Ricketts, who had an air of snobbishness about him, and right away I knew that his condescending manner would not go down well with Molloy, or the Troop for that matter. He was not that tall but to look at his thin frame, slender face, and long nose would give the optical impression of him being taller. His sandy hair complimented his blue eyes, while in contrast his large protruding teeth gave no gesture of respect to either of each. If he donned a peruke and beauty spot, he would not look out of place at the court of King Louis XVI. Just too look at the sleeveen head, and his self-righteous mannerisms gave me visions of knitting hags, and the guillotine. Pip and I were standing looking at

Ricketts putting his kit into the back of the car, and giving us a "ye should be doing this for me" kind of look. He carried on putting his kit into the car when we gave him a "bite the butt end of my bollix" kind of look back.

"What do ye make of him?" asked Pip.

"I'll tell ye one thing Pip," I said, "if he was back in the French Revolution, his head would be first to get the guillotine."

"Yeah," said Pip, "but not before the nancy fucker got gang banged by the three Musketeers and the man in the iron mask." He started to laugh.

We were standing there in the kinks of laughter when Ricketts walked over to us. "Do the pair of you find something funny?" he said, with a hand on each hip.

"Yes, Sir, we do," said Pip, straightening himself up but still laughing, and wiping the tears from his eyes.

"Well, would you like to tell me what's so funny?" inquired the bemused officer.

"No, Sir, no I wouldn't like to tell ye. Is that all right, Sir?" replied Pip.

With his hands still on his hips, Ricketts puckered his lips and turned his head to glance up and down the road, then turning his gaze back towards us, and in a sharp tone said, "Shut the fuck up laughing and control yourselves or it is going to be a very long and hard day. Now where can I find Commandant Molloy?" He took his hands off his hips.

We stopped laughing, and Pip pointed down the road. "He went down to the water truck to fill up his guillotine......oh! Did I say guillotine? ..... I meant canteen, his gone to fill up his canteen from the water truck, Sir," said a straight faced Pip. Ricketts sneered at Pip, and walk off in a huff to locate the Commandant. Pip and I went to the back of the car and out of sight to have a good laugh.

The afternoon was very clammy, and even with the windows in the car down it was very sticky sitting there as we motored along. We were travelling through one of Co. Cork's national parks, and the sandman was starting to attack, as I could feel my eyes starting to tire. Lt. Ricketts was sitting in the front of the car, while Molloy was sitting in the back beside me observing Ricketts performance.

As we were driving along I could see Pip's face in his rear view mirror, and his eyes were starting to close. Putting my hand out my window, I gave Pip's elbow, which was sticking out his window, a small shake, just enough to stop him nodding off. I had to repeat this act another four times in as many minutes. After each time that I shook his elbow, he would look in his rear view mirror and wink at me in appreciation. My own eyelids were starting to drop, so I sat up straight in my seat, and kept thinking to myself that I cannot fall asleep in front of Molloy, no matter what, I was not going to fall asleep.

"Hey!" roared Malloy. "Wake the fuck up ye dozy bastard, or I will kick the living shit out of you."

I sprang upright with a sudden fear from a deep sleep, and started to waffle. "I'm not asleep, no way was I a fucking sleep no way was I asleep no way."

"Shut the fuck up you," bellowed Molloy. "I was not talking to you; I was telling the driver to wake up. I did not mind when your head went forward as you fell asleep, but when that stupid bastard's head (pointing at Pip) came back to meet yours, and not only asleep, but putting his hands behind his head to get more comfortable, I thought I was going to die, if it had not been for Lt. Ricketts here getting his hands to the steering wheel, we were all done for."

Pip kept repeating over and over that he was sorry, and Ricketts was as white as a sheet, and not saying very much. "If I catch anybody asleep again I will make it fucking permanent, because I will make sure that they will never wake up again, have ye got that?" snarled Molloy through clenched teeth. Pip and I answered yes, and so did Ricketts after Molloy gave him a tap with his finger, on the shoulder.

After a short time later, which seemed like an eternity, I was struggling badly to keep my eyes open, as I dare not shut them in case that animalistic bastard Molloy would throw me from the car as it was still moving. Looking out the window I was glad to see a family in a car on another road adjacent to us, and though travelling in the same direction as us, they were coming down a hill in an oblique line. The children started to wave at me from their car, and then the woman in the front also started to wave.

Waving back to them, I noticed that they were going along at the same speed as us so they could stay in line to wave. Then after a short distance their vehicle disappeared behind a hedgerow which was in the thin stretch of field between them and us. Glancing ahead I could see that the hedgerow ended very shortly, and with the angle that they were travelling meant that their road was going to meet with our road at the end of the hedgerow in a v-shape, and Pip could not see them.

Danger flooded my mind, and I started to scream, "Stop the fucking car; stop the car, Pip. You're going to smash into the kids, for fuck's sake stop; their car is coming from behind the hedge."

"What car?" said Molloy. "What kids? And what fucking hedge? Ye crazy bastard ye," roared Pip, as he hit the brakes. When I looked out the window, there was no hedgerow, no car, and no road, and I realized there could only be one answer; I imagined everything. I was hallucinating from the lack of sleep. Putting my head in my lap with embarrassment I could hear Pip breaking his bollix laughing.

"It must be the strain factor," Pip reasoned.

"With you two it must be the brain factor, youse don't have any." said Molloy with a hearty laugh. We drove on.

X-RATED

There was a look of despair on the face of Pat Rush as he came down the steps of the Orderly room with a tray in his hands. On the tray there was a teapot and cups, bound for the N.C.O. mess. Once there Pat would wash the cups, and make a pot of tea for the Orderly room staff. This was a ritual every morning, so the Orderly room staff would have a cup before starting work. The morning starter of a cup of tea seemed to be a habitual pervasion of the Orderly room staff. Pat was of fair height with a brownish complexion, with faint freckles dotted around his face. He had a fierce stammer, and when he spoke, the hesitations and the repetitions would often find him saying words which he did not wish to express. Anyone would think that with a infliction of this order, that Pat would be a temperamental type, whilst in fact he was of a good natured disposition.

"What's wrong, Pat?" I inquired.

"That lo-lot in there an-anno-annoy me, they want me-me to do ever-everything, all at once." replied Pat, as he hurried away to carry out his beverage mission. I continued on into the Orderly room to get some requisitions signed by the Adjutant, as I was working in the transport office for the day, and needed the requisitions for driving details. I got to the Adjutant's office, and gave a light tap on the door and walked in. Sitting behind the desk and slinging staples off the wall from an elastic band between his fingers, was Lt. McDonald. He was of a muscular build which did not seem appropriate for his small height. He was known for his dry wit, and lack of interest in the job.

"Monotony setting in, Sir?" I said, placing the requisitions in front of him.

"The monotony, I'm afraid, set in eight months ago when I was assigned this fucking office job, which I must say has all the excitement of a eunuch swallowing a fucking Viagra," said the bored officer, as he signed the requisitions without enquiring what he was signing. I took the documentation, and before I got to the door I could hear a staple hitting the wall behind me. On leaving the Adjutant's office I cut across the hall to the Orderly room to collect some stationary for the Transport office. I had only got to the counter of the Orderly room, when from behind me came Pat Rush with the tray, which now had a fresh pot of tea and clean cups on it.

"Where's the fire, Pat?" I asked, as he rushed passed me and went through the flap door at the end of the counter. I did not get an answer, as the phone rang. Pat, with the tray in his hand's had a look of bewilderment on his face. He was all flustered, and did not know what to do with the tray, as he wanted to answer the phone. He looked from the tray to the phone to the Orderly room Sergeant and Corporal, who were not making a move to answer the phone, as they were busy at their desks. Pat hovered between answering the phone, and the tray in his hands,

"The table, Pat, the table; put the tray on the table," said the Sergeant, in a quiet but demanding voice.

"Yeah, the tab-tab- table, that that that's it, on-on the table," stuttered Pat, as he placed the tray down on the table. Picking up the phone he said, "The or-or Orderly room." Then there was a small pause, and then he said, "I- I'll get him for, for ye now, Sir." he now looked confusedly at the phone, and the tray on the table. He then walked with haste around the counter, and across the hall to the Adjutant's door and forgetting to knock, opened the door and walked straight in. Pat left the door wide open, and I could see from where I was standing that Lt. McDonald was still slinging staples off the wall.

He stopped firing the staples, but still taken aim at the wall with his forefinger, thumb and elastic band, turned his head to one side, and said, "And for what do I owe for the pleasure of this intrusion, Trooper Rush?" he then began to stretch the elastic without taking his eyes off Pat. Pat was now panicking, and his head began to go into a convulsive state, jerking back and forward as he tried to get his words out.

Then finally, and very quick and without a stutter, he said, "Lieutenant McDonald Sir, Lieutenant Murphy wants ye on the table." Standing there with the muscular spasms now gone, and replaced by a blank expression on his face.

Lt McDonald now released the elastic, and with the staple hitting the wall, he quipped, "Kinky." Pausing just for a moment, he continued, "Do you know if he wants me to wear nylons and suspenders, when I'm on the table, by any chance?" A broad grin began to show across his face. Looking out the door he could see the Orderly room Sergeant, and I in knots laughing. Laughing himself, he told Pat to transfer the call through to his office, and then, simply told Pat to fuck off.

Without realizing what he had just said to the Lieutenant, Pat came back into the Orderly room, and shaking his head from side to side in wonderment said, " I-I think he-he his a homos-homo-sex....a queer!" pointing in the direction of the Adjutant's office. After just getting over one perplexing comedy, along comes another one in the shape of Trooper Liam "Hoop" Ring.

He came rushing up to me as I rounded the corner of the Orderly room, and with a short audible intake of breath said, "Is Rush in the Orderly room?, is " Ra-Ra" in there?" He used the nick-name "Ra-Ra", which was given to Pat Rush by the Troops, because of his stammer. It was unusual to see Hoop in an agitated mood, as he was a reserved sort, and did not flap to easy. Being of an athletic build, it was even more unusual to see him out of breath. There was no need to answer him, for just then Pat came around the corner. Hoop was very relieved to see Pat, and with a look of some desperation on his face, cried out, "Pat! Good man, Pat, I'm in dire straits; can ye help me out? Would ye do me a favor, Pat? For fuck's sake, Pat, I'm in the shit." He now held Pat by the shoulders. "I need ye to go down to the X-ray department in the hospital, in the Orderly room car, and collect my medical book. Will ye do that for me, Pat?" pleaded Hoop.

"What's wrong with ye, Hoop?" I inquired.

" I-I, I know," Pat interrupted. "There was-was a phone cal-call to the Orderly r-room from the h-hospital." With a sharp intake of air, and his bottom lip flapping over his top lip, he continued on, "He, he tried to flash, to fl-flash Miss Marple. The dir-dir, the dir-dir, the filthy little swine," gasped Pat. With Pat and myself starting to laugh,

Hoop threw his hand's in the air, and with the skin tightening on his face said, "I did not flash anyone, you stupid bastard; it was all a crazy fucking mix-up, that's all, a stupid mistake on my part. Now will ye go down and get the book? Will ye? If ye don't shut the fuck up, I'll give ye such a root in the bollix, that your balls will replace your stuttering tonsils; have ye got that? Have ye?" His face now was turning red with rage. Knowing better not to say another word Pat nodded his head, and walked towards the car to go and retrieve Hoop's medical book. The "Miss Marple" Pat was talking about, and whose real name was Miss French, was a radiologist, who was in charge of the X-ray department in the General Military Hospital. She was a small frail spinster of a woman in her late fifties, and as she never married, she lived with her ageing sister. She lived for her profession, and was very conscientious of her work. Her lack of depth of character seemed to display a sheltered life. Hoop came back with me to the transport office, and told me all about his mishap in the X-ray department.

It was late yesterday evening that he went down to the hospital with an injury to the groin, which he had sustained while working out in the gym. On reaching the out-patient department he sat waiting in line to see the doctor. After sitting there for about fifteen minutes, he was ushered in to see the doctor, who, to his utter dismay was a lady doctor, Captain Little. Dr. Little was fairly young, although she had a few grey strands running through her dark brown hair. She may be "little" in name, but not in height, as she had a long and slender figure. She was accompanied in the surgery by a robust, elderly female nurse.

The blood drained from his face, when after hearing of his injury, Dr. Little told him to take down his slacks, and underwear. He told me that when he was instructed to do this, he thought he would have the biggest uprising since nineteen sixteen. When she began to check his groin, he kept repeating over, and over to himself, *Please don't let there be an uprising, please don't let there be an uprising, in the name of the love of divine Jasus, don't,* and then luck would have it. The nurse with the man features reached up to obtain something from a top press, and to his relief his uprising was quashed before it had started, because the nurse, who was wearing ankle socks, had varicose veins on the back of both muscular legs. Hoop told me that they were a junkie's dream, and that he was more intent on keeping the contents of his stomach down, than anything else coming up. Dr. Little was not happy with the examination, so she sent Hoop down to the X-ray department for an X-ray on his groin. The X-ray department was situated at the far end of the hospital. All of the other wards down that side of the hospital were closed down, thus leaving the X-ray department isolated, and a very eerie place to visit. There was only a staff of two working the department, Miss French the radiologist, and Cpl. Christy Brannan, a medical orderly who done all the book work, and any other odd jobs that had to be done around the place. He was the human equivalent of a bull dog, small, muscular, scared and fierce. He would sometimes use this canine effect to guard, and watch over Miss French if any of the lads got out of hand with her. They worked well together, him the director, and her behind the camera, so to speak. When Hoop got there, Christy was nowhere in sight, only Miss French who was standing in the middle of the room looking at some files. After she had finished looking at the files she took the doctors slip from Hoop, and after reading it she told Hoop to take down his pants, and lie on the X-ray table. She then went across the room, and behind the X-ray machine to get things ready. Ignorant to the fact that the X-ray machine could take a picture through underwear, Hoop removed his, and jumped up on the table, and stretched out. Not only was he not wearing any skivvies, but he thought by rolling his shirt underneath, and up towards his chest would make her job easier for her. He told me that unlike Dr. Little, revealing himself to Miss French would not cause him any titillating embarrassment, as he thought of her as a female suffragette Gandhi head, a fucking holdout from the early part of the twentieth century. As he was lying there on the table with one hand on his forehead, and the other holding his rolled up shirt in position, he heard a startling scream. Lifting himself up, he seen Miss French taking flight towards the office door. Just as she got to the door, Christy Brannan was coming out of it. Putting her head into Christy's shoulder, and without looking around, pointed her finger at the overly exposed Hoop. Christy calmly escorted the fragile Miss French into the office, and then came back out like a raging bull running across the room at a now bug-eyed and ashen faced Hoop. Word for word, Hoop remembered what the ranting Corporal spewed from his saliva ejecting mouth.

"Get your clothes on, ye perverted fucking bastard, ye scum bucket fuck. Do ye get your kicks from flashing old ladies, ye bollix? Ye probably have a white trench coat, and just the legs of trousers above in your locker that ye use when ye fuck off for the weekend, ye dilapidated swine ye. Did ye want a X-ray picture, or a X-rated picture taken, ye porno pig?" He then walked away towards the office to check on the injured party.

"Did you not explain yourself to him?" I said to Hoop.

"I didn't, my fuck, I ran like a bastard, and dressed myself running," said Hoop with no hard feelings!!!"

THE OFFICER'S WEDDING

I t was a Saturday morning in late June, and it looked like another scorcher of a day was in store. It was only eleven o' clock, and already I could feel my body baking beneath my number one uniform. The reason for my wearing of the good uniform being the wedding of Captain Neville Sinclair, for which I was to wait on tables at the reception. It was a great day for a wedding, but a bad one for a hangover, which most of the waiting staff had acquired from a lads' night out on the town with overindulgence of the bevvy kind. The consumption had started early last night, and finished in the wee hours of this morning, and therefore causing inconveniently turbulent heads among the waiting staff. The wedding reception itself will be held in the Officer's Mess, and this is where we are all assembled now. The staff for waiting on tables is of a workforce group of nine, consisting of one Corporal who would oversee and assign various tasks, and eight Troopers that will carry them out, myself included therein. We all came under the control of Sergeant Knight, who was the Mess Sergeant, and he in turn was answerable to the Mess Officer, Captain Darcy. We all now stood in front of Capt. Darcy in the service kitchen, for a briefing on his rules for the day. After a quick glance at our uniforms he told us to follow him across the hall, and into the main banqueting room. Once there, he again stood in front of us with his hands on his hips and legs spread apart. Capt. Darcy was a gangling type who had an absent of arrangement and neatness to his overall military attire and was conductive to inactivity. Being a sedentary person made him highly assuming of others.

Rule number one and this is first and foremost; there will be no drinking of alcohol what so—ever for the duration of the day," stated the Captain, who was talking to us all, but staring with fixed attention at Trooper Archie Lyons. Darcy was not forgetting the garden party three weeks ago when Archie was working as a drinks waiter, and had to be relieved later that night for been drunk and over familiar with the guests. Archie knew that Darcy was directing this order in a somewhat half concealed underlining threat towards him. Archie was very much overly fond of the sup, for which his face bore the brunt for his excessiveness to the bending of his elbow. He possessed large bug eyes, and broken veins which led out from a forming whiskey nose, and ran down the red cheeks of his aged, alcohol induced face, that belied his twenty nine years.

Half closing one of his bulging eyes, and shaking his head delicately from side to side, Archie peered at Darcy, and with a slight quiver in his voice said, "Excuse me a minute Sir, but by the way you're looking at me I take it that your singling out me in particular, would I be right in saying that, Sir?" His eye's returned to the floor, nervously.

"Yes! Trooper Lyons, I am," said the Captain. " I am talking to everybody, but more to the point I am stressing it especially to you considering your antics at the Garden Party a few weeks back, and I will not tolerate any shit like that at this wedding, from anyone, but most certainly you." He was pointing his finger at Archie.

"Now-now Sir, I think I'm intelligent enough not to fall foul of the same state of affairs as the last time," said Archie, somewhat grievous.

"Intelligent, I don't think so, Lyons, as far I can remember your intelligence does not even stretch as far as the ability to grasp the meaning of a simple sport," said Darcy, amid the laughter of the lads, as his sentence tailed off. The whole staff was laughing because they knew the accusation made by Darcy to be accurate, and in so being, was an awful embarrassment to Archie, who at this stage was laughing himself, but there was a self-consciousness to his giggle. The cause of Archie's discomfort came about on the Wednesday afternoon sport parade last month. During the lunch break Archie had partook a liquid lunch of beer down in the men's canteen, and presented himself for the two o' clock sport parade, a little tipsy. Lieutenant Finn took the parade, and was looking for bodies to go abseiling.

When Finn approached Archie and asked him if he would like to go abseiling, Archie's face turned ashen. "Sir, I know nothing about sailing, and besides I can't swim, not a stroke, Sir." Archie said solemnly. Lt. Finn just turned and walked away in disbelief, while the rest of the parade fell about laughing. Before long the story was all over the barracks, and poor Archie has not lived it down since. After ridiculing Archie, Captain Darcy belted out the rest of his rules, and he was adamant that they would be adhered to. When Darcy had finish his bullshit, we were told by Sgt. Knight to go to the service kitchen, and he would allot us tasks to do before the reception began, as there was still three and a half hours before the serving of the food started, and there was still a lot of other work to be done. Sergeant Knight had no sooner entered the service kitchen to assign us our jobs, when Johnny "Sponger" Boyce, the Corporal in charge for the day, verbally assaulted him about the drink. "What's all this shit about not having a drink, Sean? I mean what happened to the tradition of the staff getting a gratuity drink at the end of the shift?" voiced the perturbed and agitated Corporal.

"Look Johnny, don't worry about the Captain. I'll make sure that you and your staff are all sorted out for a couple of drinks later on, but no drinking until then, ok?" insisted Sgt. Knight with an air of reassurance. Sergeant Sean Knight and Corporal Johnny "Sponger" Boyce were the complete opposite of the work ethics and conduct befitting an N.C.O., the Sgt. being the positive, and the Cpl. negative. Sean was very diligent and conscientious about his position as Mess Sergeant, whilst Johnny was the devil may care type, who cared more about what he could get out of a situation for himself, rather than what he could put in to it. Johnny Boyce was of a slight build, with a crooked nose and strange blue eyes that were light in color that gave the impression of a manifestation of discoloring. His gift of the gab was vital to the existence of his career in the Defense Force, and his raw charm and dry wit (unbeknownst to himself) kept him in favor with the troops. Johnny received the work details from Sgt. Knight, and he in turn assigned them to us. Johnny and myself got on well together, so he gave me the cushy detail of helping Deco Lawler the barman to finish off stocking the Mess bar, and which, knowing Deco the bar would more than likely be already fully stocked. Entering the working side of the bar I could see Deco taking bottles from two crates of coke on the ground in front of him, and placing them into the cooler.

"What's the story, me man?" asked Deco from his kneeling position on the floor. I told him that I was sent to give him a hand stocking the bar, to which he replied, "It's all fucking done, get yourself a pint or an orange, and take it easy." He then stood up and took a pint glass in his hand to fill me a drink.

"I'll have the orange, Deco—because that asshole Darcy is on the prowl, and he warned us that he would lock anyone up who he caught drinking, so just the orange for the time being." I said, as I took a bottle of orange off the shelf.

"I can't stand the prick, he fucking annoys me. Every time he comes into the jasusing bar he has something to whinge about, one of these days I'll let bleedin daylight through that dopey head of his—I swear I will," raged Deco, making a fist, and with his head to one side he outwardly folded his tongue between his teeth, and bit down on it. Deco was, and maybe still is a thief who came from Dublin, and lives in the rough part of the inner city. Deco detests the army, and the only reason he was in it was a Judge's necessitating action of giving Deco a choice of joining the army or a long term in prison, so with those choice's he felt he was compelled to join up. His toleration of military discipline was of a small quantity which often found him in front of his Commanding Officer on various charges, such as, absent without leave, violent conduct, and to a larger and annoying extent to the establishment, insubordination. Deco possessed a personal façade that gave the impression that butter would not melt in his mouth. His blonde curled locks of hair and brown chocolate colored eye's complimented his twenty two year old slender frame, to which he was fully aware of, and used to his benefit in the art of deception on many occasions.

"How many people can this place hold?" I asked.

"Couldn't tell ye—and I couldn't give a bollix what it holds, but I know one thing, they'll be packed in like fucking sardines later on, and the more the merrier because I'll fucking crease them, and if I don't make anything I'll rob the place and fuck off, because I'm pissed off with this bleedin army shit in any way," said Deco with his arms folded and looking out into the soon to be crowded Mess. Then all of a sudden this small person with a large head that we could not see entering the bar because of his small size sprang up onto the bar stool displaying his large head right in front of Deco.

"Oh good fuck!!"

"What is it?" yelped Deco as he jumped backwards with spits flying from his mouth, and raising his left arm in front of himself with his hand spread out in a protective motion, and at the same time bringing his right arm back rapidly making a clenched fist to strike, and in so doing whacked his elbow off the cash register. The small person that was now sitting at the bar worked up in Dublin, in Government Buildings, I recognized him from when I was delivering a packet to the department that he works in when I was on dispatch duty sometime last year. Being so small he was someone that stuck out in the department, but it was not because of his height that I remember him, it was his Dublin accent, with his boisterous and rude nature towards visitors to his counter, including myself, not a nice small person to encounter. He now sat at the bar wearing a pinstriped suit with a white shirt and red tie, with a plastic flower in the buttonhole of the lapel. He must be in his early thirties, and his slicked back gelled hair seemed out of place with his suit.

"Pull me a pint of stout, ye little bollix ye," demanded the small person of Deco who was rubbing his elbow intensively to ease the pain.

"I'm a little bollix? I'm a little bollix? You're the only little bollix in here," snapped Deco at the small person. He then turned to me, "What do ye think of that, a fucking midget calling me a little bollix....."

"I'm no fucking midget—de ye hear me?"

"Well what are ye—a fucking dwarf?" inquired Deco, still rubbing his elbow.

The small person looked at me, and then turning his angry face towards Deco, he said "Do you know where I work? Ye jumped up little fucker, I have connections ye know," he said, with a look of importance on his face.

"There he goes again calling me little," said Deco. "So what happened? Did one of your fucking connections fall out and ye forgot where ye bleedin work—-well let me guess where ye work? Would it be the chocolate factory? Does Wonka know that ye fucked off over the wall? Ye stumpy little fuck."

"Ye want to watch your mouth, or I'll come over that bar and kick your fucking stupid barman's arse."

"Yeah right, and what makes ye think that I am going to kneel down to let ye kick my fucking arse; ye want to be fucking careful that I don't go round there and kick your bleedin umpa lumpa arse," said Deco, sharply. Bending down I let on I was putting bottles in the cooler, when in fact I was in tatters laughing. Deco saw me laughing, and began to start laughing himself.

The small person stuck out his finger, and pointing it at Deco, said, "It's well ye might laugh; I may be small, but I'm big in other places, ye dilapidated fucking bastard."

"Yeah!" said Deco. "Like your head. Look get over it; you're small and that's the way it is. I'll put it this way, Tiny, if ye were a couple of inches smaller I would have got three fucking wishes out of ye."

"Right! That's fucking it," snarled the little guy, as he got down from the stool. "Now you're in for it, ye long streak of piss; I'll be back," he said as he headed for the door leading from the bar. Sure enough, he came back into the bar about five minutes later with Darcy in tow. Darcy walked up to the bar while the small person stopped about six feet away so he could see Deco on the other side of the bar.

"Can I help you, Sir?" Deco inquired of Darcy.

"Yes you can, Trooper Lawler, this guest here, Mr. Grogan," said Darcy, pointing back towards the small person, "has made a serious complaint about your highly abusive conduct towards him, which I can tell you now that if I find any foundation to it that I will place you under arrest in...."

"Wow, hold your horses, Sir," Deco interrupted. "I was the one that was abused in the first place, and I've got a witness to that," stated Deco, at the same time turning his head in my direction, to which I stayed silent but nodded my head to the Captain in confirmation.

Darcy was quite for a moment, and then turned and looked at Mr. Grogan who by now was fuming, and speaking in a loud voice, said, "Arrest the fucker, Gary; arrest the fucking lunatic." He then threw his arms in the air and back down on to his hips in anger. Darcy knew that Deco had him over a barrel with a witness, but the small person's outburst decided his next move. He came to the conclusion that it all came down to a clash of personalities, and asked Mr. Grogan if an apology would suffice.

"Well as long as he keeps a civil tongue in his head for the rest of the day, I think as apology would do," moaned the small person. Deco looked at me, and I gave him a stern look that said quit while you're ahead. Deco smiled at me, it was a fuck this shit kind of smile, so I bent down to place more bottles in the cooler.

Deco, still smiling, looked at the small person and said "I apologize to you Mr. Groagain." He said this with his smile turning to a sneer.

Down behind the bar I was in knots laughing, as I could hear Mr. Grogan going haywire. "Did ye hear that, Gary?" Grogan roared at Darcy, "That little fucker just called me Mr. fucking Grow-again. I told ye, Gary—I fucking told ye, fuck this; I'm going out to the garden before I burst that little bollix. Will ye bring me out my drink, Gary?" he said, as he left.

Deco looked at Darcy. "Ye see, Sir, there he goes calling me little again, and that was the kind of abuse that I had to put up with when he first came in. I think it all comes down to that...short.... fuse of his, Sir," said Deco, in a derisive tone. Darcy told Deco to shut up or be locked up, and that Deco's humorless sarcasm was now starting to agitate him. He then told Deco that he was not to serve Mr. Grogan for the rest of the day, that he was to leave the service of Mr. Grogan to the other two barmen that were coming in shortly to help serve for the remainder of the day. Darcy waited until the pint for the small person was pulled, and then taking it he walked out of the bar without speaking another word. When he had gone, Deco and I had a right good laugh. Deco told me that his uncle is a small person, and that he has great respect for small persons, but the likes of that little bollix got what he deserved. Deco and I were still laughing about what had occurred when Sgt. Knight entered the Mess bar with two young looking lads of about fifteen to sixteen years of age. I wondered to myself on seeing them if the two were related in some way. Maybe brothers, as they had the same shoulder length curling hair, which was fair in color, and a choir-boy femininity about them. Sgt. Knight told Deco to give them minerals to drink, as they were videoing the wedding, and had just finished at the church. He told Deco that their father was taken ill this morning with a bug, and they were standing in for him to video the reception, and proceedings after. He was telling the two lads that they should not take too long in drinking their minerals, as the wedding party would be here soon, and that they should make sure that their equipment is set up. He then left, but not before telling me to report back to the service kitchen to prepare for the reception. Two rabbits caught in the headlights-that's the way they looked as they stood with eyes firmly fixed on Deco.

"Well lads," said Deco, "let me inform yis that you won't be getting no lemonade or orange from me, because ye see lads, that's where all my profits come from, and I'm hardly going to give ye two bottles of my profit's—now am I? Looking at the pair of ye I think that a pint of lager would do grand," he said, as he had already started to pull a pint without waiting on an answer from the two lads. By the big smile on their faces I knew that the two lads were not going to argue.

"I'm heading back down to the kitchen, Deco, I'll see ye later on," I said, heading for the door.

"Yeah, ok, I want to get a cup of coffee before all this shit kicks off, so I'll follow ye down as soon as the other two barmen come in, which should be ten bleeden minutes ago. They can look after Hansel and fucking Gretel, here," said Deco pointing at the two lads. On returning to the service kitchen I could see the rest of the lads were fell in and Sgt. Knight with his hand in the air doing a head count.

"There ye are," said Sgt. Knight, as he turned around and seen me standing there, "paddy fucking last as usual, right fall in there with the rest until I give ye all an update on what's happening." He barked, pushing me into line. He went on to tell us that it would be another half hour before the bride and groom arrived at the Mess, because they were still at the church having photographs taken. He then told us that when they and the wedding guests arrived that they would have photos taken out on the lawn in front of the Mess, and light refreshment's before the wedding meal, and therefore we could take it easy for the next hour. Just what the lads wanted to hear, for no sooner had Sean Knight left the room that they made a run for the back door, and made a beeline for the Men's Canteen for the hair of the dog that bit them the night before. Somehow or other I don't think that the lecture that Darcy gave this morning on not drinking had a lasting effect on the lads. Resisting all temptation to go, I did not venture, but instead I would have a cup of tea with Deco, who had just entered the service kitchen.

"What did you do with the two young lads?" I asked Deco.

"Who?—Hansel and Gretel?" replied Deco smiling. " I put them in the old storeroom to finish off their pints, because that fucking eejit of a dwarf came back into the bar with some other officer, and the two young lads were beginning to feel uncomfortable. So when I was coming down here for a cup of coffee I took them to the old store room where they would be away from nosey bastards, and able to finish their pints in comfort, and at the same time I was making sure I would not get into trouble for giving them the pints in the first place," he said, pouring coffee into a cup.

About half an hour later Sgt. Knight comes rushing into the service kitchen in a frantic state. "Where's them other two fucking little video eejit's gone to?" Without giving Deco a chance to answer, he continued his interrogation, "What time and where did they go after leaving the bar? Can ye tell me that, can ye?" he asked Deco, with pleading eyes.

"I haven't a clue," replied Deco, in an unconcerned tone.

"What do ye mean ye haven't a fucking clue? I left them in the bar in your care, and now the wedding party are looking for them to do some filming, and the good Captain is breathing down my fucking neck to find them, so where in the fuck are they?" inquired the agitated Sergeant.

Deco looked at me and then turning to Sergeant Knight, said, "In the first place they were not in my care; all ye told me was to give them a drink, and I did. You said nothing about watching them, who knows, maybe they had to rush off to make a bleeden film for Stephen fucking Spielberg, or something, I haven't a clue as to where they are," he lied. Sean stood there in silence for a couple of seconds staring at Deco.

"One of these days that mouth of yours will fuck you up completely, Lawler." said Sgt. Sean, speaking, as he was on the move from the room. When the good Sergeant had left, and went on his search down the long hall, Deco, walking to the sink to wash his cup, placed his index finger to his lips, and at the same time shook his head and winked at me, that silently communicated to me to not say a word, or it would be his head on the block. A big smile came across Deco's face as I nodded to him. The silence was shattered by a screech coming from down the long hall that sounded like Sgt. Knight was about to have a nervous breakdown.

Deco placed his cup in the sink, "Something tells me that Sean has found the other two," said Deco. "What's he screaming for? I'll tell ye one thing, if those two Hitchcock fucking hippie's grass me up—well I'll tell ye it will be the last film they'll make." Then turning to me he said, "Come on let's go and find what the fuck is going on." we then started for the door leading to the long hall. Looking up the long hall I could see Sergeant Knight leaning forward with his two arms folded, and placed head high against the wall with his head resting on them, and face to the floor. "What's wrong Sean?" inquired Deco as we approached.

"Take a look in there, and tell me I'm seeing things," said the Sergeant, now standing up straight and pointing towards the door of the old storeroom. Deco and I entered the room, and what we saw was maybe comical to us, but not so Sgt. Knight. For there, sitting on the floor in front of us, were the two young lads in a state of inebriation. The eldest of the two held a half bottle of wine in his hand, and was staring at us with a look of innocent guilt on his face, whilst his sibling was fast asleep with his head resting on the other's shoulder. Looking to the left of them I could see three empty wine bottles lying on the floor. Deco and I wanted to burst out laughing but did not as we were conscious of Sgt. Knight standing behind us, and very much aware of the consequences, if we did. Straight away Deco went on the defensive, "Wait a minute Sarge—I did not give them that fucking plonk, I don't know where they got there hand's on it," said Deco.

"No, it was my fault, I stored the wine for the wedding in here; I should have put a lock on the door. The two little fuckers did not even need a corkscrew as I had uncorked most of them, and re-corked them so they would be ready to serve, as it would save time when the function started," explained the Sergeant, as he pushed his way through Deco and myself, and bent down and started to shake the young lad awake. Deco returned to the bar as the Sarge and I shuffled the two drunks back down the long hall to the service kitchen. Once there Sean told me to make coffee for them, and then disappeared out the door. After sitting them down I got the kettle and went over to the tap at the sink to fill it. The screech that came from behind me made the hair stand on the back of my neck. Turning around in quick fashion I saw Mrs. Blackwell standing there with her hand to her mouth, and the other hand pointing to the youngest of the drunken pair who was standing and very much urinating all over the hot press in the center of the service kitchen. Mrs. Blackwell fled from the room stuttering Sgt. Knight's name loudly from her quivering mouth. Immediately I grabbed the young lad, and as I tried to sit him back down he was squirting all over the kitchen, so I grabbed him by the collar and pushed him by the scruff of the neck along the hall leading to the main upstairs kitchen, and out into the back yard. Placing him face to the wall I left him there and returned to the service kitchen. Returning to the service kitchen I found Sgt. Sean standing just inside the door from the long hall with a tripod in one hand, and a video camera in the other. Directly behind him but standing outside the door in the long hall with arms folded, cigarette at the side of her mouth, and with a face like a bull elephant was Mrs. Blackwell.

"I put the other one out in the back yard, Sean," I informed the Sergeant. Without saying a word Sean carefully placed the tripod and video on a dry spot on the floor. He then walked over to the urinator's brother, who was now pointing at the hot press, and laughing his head off.

"Up ye get," said Sean, as he lifted the young lad by the arm up from the chair, "Ye can laugh all ye want out the backyard," said the stern looking Sergeant.

"Do you know that we are artists?" said the young lad, pulling his arm from the Sergeant's grip.

"Is that right now—ye don't fucking say, well I'll tell ye what? Ye can wait out in the backyard with your brother Piss-fucking-casso until your father comes to get yis, I rang him, and he is on his way," snarled Sean. He then gripped the collar of the lad's shirt, and pulling upwards, walked the artist on his toes to the backyard.

"Not in all my seventeen years working in this Mess have I seen anything like fecking that," said Mrs. Blackwell, as she entered the room. Mrs. Blackwell is a little bowlegged, chain smoking woman in her late fifties of an unrefined appearance, and a harrowing disposition to all that come into contact with her. With all her fault's, she has a kind heart that stood to her with the staff of the Mess over the years. "Don't expect me to clean that up, Sean." said Mrs. Blackwell. The Sergeant did not bother to answer her, but instead raised one finger in motion for her to wait one minute.

He then stuck his head into the dumbwaiter shaft that led to the main upstairs kitchen. "Dermot! Sgt Hennessy!" he shouted up the shaft to get the attention of the cook Sergeant, Dermot Hennessy. "What ails ye, Seanie?" came Dermot's voice back down the shaft. Without putting his head into the opening Sean loudly said, "Will ye send down Scrubber to me? I have a small job for him to do."

"I'll send him down straight away, Seanie," came the cook's voice descending from above.

"What's the story, Sean? Were ye looking for me?" said Johnny Boyce, entering the kitchen.

"Good man Johnny, listen, will ye take that video camera and tripod, and go and video the bride and groom, and then just walk around filming the guests at random—will ye do that?" proposed the Sergeant. With delight on his face Johnny picked up the camera, and then went into a big rigmarole of how he had videoed his cousin's wedding, and his nephew's child's christening, and that he was a natural when it came to filming.

"That's an awful lot of videoing you've done in your fucking head and imagination, Corporal Boyce, I would be amazed if ye don't ask the people to watch the birdie or ask them to say cheese," said Scrubber Sheelan, who had come down from the kitchen, and had been standing there for the last couple of minutes listening to Johnny waffling on.

Johnny lowered the camera which he had up to his face. "And that's coming from a muck savage with the inside of his head that resembles an empty fucking shoebox—hello! Hello! Echo fucking head, do whatever shitty job that ye have to do, Sheelan, and get back up to your pot scrubbing fucking cave, and out of my sight," raged a vein popping, and crimson faced Johnny. Just before Sgt. Knight intervened between the two of them, Johnny stopped him by raising his hand in the air, and then picking up the tripod and leaving the room, but not before giving Scrubber an icy stare. Johnny was right, in a way, about Scrubber and the shitty jobs that he had to undertake. Scrubber is a big man in every way; he is six foot tall if not taller, and carries excessive weight, with legs like tree trunks. He has this wide eyed unintelligent empty stare that says it all about how he is still scrubbing pots at the age of thirty two. The hierarchy of the Mess play to, and use his lack of ability and glibness in everyday military matters to use him to do dirty jobs that the people employed in the Mess refuse to do. If there was a toilet in the Mess that was choked with crap, then they would in no doubt expect good old Scrubber to go in there and clear it, and never give a thought as to what it takes to clear it. What do they think he does? Place his big arms around the toilet bowl, and carry out the Heimlich maneuver. So here he goes again, cleaning up some other person's mess. Sgt. Knight told Scrubber, or to give him his real name, Bill Sheelan, what to do, and then left him to get on with it, and he did, without complaint. The lads returned from their canteen revival mission in great cheer, and were told by the Sarge that the wedding meal would be ready to start in about fifteen to twenty minutes, or so. He then told me to follow him. The Mess was really buzzing now, as there were throngs of people coming and going between the front gardens and the Officer's Mess, and all were elegantly dressed for the occasion. Sean brought me out into the garden, and pointed out Johnny, who was standing looking through the video lens down into the large suntrap that was situated in the center of the lawn. He then told me to stay with Johnny, and to watch that he did not fuck up as he had a habit for doing exactly that, and if he should do so, that I was to come and get him immediately. He then left me and walked over to talk to some officer that he knew. When I walked over to where Johnny stood videoing I could see that the bride and groom were standing down in the suntrap having their photos taken by the official wedding photographer, who was standing halfway down the steps that led down into the sheltered area of the suntrap, which was by now holding the heat of a furnace.

Johnny then moved down three steps, and what he said next had the muscles in my stomach and neck contracting, and my head shaking to prevent myself from bursting out laughing. "Now, Sir! Would you please grab your wife around the waist and place your lips together and give her a nice big juicy one in the hole?" requested Johnny with the camera still up to his face, and patently oblivious to the disorder of his own choice of words. The official photographer sat down on one of the steps, and took his glasses off, and lowered his head into his lap, and went into convulsions of muffled laughter. The bride dropped her head slightly, and gave a small giggle. Captain Sinclair looked up at the video holding Corporal on the steps, and gave a wry smile that showed his ironic acceptance of Johnny's altered perception of what a suntrap is. The Captain and his bride now came up the steps from the suntrap, with the official snapper swiftly moving to one side to let them pass on up. As they ascended the steps and drew nearer in a graceful motion, I could see that the bride was a lot older than the Captain, by the crow's feet at the corners of her eye's that the makeup could not hide. Other than the crow's feet, she was a stunner. She had authentic blonde hair that was styled into ringlets with a spiraling effect, and on top of this she wore a small jeweled coronet that seemed to be sparkling in tune with her blue eyes. The wedding dress she wore was a real showstopper that was off-the-shoulder and low cut which clung to her body, and in doing so, showed off her long slender figure all the way down to the ground. On reaching the top of the steps she took her arm from within the Captain's arm, and walked over to speak to two women that called to her.

The Captain walked over to face Johnny, and calmly placed his head to the right side of Johnny's shoulder, and stared out aimlessly over the garden, "Corporal Boyce, I seriously suggest that you go to the library, or buy yourself a linguistic atlas, and look up the Kildare region, or even better, buy yourself a dictionary, and locate the word suntrap, which you will find that the definition for it, is a sheltered area of bright sunlight, and not, I repeat, not, a fucking hole, Corporal Boyce." said the Captain, snidely. Then moving his head away from the area of Johnny's ear, he stood back, and then brushed the top of Johnny's shoulder with the back of his hand. He then turned and walked away in the direction of his new wife, and her two friends. Johnny stood there with the video camera across his chest giving me a bewildered stare. He then looked across the lawn to where Captain Sinclair was standing chatting to guests. He took a few paces forward to the edge of the suntrap, and looking into it he placed his free hand behind his head, and stood there contemplating for a few moments.

Then looking in Sinclair's direction with a combined look of disgust and puzzlement on his face, he said, "What in the name fuck was that stupid bastard talking about? Does he not know a cavity in any surface is a fucking hole? I mean what does he think he shits through—a sheltered fucking area? I'll tell ye? I'll pity fucking blonde when she goes on honeymoon with that dopy bastard if he doesn't know what a hole is." He then mumbled something to himself and started to walk towards the main door of the Mess. Just inside the Mess door, and coming towards us was Sgt. Knight, and following directly behind him was a tall, thin, and very angry looking middle aged man with an overly receding hairline that ran nearly half way back his head, and in doing so, made what hair he had left resemble an oversized Jewish skullcap. Left and right of him were the two drunken young lads, who were being impetuously pushed and shoved by him, rather than walking of their own accord. Stopping to explain to us, Sean told us that the man with the two young lads was their father, and that he would return to take over, and resume videoing the rest of the wedding as soon as he had dispatched the two drunken eejits to his car. He told Johnny to go straight to the service kitchen as soon as he handed over the video to the young lad's father when he returned, and I was to go there right now as the wedding meal will be starting soon. He then started to proceed along the hall, and out into the garden announcing in a loud, but gentle mannered voice to the guests to take their seats in the banqueting hall for the wedding meal.

"Fuck this!" said Johnny, switching the camera on, "if they think I'm doing this for nothing, then they have their shite. I'm off down to the bar to see if I can make anything out of this fucking lark. If that stupid fucker is looking for his video camera, tell him I'm in the bar videoing," he instructed me, and walked off in the direction of the bar. Being only back in the service kitchen a couple of seconds when Sgt. Knight followed behind me. Straight away he wanted to know if everybody that should be there was there. When someone told him that Cpl. Boyce was missing he told me to go and find him, and bring him back right away as we were about to serve very soon. Knowing exactly where Johnny was to be found, I headed for the bar. Walking into the bar I could see Johnny in conversation with the young lads' father, who was listening to what Johnny was saying but was more interested at getting the video camera from the Corporal's grasp, and by the look of Johnny's body language he was not going to relinquish it.

"Will ye listen to me? Will ye? Not only had I to get out of bed on my day off to take over the camera because I am the only one in the barracks with the experience of doing the gig, but I also had to mop up the puke after your two sons threw up. So I think that's worth a score at least for my time. Does that sound more reasonable that fifty?" pleaded Johnny, with one hand fixed firmly on the camera, and the other hand stuck out with palm facing up, towards the imitation Rabbi. Not saying a word the video man reached his hand into his back pocket and pulled out his wallet which had an imprint of Mickey Mouse on the front of it. He opened the wallet, and began running two fingers over the top of a wad of notes until he found a twenty note. He then took the twenty note from the wallet, and gave it to Johnny, who in turn handed over the video camera. Johnny, nodding his head and pointing to the wallet said, "That's an odd looking cash carrier your packing there, me man; is it Gucci?"

"No, no, it was a present the children brought back from Euro Disney while on holiday a couple of years back. Look! Mickey Mouse is on the front of...." He suddenly realized that Johnny was taking the Mickey Mouse out of him with the Gucci remark. "I have to rush as the meal will be starting, and I will have to set up for the speeches," explained the embarrassed and slightly apprehensive videophile.

"Mickey fucking Mouse, what?" sneered Johnny. "Well fuck me! And there was me thinking it was a picture of your eldest fella. Only kidding!" said the sarcastic Corporal, to the now half smiling man who was unapt to cause any trouble, and walked rapidly away, and out the bar door. After kissing the twenty note and placing it into his pocket, Johnny noticed the solemn look on my face. "What?" he snapped, shrugging his shoulders.

"What in the name of fuck are ye doing? If he tells Darcy, you're bollixed," I warned him. It didn't bother him at all; it was like water rolling off a duck's back.

"Who gives a shit about Darcy? I'll tell ye one thing though? I have got here on this piece of paper six fucking names and addresses that will get us a load of drink tonight," he said, showing me a scrap of paper that he was holding in his hand. Before I could utter a word, he told me that he had told the six people on the list that he would send them on a copy of the wedding video, and that if they wanted to show a slight bit of gratitude, then a drink later on would not go astray. Walking back down the long hall to the kitchen I could not help but laugh. The guy was implausible, he had a neck like a jockey's bollix and the audaciousness of a matador. Back in the service kitchen it was all ready to kick off. Sgt. Knight shouted up through the dumb waiter to the main upstairs kitchen for the large pot of soup to be sent down now, as it had to be ladled into the soup bowls at once, as the wedding party had already started to dine a couple of minutes ago. The starter of prawn cocktail had been previously laid out along with a couple of green salads for the guests that did not like seafood. The main course was sirloin of beef, and one vegetarian meal for an old woman who must be in her nineties. Two lads stayed in the function room during the meal in case any of the guests had any requirements, while the rest of us returned to the service kitchen.

"Bloody tough going that," moaned Archie, to no one in particular. He sat on a chair beside the open window of the kitchen wiping sweat from his brow. The look on Archie's face told me that he was under some pressure for the want of a pint, but Darcy's threat to him earlier had him in a state of anxiousness of the consequences that would befall him if he were to wet his lips. Thinking of Archie wetting his lips suddenly made me think of an overlooked, and soon to be, embarrassing failing to the main course.

"The wine!" I exclaimed to Sgt. Knight. The blood drained from his face.

"The fucking....bastering....wine!" cried the now flustered Sergeant. Telling us all to follow him, he made a dart out the door and down the long hall to the old stores. Once there he told us to take a bottle of red and white wine each, and to go to the banqueting hall and start pouring at once. Taking a bottle of white from the floor, and a red from the fridge we pulled the corks from the bottles, and walked quickly to the tables in the banqueting room to start filling the guest's glasses. The Sergeant was thanking his lucky stars that he had uncorked the bottles of wine that morning. The layout of the dining tables in the banqueting hall consisted of the top table were the bride and groom, and their special guests sat to dine. Running length ways from the top table on each side of the hall were twelve small dining tables that were adjoined in contiguous fashion to form one long surface for the remainder of the guests to sit at and dine on. Archie and I went to pour at the long table at the far side of the hall. Archie went one side of the table while I went to the other side. As I was pouring and apologizing for the delay of the wine I looked across the table, and could see that Archie was struggling with the dispensation of the wine into the glass of Captain Redford, an officer from Command H.Q. who was sitting across from his wife, who I was now pouring wine for. She was staring along with myself at Archie, who, with his hand shaking intensely, was splashing the wine everywhere, with only small amounts entering Capt. Redford's glass. With eyebrows raised the Captain looked over at his wife, and gave her a reassuring smile.

The sweat was now streaming down Archie's face, and the trembling was getting worse. "Sorry about that Sir, I don't feel very well; would ye please excuse me?" said Archie, with a voice that was shakier than his hands. Archie walked away at speed in the direction of the door where Sgt. Knight was standing, and just as he was passing the Sergeant I could see him lifting and placing the bottle of red wine to his mouth, and guzzling it down his throat. Sgt. Knight raised his hand to stop Archie drinking, but to no avail, as Archie took the red wine bottle from his mouth, and used his arm that was bringing the red wine bottle down to push the Sergeant's hand away, and at the same time brought the white wine bottle to his mouth, and continued guzzling as he walked from the room. Quickly I walked around the table to where Captain Redford was sitting and poured wine into his glass.

"What's wrong with him?" asked the Captain, just as Deco appeared from nowhere and stood beside me with a bottle of wine in each hand.

"Ah, don't mind him, Sir; he is a recovering alcoholic. Sir, and seeing the drink got the better of him," said Deco to the now bemused officer. Then Deco shared a big smile between the Captain and his wife. "Yes, Sir, a recovering alcoholic, his back up to eight pints and two small ones a night. He is trying to get back up to his normal fourteen pints and six shorts a night, and I can tell ye, Sir, his getting there slowly but surely. What can I say, but that is a real recovering alcoholic for ye, giving it one hundred percent," said Deco, and all the time smiling while he was telling the Captain and his wife. Both the officer and his wife burst out laughing, and were still laughing as Deco and myself moved on along each side of the table, continuing to pour the wine. After finishing serving the wine Deco told me that he had been walking along the hall returning from one of the stock rooms, and as he was passing by the door of the banqueting room Archie and Sean Knight came rushing out of it, and into the hall like a pair of lunatics. Archie went into the service kitchen while Sean stopped Deco and asked him to help him out with serving the wine, and that he would make it up to him later on.

"So I went inside and grabbed a bottle of red and white from the wine table just inside the door, and the rest? I will get a big favor from the good old Sarge," said a contented Deco, as we turned into the service kitchen. What I saw next was a sight, for there sitting on a chair over at the window was Archie with a glass of wine in one hand, and a cigarette in the other, and sitting on a chair alongside him was Sgt. Knight, providing solace to him. Sgt. Knight was telling him not to worry, and that everything would be alright, and for him to take it easy. Archie look relaxed now that he had a couple of nerve settlers inside him, and we were all glad and knew that Sgt. Knight always had a soft spot for Archie. Everyone knew that if it had been anyone else other than Sean, then Archie would have been placed under arrest, and locked up.

The atmosphere in the kitchen was broken by the voice of the cook Sergeant coming down through the shaft of the dumb waiter from the main kitchen, "Here!" he shouted down. "How did they find their beef?" He then went quiet, waiting for a satisfactory answer to his inquiry.

"With a map and a fucking compass, Dermot, some of them could not find any fucking meat on their plates at all," shouted Dick Core back up to him.

"Very funny," said Dermot, amid laughter from everyone in the service kitchen. "I know it's you, Core, ye little squeaky voiced fucker ye. Let's see how much meat is on your plate when ye come up here to get something to eat after ye finish down there," said the cook, half joking and half in earnest. Either way I don't think that threat would bother Trooper Dick Core, because he was as thin as a whippet, and I never knew him to have a big appetite. He was like most of the young lads in the Unit, who would have the odd burger and chips after a few pints, but essentially they would eat healthy, and never overindulged.

Dick pushed himself up to sit on the counter top that was running adjacent to the kitchen sink, and then closing and resting his lazy eye, he said, "Here, boys, did ye see the old woman sitting at the top table? She must be over a fucking century old. I mean, how did she get here? She must have come here in a hearse after getting permission from the morgue to attend the wedding. I honestly thought that she would be dead before the main course, and did any of yis see the size of the false fucking teeth on her; I mean they looked like they were made from big giant lumps of white fucking leggo, and the size of her little mouth. I mean how does she get them in?" He then began to laugh with embarrassment because we were all looking stony faced at him.

"The things that go through your fucking head, Core," said Sgt Knight.

"Ah I was only having a bit of a laugh Sarge," said Dick, trying to vindicate himself. Everyone then started to laugh, but this soon ceased when a voice, in between alternated laughter, said, "Yeah, maybe she has to force them in with a fucking shoehorn?" It was the voice of Johnny Boyce, who was now going into a manic giggle fit.

The Sergeant jumped from his chair. "My jasus, Boyce, you're as big a sick fuck as that demented fucking eejit over there," said the Sergeant, pointing over at Dick. Johnny tried to explain to Sean that he was only messing with Core, but the Sarge was not listening to him, and told him to get his staff into the banqueting hall to collect the finished plates and cutlery and to get ready for the sweet course. Sean grabbed me by the shoulder as I was leaving the kitchen, and told me to stay there to give him a hand taking the desserts off the dumb waiter. Sean shouted up to Dermot to start sending the desserts down. When he turned around he saw Deco standing in the doorway.

"Well Sarge, about that small favour ye mentioned when I done ye a turn there, well it's like this. Sarge. I have to go to a civvy dentist on Monday morning to get root canal in my mouth done, so if I could have Monday off, Sarge?" said Deco, showing Sean his begging face.

"With a mouth as big as yours, Lawler, are ye sure it's not the fucking Suez Canal? Go on, I suppose I owe ye one; get the fuck out of my sight before I change my mind—go on," said Sean, as he turned away smiling to himself. Looking over at Archie I could see that he was as happy as a gay jockey coming last in a five furlong sprint. After a time he got up from his private bar, and gave Sean and myself a hand at taking the desserts off the dumb waiter. Everything else went grand, the wedding meal and the speeches were now over, and all the guests were either in the bar or the ballroom. When we had cleaned up and put everything away, all the staff was waiting in the service kitchen for Sgt. Knight who had gone to find Capt. Darcy to get the go ahead for a free drink for us. We had been waiting about fifteen minutes when Sgt. Knight walked into the service kitchen.

"I'm sorry, lads, but the Captain said that you are soldiers twenty four hours a day, seven days a week, and that's what ye get paid for, but he said he will get a drink later on for anyone that stays back to collect glasses throughout the evening. Now! If no one is not willing to stay back, then I have to detail four bodies, his words, lads, not mine," said a disgruntled Sergeant. The lads started to shuffle about the room somewhat edgy as they tried to avoid eye contact with the Sergeant in case of getting caught to stay behind.

"Fuck that." said Johnny, "we'll all have to think about that over a drink, so I'm getting them in, so what are ye all having? Come on-; come on lets have yis," enthused the Corporal, as he clapped his hand's together. Shock!! There was no other word for it as the lads stood there with blank expressions on their face's staring at Johnny, and all thinking the same thing (Johnny Boyce buying me a fucking drink???) to themselves. All of us, and even the Sarge, told Johnny what they wanted to drink, which he wrote down on a piece of paper, and then disappeared out the door. Within ten minutes he was walking back into the service kitchen with a tray full of pints. Following directly behind him carrying a second tray of drink was Mrs. Blackwell. Johnny gave everyone the required drink that they had asked for, and even Mrs. Blackwell got an orange juice. Sgt. Knight was still in disbelief, he gave Johnny a disconcerting look before he left the room to take his usual seat with the cook Sergeant, Dermot at a small table out in the large entrance hall. Sean and Dermot always perched themselves at this table after every function to receive compliments, and gratuities of free drink from the hierarchy and guests alike, on a job well done. Besides all the generous lavishness and statements of praise from the party-goers, I think the main reason for them sitting out in the foyer was the nosiness of two old monitors watching out for improper conduct of those coming and going. Pulling Johnny to one side in the kitchen I asked him if he had got the drink from one of the guests that he had promised to send a video on to. "I didn't my bollix!" He exclaimed, "I mean, what do you take me for? No! I put it down to Darcy. I told Deco to put the damage onto Darcy's Mess bill, and let him sort it out with the Mess office; fuck him. Ye don't really think that I was going to waste one of the video fucking idiots, do ye? No, me man, they're for later on tonight," he expressed with a look of delight on his face.

"Yeah! But won't Darcy figure it out when he checks his Mess bill?" I asked him.

"Oh yeah, oh fuck yeah! He'll figure it out alright; he'll figure out that his is a fucking eejit twenty four hours a day—seven days a week, and that's why he is paying for it. Now come on, drink that up, there's more where that came from," he said, in a factually manner. True to his word he was back and forth with trays of free drink for all the lads, and none more happier than Archie, who was now verging on the edge of drunk, and kept informing Johnny that he was the best N.C.O. in the Unit. Now and again Johnny would send two of the lads on walkabout to collect the empty glasses from various places around the Mess to justify our presence there, as he had earlier told all the lads that if they wanted to stay on, that they could, and if any of them wanted to leave, then they could go. Five of us opted to stay to collect the glasses. Besides Johnny and I staying behind, there was Dick, Archie and Joey Donavan. Joey only stayed behind because Dick did, because most of the time, where you would see one, you would see the other. Joey was similar in appearance to Dick, they were both tall, and as thin as laths, and into fitness in a big way. Joey looking the more fitter of the two, because he possessed a square jaw and a tautness to his face and neck that Dick was lacking. Joining Johnny on one of his trips to seek out another video club member to extract free beer from, he stopped me in my tracks as we walked down the long hall leading to the bar.

"What's wrong?" I asked him.

"There's that fucking oul one," he said, nodding down the hall in the direction of a well-dressed, elderly, and very elegant looking woman who was standing with her back to the wall across the hall from the bar. She had short dyed copper red hair that was curving inwards at both sides at chin level, and was held stiffly by an overindulgence of hairspray. Being only a few yards from where the woman stood, Johnny lowered his voice and whispered, "I think she fancies me? She had me fucking pestered at the meal, I mean at one stage when I was placing her plate in front of her. She grabbed my hand, and would not let fucking go of it, and all the time her big fucker of a husband staring across the table at me. I remember him from years ago, he was a Colonel, and a tough fucking nut at that, so I'll be keeping out of her and his way." He then nudged me, and said, "Come on." As he moved forward towards her, he avoided eye contact with her. It was in vain, because as Johnny neared her, she stood away from the wall, and in doing so she was now standing directly in front of him, with what looked like a tall glass of champagne she was holding in her hand.

She then switched the glass from her right hand to her left hand, and placing her free hand on Johnny's shoulder, said, "Why, Corporal, are you not going to say hello? Don't tell me that you forgot me already?" She then moved her hand to the side of Johnny's face, and gave him a playful pinch to the cheek.

Johnny started to giggle like a school girl. "Ah Jasus, I didn't see ye there.....how are ye getting on?" he said awkwardly. Without moving his head, his eyes turned sideways towards me with a pleading look in them for me to intervene, and get him out of there.

Looking at him I nodded and said, "Is this the gorgeous looking woman that you were telling all the lads about, and could not take your eyes off her every time that you went in to serve her?" I then stuck out my hand towards her. "I am very glad to meet you; he (I now pointed to Johnny) was doing nothing but singing your praises all evening. All the lads think that the only reason that you were being nice to him was because of his face, you thought he was touched in the head, and took pity on him. I have to say that he does have that effect on people he meets for the first time." I told her without laughing out loud.

"Don't mind that sappy bastard....excuse my French," he said to her. She just stood there with her head to one side staring at Johnny.

"I don't care what the boys say about you..... I think you're adorable," she said, whispering the last few words of her sentence to him. Before Johnny could get a word in she accidentally on purpose spilled her drink down the front of her blouse. "Oops, how clumsy of me, I'm absolutely drenched—just look at my blouse," she said to Johnny, and at the same time pulling the top of her blouse outwards to show some of her cleavage to the unsuspecting Corporal. "Could you show me somewhere that I could dry myself, Corporal?" she asked. It was the biggest come on that I ever seen, she was as much as telling Johnny to take her somewhere and do the business. Johnny being totally oblivious to this reached into his pocket, and pulled out a large serviette that he must have retained from the meal, and proceeded to wipe the front of her blouse. With him dabbing away at her blouse, I was standing there in a state of embarrassment. We did not see the giant of a figure that was now standing there watching Johnny innocently molesting his wife's breast area through her blouse with a large napkin.

"Just what in the name of fuck do you think you're doing to my wife?" growled the red faced Ex. Colonel. When Johnny looked up and seen the stern, grave and pock marked face of the retired officer staring at him, he panicked, and immediately shifted the napkin from the woman's loose fitting shirt to her face, and continued dabbing for a few seconds until she withdrew her face away from the napkin, and told her husband how Johnny was a true gentleman that came to her rescue when she had spilled her drink onto her blouse.

"Look Sir, she was the one that asked for some help, the Corporal was just......"

"Right!" said her husband, interrupting me as I was about to explain on behalf of Johnny. Then grabbing his wife by the arm, and clearing his throat he said to her, "Let's go, the Hudsons are inside waiting for us to join them."

"Oh shag the Hudsons; why don't you go and join them? I'm going to stay here and have a drink with my new Corporal friend," she said, pulling her arm from his grip. It was like a red flag to a bull, he sent a ferocious thump with his fist to the side of Johnny's head that sent him reeling into me and landing the two of us on the floor. Johnny did not wait to pick himself up off the floor; he was up that quick and ready to run. There was no need to run, because the Ex. Colonel was pinned up against the wall by Capt. Sinclair, and some guests who had come out from the bar just as Johnny got the punch.

"What the bloody hell is going on here?" inquired the puzzled Captain to Johnny and myself, as he released his grip on the now simmering husband.

"Fucked if I know, Sir," said Johnny, rubbing the side of his head.

"That N.C.O. had his hands all over my wife's body; I'll kill the little fuck." ranted the now boiling over again Ex. Colonel, still having to be restrained by some guests. Johnny and I quickly put our side of the story to the Captain, which was verified by the wife of the retired Colonel. Sinclair walked over to where the guests still held the jealous husband, and motioned for them to let him go. He then explained to the guests that it was all a big misunderstanding, and thanked them for their help. Gripping the now disheveled Ex. Colonel by the arm, and nodding for his wife to follow, Capt. Sinclair led them down the long hall. After having words with the two of them down the hall, he returned to Johnny and me, leaving the husband and wife where they were. He asked Johnny if he could forget about the assault by the retired officer, and by doing so would not put a dampener on his wedding day.

Johnny, never one to miss an opening, said, "Well, Sir, if that man could see his way to buying the lads and myself a drink of contriteness then the matter will be forgotten." He lifted his hand up to the side of his head and rubbed it.

"I get the message, Corporal Boyce, go to the bar, and order the drink, tell the barman I said it will be fixed up shortly," concurred the Captain, who then made his way back down the hall to the odd couple. Standing at the bar waiting on the pints to be pulled off, I asked Johnny what did he think of the Ex. Colonel.

"I'll tell ye something for fucking nothing, I won't be sending a video of the wedding onto that bollix; that's for sure," he proclaimed, winking, and the two of us had a right laugh standing at the bar.

"I thought yis went to Guinness's fucking brewery for the drink." said Archie, as we returned to the service kitchen. The craic was great in the kitchen, as we lashed back the free gargle, and Johnny was as good as his word, as time and time again he went to the bar, and never returned without a tray of drink. We would take it in turns to go out and about to collect glasses, except for Archie, who was starting to get rat arsed, and we did not want to take the risk of letting him go out into the Mess. On one of my glass runs I was collecting at Sgt. Knight's table. He was with Dermot and Mrs. Blackwell, and they were still sitting out in the entrance hall. He asked me if everything was alright, and I told him it was (if only he knew) and carried on my way. The bride walked into the kitchen and asked us if we could give her a tablecloth so she could cover the wheeled table that would be used to bring the wedding cake from the banqueting room to the main ballroom for the cutting of the cake.

"I'm sorry, Ma'am," said Dick Core, "but all the tablecloths are kept in a press, up in the kitchen, and the kitchen is locked up for the night." He stood there looking awkward.

"Oh damn it! I really need a tablecloth to cover......wait a minute?" she said, with her face lighting up, and her finger pointing at the dumb waiter. "The kitchen is upstairs? Is that right?" she asked, of no one person in partic-ular. "So if the kitchen is upstairs then that dumbwaiter goes up there, is that right?" she asked. I told her that it did, but if any of us were to be caught up there, we would be in a whole lot of trouble. She walked over to the dumb waiter, and opened the doors of it. "I'll be up and down in a flash; right, boys, get ready to hoist me up." she said, lifting up her wedding dress to her knees so she could climb into it. Dick and Joey gave her a hand to climb into it, and were careful where they put their hands, as it was a tight squeeze to get her in. Luckily for her that her wedding dress was not the big flowing kind, but was slinky and loose enough at the bottom to be pulled up to her knees. Dick and Joey then got hold of the rope, and started to pull. Just as the dumbwaiter passed the opening to the service kitchen, the sound of her voice came into the kitchen, "Let me tell you, boys. This is not the first dumbwaiter I've been in," she called down, with a sound of laughter.

"I bet," whispered Dick, "I bet it's not the first dumb fucking waiter that was in her either. That one must have been around the block once or twice, what do ye think?" he asked Joey.

"Shut the fuck up and pull ye dozy bastard," replied a perturbed Joey. She was about half way up to the kitchen when we got the shock of our lives, for into the kitchen walks Captain Sinclair.

"My wife didn't pass this way looking for a tablecloth? Did she, lads?" inquired the Captain. The two lads stopped pulling on the rope, while Archie and I just looked at him in dumbstruck fashion.

"What's keeping you? Come on—come on—lets go," her muffled voice came from the now stalled dumbwaiter.

I was just about to explain to Sinclair, when he said, "Ah! I think I hear her calling me from the hall to come on—she must have found one, well carry on, lads." He then walked with great haste from the kitchen.

"Un-fucking-believable or what?" gasped Joey. The two lads started pulling on the rope again, as Archie and I took a big swig from our pints. She shouted down that she was now in the main kitchen, and wanted to know where the press with the tablecloths was. Dick shouted directions up to her through the shaft.

"What's going on?" asked Johnny as he entered the room.

"Where were you?" I asked him.

"I was down in the bar talking with my teacher friend, what in the name of the Sergeant's arse is going on here?" said Johnny, walking over to the dumbwaiter. After I told him of everything that had happened with Sinclair and his wife, Johnny told Joey to bring down the dumbwaiter. When Joey brought the small lift back down, Johnny got into it. He then told the two lads to pull him up to the kitchen, as he wanted to make sure that Mrs. Sinclair was alright. About twenty seconds after Johnny shouted down to us that he was now in the kitchen, Capt. Sinclair and Dermot walked through the service kitchen.

While walking through, and without stopping, Dermot said, "Just going up to the kitchen, lads, for a few minutes, the Captain wants to get a tablecloth." He followed after Sinclair. Dick, who was standing beside the dumbwaiter immediately started to shout up the shaft, calling Johnny's name at the top of his voice.

"Will ye shut the fuck up, ye can hear ye all over the bleeden shop—ye fucking mouth ye," shouted Johnny back down the shaft. Dick told him that Dermot and Sinclair were on their way up, and that they should hide straight away. The last words we heard from up the shaft were, " O sweet loving mother of fuck," and then there was silence. Gathered around the opening to the shaft we were straining our ears to hear of any sound of violence coming from the upstairs kitchen.

"It's very quiet up there, I don't think that they found them." No sooner did the words pass my lips when we heard raised voices with argumentative tones coming from upstairs. "I think the good Corporal is in the shit?" I said.

Dick let out a short sharp whistle. "Is he gone this time, or what?" He put forward to the rest of us. "Betcha Sinclair thinks Johnny was up to no good with her, up there?" reckoned Joey. They soon forgot all about Johnny's perilous predicament when I reminded them that we also were in the shit for our part in it. Quickly I told the lads to hide their drink, as we could hear voices and footsteps coming in our direction from the stairs leading down from the kitchen. First to enter the service kitchen was Mrs. Sinclair with a look of rage on her face. Following hot on her heels was a sheepish looking Captain carrying a tablecloth, and then came Dermot scratching under his chin with one of the kitchen keys, looking puzzled about the whole thing. We were waiting for Capt. Sinclair to lay into us, but it was his wife that spoke to us instead.

"I would like to express my thanks to all of you for going out of your way to help me, and I would like to show my appreciation by leaving a drink of your choice behind the bar for you all," she said, with a smile on her face, and walked from the kitchen. Sinclair himself did not say a word to us, he took flight after his bride, and something told me that it would not be wedding cake that he would be eating, but humble pie. Dermot headed out the door mumbling to himself, no doubt heading back to his reserved "spy" table in the entrance hall.

"Where the fucking hell is Johnny?" asked Archie in a loud drunken voice, retrieving his pint from its hiding place.

"I'm up fucking here—that's where I am; is the coast clear?" called Johnny, from up the shaft. After he came down and out of the lift, and taking a big drink from my pint, he began to explain to us all just what took place up in the kitchen? "After ye told me Sinclair was coming up, I quickly walked across the kitchen to hide in the piggery. Before I went in the door of the pot wash I turned to her, and without saying fuck all to her I pointed at the kitchen door, then I put my finger to my lips to tell her not to say a word. I then slipped into the piggery and started to pray like a monk on the altar wine. Well the whinges from the other fella when he walked in the door to see her standing there. He asked her how did she get into the kitchen, and when she told him that she came up in the dumbwaiter, he went fucking ape shit. He told her that only a slapper would do something like that, and it was improper conduct for the wife of a Captain in the Irish Army..."

"What did she say?" interrupted Archie.

"Shut your fucking drink hole, Archie—carry on, Johnny." said Joey, insistently. Johnny gave Archie a sinister look, and then carried on.

"In anyway, before I was rudely stopped by the village drunk...." he gave Archie another dirty look, " she told him to forget about the tablecloth as she would be cutting no cake tonight, and the only thing that would be cut tonight, would be his balls off if he tried to get into bed with her. I then could hear her leaving; he must have followed her because I could then hear the door being locked," said Johnny, with his face now acting out the expression of relief that he must have felt when he heard the door being locked.

"Well, that was one short marriage, what?" said Joey.

"Yeah!" said Dick, "it's about as short as that little fucking irritating midget that's been going around tormenting everyone all day." He quipped, and we all started to laugh. Johnny was delighted when I told him that Mrs. Sinclair had left a drink behind the bar for us all, for helping her out. He told me that the free drink had just come in time, for he did not think that there were any video buffs left that could be fleeced. Later on I was standing at the bar having a yap to Deco while Johnny was down the way talking to his new found teacher friend. The other two barmen were giving Deco dirty looks as he stood talking to me while they were flat out, as the bar was packed to the hilt. Deco noticed me noticing them giving him the dirty looks, and turning his head in their direction and in earshot of, and meant for them, but talking to me,

"Them! De ye know what? If they were shooting barmen in the morning, them two bastards would die fucking innocent. Fuck them! Their getting paid enough, their probably robbing me fucking blind as it is?" he voiced, rebuffing the now heads down and retreating barmen.

"What's wrong Deco? Are ye fed up?" I asked him.

"Ah its this fucking army, it has me browned off, but what can I do? I mean, if I left the shit hole I would more than likely end up in prison. So it's the bar here or the bars in prison, and I think I would rather the bar here, because if I go to prison them twenty five to lifers would pass me around like a fucking collection plate at a Sunday mass, I would come out of the fucking place with me hole as big as the Grand-bleedin-Canyon. So I'm stuck here for the foreseeable future," he said, with resentment, and a note of conceding in his voice. Deco suddenly stood upright from his slouching position across the counter. "Now here's a cloth, I want ye to go around and give the tables a rub, and collect whatever glasses are out there," he ordered. Deco's action had me puzzled until I got a tap on the shoulder from behind. Deco could see him coming, whereas I could not, for there standing looking at me when I turned around, was the C.O. of the barracks, Lt. Colonel Pearse, in civilian attire.

"Trooper, where is the N.C.O. in charge of the Mess staff?" he asked me.

"If you would please follow me, Sir?" I said, taking the cloth from Deco, and walked off down the Mess in the direction of Johnny and his Welsh school teacher friend, with the C.O. following right behind me. After I pointed out Johnny to the Lt. Colonel, I had this vision of the Garden of Gethsemane, all I was short of doing was kissing Johnny on the cheek. Taking hold of the cloth

I started to wipe a table right beside where they stood, because I knew that this was going to be good, as Johnny Boyce did not know who this man standing in front of him, was. The reason Johnny did not know Lt. Col. Pearse was because Johnny had just transferred into the Unit a couple of months ago. He would have only dealt with, and known our own Unit Commanding Officer, as the barrack C.O. was rarely seen.

"Excuse me Corporal, are you in charge of the troopers that are working here tonight?" the Lt. Col asked Johnny. Looking into the man's thin, compact and solid face, Johnny held his hand up shoulder high in front of himself in a motion to stop the man from proceeding any further with more questions.

"I will be with ye shortly, my good man—can't you see that I am in a conversation here with my teacher friend? Don't ye know that it is very rude to interrupt when I'm in a private conversation?" rebuked Johnny. The C.O. took a pace back and looked at the Corporal in disbelief. He tapped Johnny on the shoulder once again, for Johnny had turned away from him to continue his chatter to the now bemused looking teacher.

"Do you know who the fuck you're talking to, Corporal?" asked the irate C.O, of Johnny.

"Who am I talking to?" replied Johnny.

"I am the C.O. of the barracks, and I will ask you one more time Corporal; are you in charge of the Mess staff?"

"Well, Sir, C.O. and all, I think that does not give ye the right to embarrass me in front on my Welsh teacher friend. I think that we should go out to the privacy of the hall to continue on this question from ye," came Johnny back at him.

The C.O. stepped back and stretched out his arm with palm up and pointing towards the door leading to the hall, and said, " Right Corporal, let's go and sort this out in the hall, or I will end up doing something that will embarrass myself." Then the two of them walked to the door. Like a shot I quickly passed them out before they got to the door, as I wanted to get to the toilet, which was in the long hall, and listen from the toilet door for what Johnny was going to come out with next, and I was not going to miss that. Standing just inside the open toilet door which was only a couple of yards from where they now stood in the long hall, gave me a perfect position to hear the final words of a soon to be assistant to Scrubber Sheelan in the kitchen for the remainder of his military career.

"Now then Corporal, I....."

"Hold it right there, Sir," said Johnny interrupting the C.O., " before we go any further, Sir, don't ye think an apology is in order?"

"An apology for fucking what? It should be you apologizing to me for the way that you talked to me in there, Corporal."

"Well Sir, with all due respect to your rank, Sir, if ye had the decency in the first place to introduce yourself to me....then I would not have spoken to ye in which the way I did. Come on, Sir, I mean ye were standing there with civilian clothes on, for all I knew ye could have been a sheep dipper from Wicklow, Sir," said Johnny.

That's it, I thought to myself, you're gone, Boyce, then I could not believe my ears when I heard the C.O. saying, "Right so, Corporal, I was not thinking in there, so I apologize. Now! Are you in charge of......" there was silence for a moment, and then the C.O. said, "A fucking sheep dipper from Wicklow?" then more silence until once again he carried on. "Look here; are you in charge of the waiting staff? Yes or no?"

"Yes I am, Sir, and thank you for the apology."

"Never mind that for now, Corporal, who is the officer in charge?"

"You are, Sir."

"No-no, not fucking me, Corporal; who is the officer over you and the rest of the waiting staff?"

"Sorry Sir, eh, its Captain Darcy, Sir," answered Johnny. Standing just inside the toilet door I had to control myself from laughing out loud.

"Right!" said the C.O. " I am going to go and find him, and in the meantime Corporal I suggest that you proceed to the main ballroom and remove the two troopers that are in there dancing with the guests' wives and their girlfriends. Do you comprehend that, Corporal?"

"No I don't Sir, I don't encourage that kind of thing at all. Sir, troopers should not be in there dancing with the guests, at all Sir."

"Corporal, you really don't have a fucking clue, do you? The word "comprehend" means understand, so do you understand—understand Corporal, do you?"

"Of course I do, Sir; I just did not catch what ye said, Sir," said the embarrassed and worried voice of the Corporal.

"Listen!" said the C.O. raising his voice slightly. "Just get it done, will you Corporal?" He then walked away down the hall without waiting on Johnny's reply. Coming out from the toilet door, I could see Johnny standing in the hall with one hand on his hip, and the other hand caressing the back of his neck, as he was deep in thought and probably wondering what hell had just happened.

On seeing me he said, "Quick, come with me, them two fucking eejits, Dick and Joey are in the ballroom trying to shift the women." He then started to walk at pace down the long hall towards the ballroom, with myself following. Right enough, when we got to the ballroom, there was Dick and Joey out on the dance floor dancing with two women, who seemed to delight in the attention of two soldiers. Johnny immediately went out onto the dance floor while I stayed by the door. Whatever Johnny whispered into their ears had an alarming effect on them, as they walked off the floor leaving the two women stranded, with one woman looking at the other with eyebrows raised and eyes wide open in mutual mystification. When Johnny got the pair of them outside in the hall, he gave them both a right rollicking, and told them that the C.O. of the barracks had seen them.

"Lads, for fuck sake keep a low profile, stay in or around the service kitchen, can yis comprehend that? Com-pre-hen-d!!" Johnny said, intensely stressing the word "comprehend" to them. By the sound of him I think Johnny got a guilty uneducated complex of not knowing the word when the C.O. had used it earlier on, and he was now picking it out on the two lads. The two lads shrugged their shoulders, and nodded to him. " Yis don't even know what comprehend fucking means, do yis? Well it means…."

"Yeah, I know what it fucking means." said Dick, halting Johnny's flow of explanation of the word.

"So do I comprehend what comprehend fucking means, does that seem inconceivable to you that we understand what under-fucking-stand means, Corporal?" said Joey, vexed.

Cutting in straight away at this stage before it got out of hand, I said, "Look, we're all getting a little tipsy, well, to tell the truth, we're all fucking pissed. Johnny just got the living bollix eat out of him by Lieutenant Colonel Pearse, over you two. So come on let's collect a few glasses, and get on with enjoying the free gargle, what do youse think?"

"Yeah!" said Joey. "We'll go and collect a few glasses Johnny, and meet yis back in the kitchen for a few pints and a laugh, and if that fucking dope Pearse says anything, just tell him that the women forced us to dance, and that we did not want to embarrass them, if he doesn't like that, tell him we said to go and fuck himself," he said, as the two of them, one after the other patted the side of Johnny's shoulder as they walked off to collect glasses. Joey turned around as he got down the hall, and walked back to tell Johnny that he was only joking about the last part of what he had just said, about telling the C.O. to go and fuck himself. " I'll tell ye one thing," said Johnny, as he leered in the direction of Joey fading down the hall, "only for you stepped in there, I was going to lock the pair of them up, I swear I was." He turned to look at me, doe eyed, and scratching the back of his head.

"Don't talk shite!" I said, and half smiled at him.

"Yeah, your bang on, I don't have it in me, I never had the balls for that kinda thing, what de ye think?" he asked me.

"No ye don't have the balls for that kind of thing, but ye have them for every other fucking thing that ye can get your hands on for nothing," I expressed factually.

He looked at me for a moment, and then broke out laughing, with myself joining in. "Speaking of which," he said, as he stopped laughing abruptly, "them two fuckers are going to buy me a drink later on for covering their arses, and I will make sure of that. Now let's go and find the main man Pearse, and lay it on the line to him." he said, as we set off in pursuit of the C.O. of the barracks. Johnny suddenly stopped as we headed for the bar, and asked me, "Where in the name of jasus did a dopy bastard of a fucking eejit like Donavan come across a big word like that?"

"What word?" I asked him.

"That fucking word he laid on me back there, "inconceivable," yeah, that was it alright, " inconfuckingceivable" I mean where did he dig that one up?"

"I don't know? I think he plays Scrabble all the time." I said to him, just to shut him up.

"Wouldn't that just fucking sicken ye, the fucking asshole is not only brainy, but is also the athletic type as well," he said, with a contorted look on his face. I was astounded by what I heard, I suddenly got this vision of Archie and himself on two windsurf boards abseiling down a steep rock face doing a crossword puzzle. What goes through the guy's mind, or my mind for that matter.

"Listen Johnny!" I said, about to tell him that I was calling it a day but did not get the chance to, as he cut me off and told me to hang on as he had to go to the toilet. Talk about timing, just as Johnny came out from the toilet the C.O. was approaching us from down the hall. Johnny raised his hand at the Lt. Col. in stopping fashion so he (Johnny) could have the first say. Johnny lowered his hand.

"Now Sir, I went down to the ballroom and dealt with that matter that ye told me to get sorted, and I might add Sir, that when I got down there the two troopers were not dancing with wives and girlfriends, but were dancing with two fat chicks that forcedly embarrassed the two troopers to dance with them. I took the troopers to one side and gave them a severe reprimand, and I can ensure ye, Sir, that it will not happen again. All that aside, Sir, does it seem inconceivable to you, Sir, that I can't comprehend the situation and control my troops?" rebuked the now slightly shaking Johnny, who was off on another uneducated guilt trip.

The C.O. stared at the Corporal for a moment, and then said, "Is your arsehole blocked up, Corporal?" he then went quiet and continued to stare at Johnny.

Johnny seemed confused by the question, and glanced back at the toilet that he had just come from, he then said, "No, Sir....what do ye mean, Sir?"

" I mean, Corporal, I was just wondering if your arsehole is blocked, because the shit seems to be overflowing from your mouth, and I would say that you are in dire need of a good shit plumber, so I suggest that you just stand there and not let any more shit come from your mouth, and listen, ok? Now I was talking to Captain Darcy before he had to rush away to deal with an emergency at home, and he told me that you and your staff have done a superb job all day, and that all of you willingly gave up your own time to volunteer to collect glasses and empties for the night. Well I would like to express my appreciation to yourself and your staff, and I would be grateful if you would pass that on to the rest of them," said the C.O, as he took Johnny's hand and shook it. Johnny stood there shaking the Lt. Colonel's hand with a look of utter astonishment on his face, but Johnny being Johnny said, "Thank you, eh—Sir, Captain Darcy told the lads that there would be a few free drinks for them for the work that they have put in, and as he has left....I was wondering, Sir, if you could ok it with the barman, Sir?"

"I can see no problem there Corporal, I will do that now before I leave," said the C.O. turning and walking into the bar. Johnny went into the bar to order another round of drinks for the lads, but only after the C.O. had departed, as I returned to the service kitchen to sit down, and take a little time out from Johnny dictionary. The kitchen was empty except for Archie, who was slouched on the armchair in the corner of the room in a drunken sleep. No sooner had I plonked myself down on a chair when Mrs. Blackwell and Sgt. Knight entered the room.

"Where's the lads?" enquired the Sergeant. I did not have to answer him, first Johnny walked in carrying a tray full of drink, and right behind him came Dick and Joey, both in possession of a tray of pints.

"Are yis having a hooley, lads?" asked the Blackwell one on seeing the gargle. "Is it free drink?" she asked.

"Why do ye ask that?" inquired Johnny of her.

"No reason," she replied, folding her arms across her chest.

With a look of discontentment on his face, Johnny said, "Let me ask ye, Mrs Blackwell. Does it seem inconceivable to ye that we can't pay for our own drink? Well, let me assure you ...."

"Will ye shut the fuck up, Johnny?" I snapped, "You're starting to sound like a fucking educated parrot—if I hear that word again—I won't be responsible for my actions, I'll..."

Ok! Will everyone just shut up?" the Sergeant shouted, cutting across me. There was complete silence in the kitchen. The Sergeant then told us that the wedding cake was going to be moved from the banqueting room to the main ballroom for cutting, and that he would need two lads to do the job of wheeling in the cake, one at each end of the wheel table. Johnny put his hand up in the air like a schoolchild that knew the answer, but Sean Knight ignored him, and picked Joey and Dick to do the job. He then told Johnny to take the two lads and the wheel table across to the banqueting room, and carefully take the cake from the top table and place it onto the wheel table. He told them that when they had that done, they were to leave the cake there, and Johnny was to lock the door, and return to the service kitchen and wait there until he came and got them when the wedding cake was ready to be presented to the bride and groom. "And another thing? Go easy on that fucking drink until this task is carried out, and then I couldn't give shite if yis go and get rat arsed, as long as that cake gets delivered to the Captain and his wife without any fuckups. Do I make myself clear?" said the flustered Sergeant. We all nodded in agreement to his demands, and he then left with Mrs. Blackwell in tow, but not before she gave Johnny dagger eyes. Johnny and the two lads went across to sort out the cake over in the banqueting hall while I took a pint from one of the trays for myself, and sat down once more to relax. Looking over at Archie I wondered how he could sleep through all the commotion that had just happened in the kitchen. Looking at Archie I started to feel tired and sleepy, but that was short lived when I was stirred from my rest by the sound of the backdoor slamming shut. The noise of the backdoor aroused Archie from his drunken slumber as he sat upright and startled in his chair, looking around the kitchen to get his bearings.

"What the fuck?" said Archie.

"Relax, Archie, it's only the backdoor shutting," I told him, putting him at ease. From down the back hall I could hear someone coming towards us clearing their throat in between mumblings.

"Who the fuck is there?" Archie called out, whilst staring at the entrance from the back hall into the service kitchen.

"'Tis I, and I've come to drink the fucking place dry," said the recognizable and distinctive voice of Scrubber Sheelan. "Where would a man get a drop of porter around here?" asked Scrubber, who was now standing in, and taking up most of the back doorway into the kitchen with his giant frame. Scrubber's face lit up when he seen the trays of drink. "Now that's what I call service, what?" he said, taking a pint of stout from one of the trays, and taking a large gulp from it, which seen half the pint disappear.

"Where in the name of jasus did you spring from?" asked Archie of Scrubber, who was now wiping white stout froth from around his mouth with the back of his hand.

"I was down the men's canteen playing poker, lost me bollix, and had no money left, so I ventured up here because I knew that there would be free drink flowing, so—all in all, I'm doing the same fucking thing you're doing—now does that answer your question?—ye goggle eyed prick," said the drunken pot-walloper. Scrubber looked in a mess, he still wore the same clothes that he had worn washing pots all day, which consisted of army green slacks and beige coloured shirt, which had grease stains all over them, the front of the shirt having the majority of the stains. As I was sitting there staring at the state of Scrubber, my immersed concentration was broken by the dull sound of Mr. Grogan, the small person, hitting the floor, as he had slipped on entering the kitchen.

"That floor is fucking manky. I nearly broke me bollix there; do yis ever clean the fucking thing, yis scumbags? And what the fuck are you laughing at—ye big bag of shit?" roared the small person at Scrubber, who was laughing his head off. "Looking at the state of you, I think your filthier than the floor; what do ye think ye long streak of piss?" said the irritated Mr Grogan to Scrubber.

"Yeah I know!" said Scrubber, still laughing, "But wouldn't ye think it would be the other way around? That it would be you that would be filthy, because you're closer to the floor than I am, ye sawed-off little fucker," he said, and still continued to laugh. Scrubber stopped laughing, and with a serious look on his face said, "No-no I'm sorry about that, I was only messing, I am truly sorry. Is yourself in the army, by any chance?"

"No I'm not, thanks be to fuck, with big sappy bastards in it like you," replied the small man.

Scrubber took a step back with a look of wonderment on his face, and with his index finger wagging at Grogan he said, "Now isn't that a pity that you're not in the army? Because I'll tell ye one thing. Ye would have made a great tunnel fucking rat, ye little aul shite ye." He once again broke into laughing, and this time Archie and myself joined in.

"I'll have your balls for that—do ye hear me?" shouted Grogan, standing on his toes, and pulling down on both ends of his little waistcoat in a fierce strop. Scrubber took two steps forward, and was now right in front of, and looking down at Mr Grogan.

"Be off with yourself now me little aul man, before I take my army issue boot and place it on the top of your pumped up head, and scrunch ye into the filthy floor like the bugging little bastard that ye are, how about that?" said Scrubber with a snarling voice.

The small person started to walk backwards towards the door, and with his face now looking devoid of blood from the shock of Scrubber's threat, said, "Listen! I only came in here to tell the staff that Captain Sinclair wants the cake to be brought to the ballroom as soon as its ready, so back the fuck off—ok?" He quickly turned, and walked from the kitchen without waiting on an answer from any of us. Johnny and the two lads appeared thorough the kitchen door to the sight of us having a good laugh.

"What's going on here? And what the fuck are you doing here?" Johnny queried, pointing his finger at Scrubber.

"I'm here Corporal Boyce at the request and pleasure of the master chef, Sergeant Hennessy, and I'm going to be doing the same thing that the rest of yis are doing, drinking fucking gratuitously, thank you very much," said Scrubber as he raised his pint glass in the air towards Johnny, then in two gulps, the half pint that was in the glass was gone. The disparaging Corporal leaned slightly backwards, and with a look of disgust on his face he began to repeatedly look Scrubber up and down from head to toe in exaggerated fashion.

"I'll tell ye what," said Johnny to Scrubber, "if ye think your stepping outside this door, well let me tell ye, your fucking mistaking. Look at the state of ye, I mean ye look like ye got dressed in a fucking dumpster; there's enough food mashed into your trousers that would feed a man on the ground for a fucking week. And look at your shirt….look at your shirt…the stains; it looks like an sad over used beer-mat. Oh-no, I'm afraid you're not budging from this kitchen ye big abattoir scented fuck; you'll wait here until I get Dermot, and he can decide what to do with ye—have ye got that?" spewed Johnny, somewhat condescendingly, and most certainly, hurtful to Scrubber.

With his face showing no emotional pain, Scrubber replied, "Well Corporal, if that's the case I'll have a drink while I'm waiting on ye to come back with the Sergeant."

"Ye aren't your bollix going to have one of our drink's—ye can wait on Dermot to get ye one," said Johnny, as he moved very swiftly across the floor, and placed himself between Scrubber and the drink trays, that were situated on top of a large table. With Johnny now standing in front of Scrubber he did not notice Archie sitting behind his back at the table, removing a pint of the black stuff from one of the trays, and placing it on the ground between his feet.

"Listen, Johnny! Sean Knight is going to go ape shit if that cake is not in the ballroom very soon, so I suggest ye put a move on," I said, to break the icy atmosphere between him and the Scrubber.

Johnny looked at me, and by the expression on my face, the seriousness of the cake situation kicked in with him, and he said, "Right, Joey; Dick, grab a tray of gargle each, and I'll lock them up across the way in the banqueting hall until we're finished with this cake business, because that covetous bastard (pointing at Scrubber) will have them all drank by the time we got back." He then, with Dick and Joey picked up a tray of drink each, and left the kitchen for the banqueting hall. After they had left the room, Archie lifted the pint of stout up from between his feet, and presented it to the now smiling Scrubber. Oddly enough, Scrubber did not guzzle the pint down, but un-characteristically, he placed it on the table untouched. The reason for this abstention became apparent when Johnny and the two lads came walking past the kitchen door a few minutes later, wheeling the table with the cake on it towards the ballroom.

"Take it nice and handy, lads." said Johnny, as Dick and Joey wheeled the table at a very slow pace. Looking down at the wheel table I could now see the reason for the snail's pace, there was a wheel missing from the rear of the table.

"Where's the wheel, Johnny?" I asked him.

"Inside, in that fucking place," he said, nodding towards the banqueting hall. "The bastering thing fell off, and we could not get it back on, so we will just have to take it easy, and balance it until we get it to the ballroom," he said, frustratingly.

"Well fair dues to ye boys!" expressed Scrubber. "I'll toast your mission, and your safe return." he said, mockingly, as he raised the pint tumbler (which was still full) upwards and then outwards, towards Johnny and the two lads. He left his arm stretched out with the pint in it, making no attempt to move it towards his mouth. Johnny halted the two lads pushing the three wheeled table, and then walked through the doorway from the hall, into the kitchen.

"Where did ye get that pint?" the now, very much irritated Corporal asked Scrubber. Before Scrubber could utter a snide reply, a voice from the back of the kitchen conveyed to Johnny that it was him that gave Scrubber the pint— it was Archie. Johnny turned around, and with a slow disbelieving shake of his head from side to side, and with a solemn look on his face, he stared at Archie, who was now sitting back in his chair lighting a cigarette.

"Why in the name of fuck did ye have to go and do that for?" ragingly asked Johnny, as he moved a little closer, with arms stretched out towards Archie. Sitting up nervously in his chair, and before the stern looking Corporal got any closer to him,

Archie said, "I had to give it to him, Johnny; I mean he saved my life overseas in the Lebanon—I mean—what the fuck was I supposed to do? What, Johnny?" He then sat back in his chair. There was an eerie feeling in the kitchen as everyone turned to look at the Scrubber in total awe, mouths agape. Johnny looked long and hard from Archie to Scrubber before he finally spoke.

"Right!" he said, to Joey and Dick, who were still holding onto the wheel table in the doorway, " grab that piggy fucking table, and let's get this over with." He then walked out to the two lads, and the three of them continued on down the hall. Looking over at Scrubber I could see that he was more amazed by Archie's statement than anybody else, as he was not really looking at Archie, but moreover, was staring through him.

"Truly, Archie, did Scrubber save your life overseas?" I insistently asked. From the corner of my eye I could see Scrubber moving slowly across the floor, full of attention, and showing excessive eagerness for Archie's reply.

"He did indeed, by jasus he did," said Archie, now standing to his feet. "Wasn't I dying from the drink one morning, and the bold Scrubber here gave me two of his cans—well I can tell ye—them two cans save my fucking life that morning, but we won't tell Johnny though?" He then started to burst out laughing with Scrubber and myself joining in on it. When we eventually stopped laughing Scrubber told us that he was going out to the foyer to see Dermot to mooch a few pints off him, so Archie and I went along with him, as we wanted to see the wedding cake being wheeled into the bride and groom.

"Get over there, you!" snapped Sgt. Knight on seeing Scrubber coming into view. "Sit down there with Dermot, and keep out of sight; do ye hear me?" he quietly said, pointing over to where Dermot was sitting at his table, that was situated just inside the main door. The Scrubber nodded, and took a mouthful of the pint that he had brought with him from the kitchen. As he did not want to approach Dermot looking like he was alright for a drink, he placed the pint glass with the remainder of the drink in it on top of the big oak table across from the twin doors of the ballroom, that were shut for the moment, and would be opening soon for the cake to be wheeled in for the cutting. Mrs. Blackwell was over excited, and was behaving like a giddy schoolgirl. She was telling anyone and everyone that would listen to her that the cake was majestic, and pointing out Dermot to all that stood in the foyer, as the cake's creator, much to Dermot's uneasiness and deep embarrassment. Dermot had nothing to be embarrassed about, as it was a well-made beautiful, white icing covered three tier cake, with tiny pink roses around the bottom, and silver beads around the top of each tier, and a small bride and groom standing on the very tip of it. There were a lot of guests out in the foyer with their cameras at the ready to take photos of the cake being provided to the bride and groom. Dermot's frantic waving caught my eye, and he was beckoning me to come over to him.

"What's up, Dermot?" I asked, on reaching his table.

"Did someone feed that fucking Blackwell one magic fucking mushrooms or what? Go over to Johnny Boyce, and tell him to shut her to fuck up, and if that does not work, tell him I said to put his fist in her blabbering fucking mouth?" Dermot said, with an insincere one sided facial smile. "Listen!" he said, rising from his seat. "I'm going outside to the garden for a while to get away from her pointing and fucking yapping. If ye see Scrubber coming back with the drink, could ye tell him that I will be back shortly?" he then walked through the main door, out across the driveway, and into the garden. No sooner had I sat down in the chair that Dermot had vacated when Scrubber arrived back with the drink. I told Scrubber the reason for Dermot leaving, and what he had told me to tell Johnny Boyce, and he started to laugh.

"Here! Are they ever going to bring that stupid fucking cake in?" said Scrubber. No answer had to be given, because just then Sgt. Knight came around the corner into the foyer, and announced that the twin doors would be opening soon, and that the two lads were to get themselves ready to wheel in the cake. Looking over to where the two lads stood, I noticed that Dick's head kept turning around to stare at the half pint that Scrubber had left on the big oak table.

"Dick must be under some pressure; he keeps looking at that pint ye left over there, what do ye think?" I said to Scrubber. The words were only out of my mouth when, simultaneously Dick left the wheel table to go and get a mouthful from the pint glass on the oak table, and the twin doors opened. Mrs. Blackwell was the first to scream as the wheel table leaned to one side, and the cake started to shift in a fast downward motion. Then the screaming started to come from inside the ballroom, as everyone in the vicinity of the cake rushed and tried to grab and straighten the wheel table, including Mr. Grogan, the small person, who had opened the twin doors. Too late, the cake was now sliding from the table, and heading for the floor. Mrs. Blackwell was like a ninja as she dived through the air to save the cake hitting the floor. She met the cake coming towards her at an angle, and in so doing, she wrapped her arms around the middle tier with a grip that a Beirut wrestler would have been proud of. Mrs. Blackwell hit the floor still holding the squashed middle tier, with the other two tiers shattered all over hall. Then the wheel table turned over and fell on top of Mrs. Blackwell, and like a human avalanche, everybody that was trying to catch the table, fell onto the floor.

"I only wish that I could see that again in slow fucking motion," Scrubber said to me as we hurried across the foyer to help out. Scrubber helped Johnny to turn the wheel table back upright. With the table now pulled away, the scene on the floor was pandemonium. The sheet from the table was covering a screaming Mrs. Blackwell, while other bodies lay crumbled on top of one another. Looking into the ballroom I could see that the bride and groom stood lifeless at their table staring out at the mayhem, in complete shock. Scrubber made his way around the wheel table, and reached down and lifted Mr. Grogan up from the floor without any effort, with one hand.

He now had the small person held up off the ground by the collar of his jacket, and looking in the direction of Mr. and Mrs. Sinclair, he declared, "The cake is fucked, Sir, but the little lad from the top of the cake seems to be alright." He then released Mr. Grogan. Sgt. Knight heard and seen it all, as he was shutting the twin doors.

"Do something about that muck savage bastard," growled an anger inflamed Grogan to the Sergeant. Sgt. Knight gave Scrubber a dirty look, and told Grogan that he would deal with the matter when he had the doors closed. Just then Dermot came rushing up the foyer, feverishly.

"What the fuck happened?" he said, almost panic stricken. Before I could say a word, I could see Scrubber with an evil grin on his face staring over at Johnny, who was trying to calm Dick down.

"Boyce gave Mrs Blackwell a roundhouse to the side of the head that sent her flying into the cake." Scrubber told Dermot.

"I don't fucking believe it!" said Dermot as he ran across the hall to an un-suspecting Johnny. "I was only fucking joking ye stupid bastard ye when I said put your fist in her mouth, ye dopy bastard."

"What?" said Johnny, before he was knocked unconscious by a haymaker of a punch to the side of the head by Dermot. Scrubber made a quick exit out the main door, while I went over to Dermot and explained what had hap-pened. I thought Dermot would run riot, but no—he calmly walked past Mrs. Blackwell, who was standing in a dazed state in the middle of the foyer, still hugging the middle tier of the cake into her chest. He then walked out the main door, and into the night, no doubt disgusted with himself.

"Where the fuck is Sheelan?" asked Sgt. Knight, who had now appeared, along with Capt. Sinclair, onto the scene.

"I want him strung up by his balls, Neville—by the balls," roared a di-sheveled Mr Grogan, who was following behind.

"For heaven's sake, stay quiet for a moment, Tim," rapped Capt. Sinclair to Mr. Grogan; he then brought Sgt. Knight to one side, and started to talk to him in a hush-hush tone, and all the time pointing over towards the de-bacle across the way.

"Tim! Fucking Tim!" said Deco Lawler to me, in a whispered voice. Deco had come down from the bar to see for himself the chaos in the foyer, and the bits and pieces of wedding cake that lay in front of the ballroom doors. "I'll tell ye one thing," said Deco, " that little fuck's aul-fella and aul-one must have had some sense of humor, or they were really into Charles fucking Dickens. I mean, think about it. Tiny Tim….. out-fucking-standing," he chuckled. After I gave Deco a rough outline on what had taken place he went to comfort Mrs. Blackwell, who was still standing in a dazed state in the middle of the foyer. Deco had great time for Mrs. Blackwell, as she cleaned up the outside of the bar each morning for him, which she did of her own accord, as cleaning the bar was not part of her duties in the Mess. He would always reward her at the end of her week on duty as barman with twenty cigarettes and a small baby whiskey, which she was very content with. Johnny, who was only out cold for a few seconds, was now standing in a small huddle with Capt. Sinclair and Sgt. Knight. After a few moments the Captain and the Sergeant shook hands with Johnny, and then they parted ways with Sgt. Knight and Johnny moving to the shambolic location outside the ballroom doors, while Capt. Sinclair, no doubt made his way back to the ballroom to console his wife, and probably try to convince her that the mishaps of the day were not signs to an inauspicious marriage, but just human error. Sgt. Knight called Dick, Joey, and me over to where Johnny and he were standing. He told us to pick the cake up off the ground, and that he would go to the kitchen to get small plates, and a large knife. He explained to us that the Captain came to a decision that what's left of the cake was to be cut into small pieces, and put on small plates, and was to be given out to the guests. So the Sergeant headed off to the kitchen to get the small plates and knife while the rest of us went about gathering what cake was left to salvage.

"I seen ye talking to Sinclair and Sean, what was that all about?" I asked Johnny, as we went about picking up the cake.

"They asked me would I be willing to forget Dermot thumping the fucking head off me—well they did not exactly use them words, but ye know what I mean?" he said, reaching his hand up and rubbing the side of his head. "I told Sinclair," he continued, "that was two punches that I got at this wedding today, and I told him straight out that I would forget about it if the three lads and myself got twenty smackers each for the work that we put in during the night, collecting glasses. Well, I can tell ye the fucker never even hesitated; he said yes, and that he would give me the money shortly. Am I the man, or am I the fucking man—or what?" he said with elation, and a look of triumph on his face.

"That's great, Johnny, I'll tell the two lads, they will be delighted," I said. The look of joy on his face now turned to a frown.

"Ye aren't your bollix going to tell them fuck all; no, me good man, It's forty each, and fuck them pair of shit-heads. Besides I've been getting them drink for nothing all day, so that's their lot, good luck them," he said, with a smile now back on his face, as he continued to pick cake from off the floor. Sgt. Knight came back with the plates and knife at the same time that the four of us had retrieved all the cake that was retrievable, and placed it onto the wheel table that Joey had put cardboard under to stabilize it. Sgt. Knight told me to go over to Mrs. Blackwell and take the middle tier from her so it could be cut, and placed on plates. Mr. Grogan got to Mrs. Blackwell's table before me and took his jacket off and threw it to the floor.

"You!" he rasped, to Mrs. Blackwell. " Mrs. fucking Doubtfire, what the fuck did ye think ye were doing flying through the air, and squashing the fuck out of the cake? I mean who the fuck do ye think ye are, super granny or something?" he snapped at her.

Deco, who had been sitting down with his arm around Mrs. Blackwell consoling her, now jumped to his feet. "Hey, Sergeant!" Deco called out to Sean Knight. "Ye want to tell fucking stretch here to watch his fucking mouth, or I will break it for him," he warned, as he gently took the cake from Mrs. Blackwell's lap and walked towards the small person and me.

Tapping Grogan on the shoulder, I said, "There's no need for that, she—"

"Shut the fuck up, bum boy," the insulting little shit head interjected. Because he was looking at and insulting me, he did not see it coming. The cake being slammed with force into his face lifted Grogan right off his feet and onto the broad of his back. The Sarge and I quickly grabbed Deco before he did any more damage to the small person.

Mrs. Blackwell was sitting on her chair laughing and clapping. "What have ye done, Lawler?" asked Sean.

"Well, Sarge, it looks like I turned a wedding cake into a shortcake," quipped Deco. Everyone started to laugh, even Sgt. Knight, everyone that is, except for Grogan, who was still sitting on the floor, stunned. Capt. Sinclair arrived just then holding four twenty notes in his hand. He looked down at Grogan who was shaking his head trying to get his mental abilities back.

"What the hell happened him?" the Captain asked, pointing at Grogan.

Johnny, taking the money from Sinclair's hand, said, "I think he is drunk, Sir, and must have fell over with the cake in his hands, and to tell ye the truth, Sir, I don't really care, because he is one disturbed little man, and anything bad that befalls him, then all as I can say is up his sheltered area, or would that be up his suntrap, Sir?"

"No need for the cutting language, Corporal," said Sinclair to a walking away Johnny. We all followed a smiling Johnny to go and distribute the plated wedding cake to the guests.